INTRODUCTION

Everyone is on a journey from the day they are born to the moment they die. Some believe it is predestined while others believe that they make their own path. Whatever drives or guides you, always find joy in being yourself, enjoy what has passed, live in the moment, look forward to what may be and always strive to be the best you can.

Joseph Leon Anderson is on an unexpected journey north as he reflects on what has brought him to this place in his life. Reliving memories as he tries to unravel and make sense of the web of what might have been.

Harriet Lucy McIntosh gave up her dreams of becoming a professional dancer to be with the man she loves but will that love be enough to keep her warm in the darkest of days?

Howard James Morris harbours feelings for his best friends' wife and is on a journey of self-destruction as he tries to ignore that which drives him forward and which holds him back.

Three journeys intertwined with love and betrayal. All leading to one ending which is the beginning of lives yet lived.

ISBN-13: 9781800684393

Cover design by: DMWilson
Library of Congress Control Number: 2018675309

Thanks, and Love:
Hayley for her unending love, support and encouragement.
Gregory, Rosalie and Carys for keeping me smiling without even realising it.
Sam Oulaid and Trevor Gordon, without them this book may have been lost forever.
Michelle Allbones for agreeing to endure the first read spelling mistakes and all.

CHAPTER ONE

17:31hrs Friday 23rd March 2018

Darkness surrounds him, eyes screwed shut just for an instance, breath short, sharp.

Calm Down.

Calm!

Down!

Eyes open, metaphorical darkness surrounds him.

The piercing lights from the car's headlights seemingly the only illumination on the empty journey ahead. A journey to a distant almost long since forgotten place.

How long had it been since he moved away? Since he'd left it all behind.

Twenty-six years?

Monday 27th November 2017

"Relax." Whispered Joe to himself. "Just fucking relax Joe." He slouched his six-foot frame a little further into his chair in the dimly lit corner of the hotel bar and pulled his cap just a little further down over his short dark brown hair on his forehead. Joe checked his watch for the tenth time in as many minutes. Twenty-two minutes passed seven. Another eight minutes, Eight minutes. Joe took a sip of his whiskey. He didn't think he could last another eight seconds let alone another eight minutes. Joe looked down and put his thumb in his waistband in an attempt to adjust how his jeans sat. He needed to lose a few pounds. If he was being honest with himself he probably needed to lose a stone, his belly was a little rounder than he'd like and his belt was digging in. Over the past couple of years, he'd let himself go a little. Not exercising quiet as much as he probably should do, eating a few too many chocolate bars and bags of crisps. Deciding on pizzas, fish and chips or burgers instead of cooking healthier options for his evening meals when Harriet was away on business, which recently seemed to be getting more often. Was that what had led him here to this point or was his current predicament the cause of his lack of empathy for his body. Another sip of his whiskey and Joe scanned the room yet again. Under different circumstances the Double Tree bar at the Hilton Woking might have been a nice place to spend an evening. Drinking with colleagues, friends or his wife. Different circumstance. How different they would have to be for him to feel happy.

He felt lost and alone.

Relax Joe. She probably wasn't even going to turn up. Why would she? Joe had long speculated that Harriet had been having an affair but the phone call he'd overheard last week had all but confirmed it. Joe hoped more than anything that he'd misheard her or had come to the wrong conclusion. Hoped that he was wrong and what he had heard wasn't what he was expecting but, in his heart, he knew what was going to happen, how the night would play out. His heart beat fast in anticipation of the betrayal that would play out in this bar in the coming minutes.

Joe checked his watch again, well in six and a half minutes he'd find out one way or another.

He so desperately wanted to be wrong.

Joe's attention was distracted from the bar by his phone buzzing on the table in front of him. He retrieved his phone and unlocked it with his thumb print. A text message from his mother. She seemed to have a knack of calling or sending messages at the most inconvenient or inappropriate times. Why was that? It was as if she knew and was doing it on purpose. It was too frequent to be a coincidence. What did she want? Christmas. Was he and Harriet still coming to spend the holidays with her in Dundee? How could he answer? Joe didn't know. He replied with one word, yes. What else could he say? If he said no she'd call him and start asking questions, questions for which he didn't have the answers to at the moment. If he didn't answer the message, she would call him and start asking more questions, and he didn't have the answers to those either. Hopefully he would have those answers soon enough and could have that conversation at a time that was more convenient for him. Joe didn't want to get distracted, not now. He slipped the phone in his jacket pocket and picked up his glass. It almost reached his lips before it stopped. She was there, at the bar sitting down with her back to him. He hadn't seen her come in and she had obviously not noticed him otherwise she'd have either made a hasty exit or come over and asked what he was doing this far from home.

Now what? At that point Joe seemed to notice the glass by his lips and finally took a sip, the golden liquid flowed down his throat and into his stomach giving him a warm and relaxed sensation for the first time in a long time. Now he would wait, wait and see if anything happened. There was nothing else he could do. He hoped so much that she would have a drink then head to her room alone to sleep before she left for her supposed meeting in Exeter the following morning. Joe checked his watch again. Relax Joe. He decided that he would wait another fifteen minutes then make a discreet exit.

❖

Harriet sat at the bar and flicked several glances over her shoulder, through her long auburn hair that cascaded down her back, in the direction of the entrance and waited for the barman to get her drink. Her fingers tapped the bar top nervously while her jiggled foot on the stool step. She felt like she was nineteen again waiting for Joe to turn up for a date. Where had things gone so wrong for her and Joe? That was a silly question, she knew exactly what had brought her here, where her and Joe had '*gone wrong*' and what she was doing. She watched as the barman placed a coaster on the bar in front of her and then a gin and tonic on top of it. She thanked the barman and sipped her drink noticing that his gaze lingered on her chest, her crimson dress exposing her cleavage, admittedly for the person she was meeting and not the barman but still, it was nice to be noticed, to still feel attractive and have some attention.

She had so desperately wanted children. Joe had said that he did too but she never really believed it. They had tried for years but circumstances had conspired against them and apart from one miscarriage they had not had any children. Their love life, once passionate and spontaneous, had become routine and methodic and a means to an end. Neither happy nor engaged both her and her husband had spent less and less time together and the time they were together was becoming less special, becoming trite and argumentative. She wanted a family, a loving family with a husband that saw her, took notice of what she was wearing, gave her the attention she desired and took the attention she gave. She had thought Joseph Anderson was the man to give her all of that and for a time it seemed he would be, but not recently.

Harriet had not considered herself beautiful in the way that a supermodel was but she was attractive, five foot ten and a curvaceous size ten. She worked out, ate healthily and ensured she always looked good, always made the effort, especially for Joe, not that he seemed to notice.

Harriet felt her hair move gently from her shoulder, a finger tracing behind her ear sending an electric tingle of expectation down her spine. A hand rested on her left shoulder and warm breath tickle her right ear jolting her from her thoughts, making her smile and causing her to tilt her head slightly exposing her neck.

"Hello beautiful. Fancy meeting you here."

"Hmm, fancy that." Harriet's smile broadened. "Why don't you sit down and have a drink?" Harriet patted the stool next to her then took another drink. She turned to her right and watched as Howard sat next to her. "What do you want?"

"You." Came the reply.

"I mean to drink." Harriet's cheeks flushed slightly.

"Nothing."

"Are you going to sit there and watch me drink?" She asked.

"No, I thought we could go up to our room and watch each other."

"You got us a room?" Harriet giggled.

Howard loved Harriet's silly sense of humour. "Yes I got us a room." He loved everything about Harriet and always had. He got the barman's attention and showed him his room key. "Shall we?"

Harriet took one final drink from her glass and followed Howard, all six feet two inches of him out of the bar.

❖

Joe sat mouth open. He took his cap off his head in a slow deliberate movement, placed it on the table next to his empty glass and ran his fingers through his flattened hair. So, it was true. His worst nightmare was a reality. Harriet was having an affair. His wife was sleeping with another man. But the worst thing was that the man she was sleeping with was Howard, his best friend. How could they do this to him? His best friend and his soul mate. The reality of it made him feel sick. They had lied to him, they had both lied to him.

Harriet had told him that she was in Exeter on business and Howard was supposed to be in Dundee visiting his mother on the anniversary of his father's death.

For the briefest of moments Joe's mind wandered to that cold grey November day twenty-nine years earlier when Howard had found out that his dad was dead.

Joe stood and walked, head in a daze, out of the bar, through the hotel lobby, out of the main entrance and ambled round the side of the building to the car park. Joe climbed in to his car and sat in the driver's seat staring out of the front windscreen into the partially lit darkness tears forming in his eyes.

His head slumped forward and hit the steering wheel. Joe let out a cry. "Why?!"

Joe punched the steering wheel and had a sudden urge to drink, a lot. He thrust the car keys into the ignition and started the engine. A screech of tyres and Joe left the carpark in a cloud of dust.

He needed a drink and to think. To think about what he's just seen, his wife and best friend meeting in hotel bars. The fact that they had both lied to him, lied to his face. He needed that drink. The drive would take about twenty minutes and he could drop his car off at home and head down the Royal Oak, Dave had finally got a couple of decent guest ales on tap.

Joe slowed the car, swung round the roundabout and exited onto Egley Road leaving Woking and the two people who had once been the most important things in his life behind him. He leaned over and opened the glove box rummaging inside. He knew they were in there somewhere. Joe's hand came out holding a battered packet of cigarettes and a lighter. He had been trying to stop for the past two years and by trying it meant that he had told Harriet he was trying and cut down on the amount he smoked at home.

❖

"Same again Dave." Joe placed his empty glass on the bar with a slightly unsteady hand.

A quizzical look came back from the middle-aged man behind the bar but he didn't speak, he just moved slightly to his left, pulled another pint of dark ale and placed it on the bar in front of Joe.

"Thanks." Joe took a sip and placed his bank card on the proffered contactless card reader.

"So, What's on your mind Joe?" Dave finally asked the question that had been on his mind for the past few hours his voice still tinged with his old west midlands drawl.

"What do you mean?" Joe answered with a question of his own.

"I mean you've been here over two hours, that's your seventh pint and you've barely said twenty words to me." Dave paused and scratted the top of his head, the thin greying wavy hair seemed to ripple like a gentle breeze caressing the surface of a pond. "There's something on your mind."

"Maybe." Joe conceded. He still wasn't sure he knew what had happened earlier. No he was lying to himself, he knew exactly what had happened earlier. His wife and his best friend had lied to him and arranged a clandestine meeting that could mean only one thing. He just didn't want to believe it. "Harri's away on business for a few days, that's all." He said trying to deflect. Joe looked at the

"So, where's that gobshite of a friend of yours?" It was no secret that Dave didn't like Howard, he'd made it plainly obvious on numerous occasions how he felt.

"He said he was heading up to Dundee for a few days to see his mother, had a flight around three." Well, that's what Howard had told him.

"So what's this then? You don't normally let your hair down on a school night." Dave took off his thick black rimmed glasses and looked around the almost empty bar then back to his friend in front of him. "Special occasion or just celebrating having a day away from the gobshite."

"Something happened earlier that I'm trying to get my head around. I just need time to think about it or maybe not think about. I haven't really made my mind up but I don't really want to talk about it." Joe looked at his friend behind the bar. It just dawned on him that without the glasses Dave looked a lot like Howard even down to their height. Admittedly Dave didn't dye his hair, letting the natural grey show and Howard would never be caught wearing glasses. Aside from that, they could be brothers. Well that, and their personalities.

"Fair enough." Dave turned and poured two large whiskeys. He knew when Joe said he didn't want to talk about something that there was no use even trying to pry it out of him. "I take it you watched the rugby at the weekend. A good win for

Scotland and they set some records didn't they?"

"Yeah." Joe smiled for the first time in three hours, probably for the first time that day. "It was a great team effort. Fifty-three. The most points scored against Australia in an international. Twenty-nine. The biggest winning margin against any of the big three. Did you see it?"

"We had the England game on live here but I did manage to see some of the highlights."

"Did you see the red card?" Joe asked as he took a long draw on his rapidly disappearing fifth pint.

Dave nodded and replaced his glasses onto the end of his nose.

"Tell me, from a neutral perspective, harsh or fair?"

"It was a red. No doubt about it. Kepu lead with the shoulder deliberately to the head. He didn't even try to wrap his arms around Watson and make it look like a tackle. Watson had the better of him for most of the first half and in my opinion Kepu was getting pissed off and snapped, made a stupid decision to try and exert his authority and take Watson out of the game." Dave pushed a whiskey glass towards Joe. "On me."

Joe woke to the sound of his alarm buzzing loudly in his ear. He rolled over still half asleep and hit his head on the bed side table, swore then hit the snooze button hoping to get another ten minutes sleep but the noise seemed to persist in his head.

How much had he consumed last night? His mouth was dry and his head screamed at him. Joe sat up slowly so as not to disturb Harriet and drank some water from the glass by his side of the bed.

Wait.

Harriet wasn't there.

The memories from last night came flooding back like water crashing over a broken dam. He needed time to think about things properly, with a clear head. Joe swung his legs out of bed and padded into the bathroom.

Half an hour later he was showered, dressed and heading down stairs for breakfast. Coffee and poached eggs on toast. In his mind he knew what he wanted to do, he just needed to psych himself up and make a few preparations. Until he was ready however everything had to carry on as normal, as if he still didn't know what was going on.

Joe poured himself a coffee, the bitter aroma seemed to caress his nostrils and fire his determination. It brought back memories of when he and Harriet had been happy. Coffee in the morning, a laugh and a joke over breakfast.

He slammed his mug down on the counter splashing hot dark liquid across the white speckled surface of the kitchen counter. If he was being honest with himself, he had suspected something had been going on for a while but had not connected the dots before yesterday. Why? He asked himself not for the first time. Why? Why had she done what she had done? Questions whirled around his head. Maybe it was his fault. What had he done to cause Harriet to run into the arms of another man? A man that was supposed to be there for him, to look out for him, was supposed to be his friend. His best friend. Best friends didn't do that to each other. They'd known each other for over thirty years, grown up together in Dundee, chosen the same university, took jobs at the same firm on graduating. There was so much history between them and Howard had thrown it all away. He knew what Howard was like, a lady's man, one girlfriend after another. He always seemed to be getting serious before it fell apart, but Joe had never thought, not for one second that he would try anything with Harriet. Obviously Joe had been wrong. He'd trusted Howard and he'd betrayed that trust in the most heinous way. It made more sense that Howard had been the one to do the chasing, it fit with his character. But then Harriet had let him and had reacted to his advances, she'd let him take advantage of her. Joe didn't know if that was true but for the moment it made things easier to bear.

Joe grabbed the cloth by the sink, wiped the breakfast bar and began to drink the now barely warm coffee.

Was he being hypocritical? That night in December two thousand and three with Stacey suddenly jumped into his head. Harriet had been away on business and Stacey had been drunk when she had arrived on his doorstep. Howard had sent her one of his texts ending the relationship in his usual cowardly way. Stacey had come to cry on his shoulder and they had drunk wine and chatted for hours. They both were feeling lonely, in need of physical affection and it just seemed to happen. It was one night that he swore he'd make up for even if Harriet didn't know about it. Stacey hadn't said anything to anyone probably more out of embarrassment than anything else and over time it had faded from his memory. He had said that he would be able to forgive Harriet of an indiscretion but now he was here, in this situation, knowing what he knew, could he? Could he forgive her?

No, was the simple answer. The situation was completely different. His had been just one night, Harriet's affair was just that. A prolonged, sustained affair. He knew for sure that it had been going on for at least eighteen months and was fairly confident that it probably had been going on for longer, so what did he have to feel guilty about.

A drunken one-night stand?

No. Joe shook his head, when he put everything into context, he had nothing to feel guilty about.

Nothing at all.

He had the beginnings of an idea of what he was going to do and a rough idea of when he was going to do it. He needed to remain calm and bide his time. Joe checked his watch. Seven twenty-five. Time to head into the office.

CHAPTER TWO

18:04hrs

The ten miles from the factory to junction ten of the M25 had taken him a little over fifteen minutes. It had taken a further fifteen to traverse the slip road off the A3 and onto the motorway. The M25 was, in Joe's opinion, nothing more than a glorified carpark.

Joe sighed. God, he hated the M25.

Tuesday 02nd January 2002

"You know if we worked in Scotland we'd be on holiday today for Hogmanay." Joe talked quietly out of the corner of his mouth as he surveyed the room then looked at his friend stood next to him, a distant look on his face. "Sometimes I wake up in the mornings and think I would like the paint to stay pink."

"Yes." Came the one word whispered answer before Howard turned slightly towards Joe. "Pink?" The distant look was replaced by a quizzical one. "What do you mean pink paint? What pink paint?"

"Forget the paint. What's on your mind?"

"What?" Howard Morris fully turned to face his oldest and closest friend. "What are we talking about?"

"I asked what was on your mind. You look distracted." Joe knew Howard better than anyone else. The two men were twenty-eight, twelve and six weeks, respectively, away from their twenty ninth birthdays. They had known each other for almost twenty years having met at school when Howards parents had moved to Dundee from Glasgow in nineteen eighty-one. They had stuck together since, going to the same secondary school, the same sixth form college, the same university and finally getting jobs with the same firm, Guildford Engineering Technology and Aerodynamic Systems, where they were stood now, in the boardroom. They were waiting for a meeting with about fifteen other employees, all were milling around whispering trying to guess what it was about.

"This meeting." whispered Howard. "I think I know what it's about." His voice barely audible above the hissing throng of muffled conversations. He walked slowly to an empty corner of the room and surreptitiously beckoned for Joe to follow him.

"Well?" Asked Joe as he arrived next to his friend again.

"Think about it. GETAS is going places, and going places fast. Everyone in this room has invested in the business and owns shares in the business. Right? Which means it's something big. I saw old man Thompson in the building earlier so I'd say he's going to chair the meeting for a change. I don't think old man Thompson is the man to take the business any further forward and he knows that so he's wanting to sell. He needs our nod to sell up."

"What?" It was Joe's turn to look distant.

"You said it yourself. The company needs a massive injection of cash. The last three years we've not really done anything except tread water. Your new engine design is good to go but needs financing to get it off the ground, no pun intended. Old man Thompson has finally admitted that he's taken the company as far as it can go and decided to sell up. It's the only thing that makes sense." Howard scanned the room looking at fifteen other nervous faces all engaged in frantic nervous conversations. He looked back at Joe. "Your tie's not straight."

Joe absent mindedly straightened his tie. "I suppose it makes sense. The only question is to whom will he sell? BAE?"

"No, BAE would be the last company he'd sell to. Remember Thompson used to work for BAE before he set up GETAS and always complained about how impersonal the place was, and how entrenched in red tape it is. For all of his faults he's kept this place friendly, like a family."

"Ok, then who?" Asked Joe. He too had started to notice all of the nervous faces. The sideways glances, the shuffling of feet, the unconscious playing with ties and earrings, the adjustment of hair and glasses.

Howard shuffled so he could see the rest of the room and spoke out of the corner of his mouth. "It'll be UAE."

"The United Arab Emirates?" Joe's eyebrows pinched together. Joe knew who Howard was actually talking about and was taken aback for the second time in as many minutes.

"UK Aeronautical Engineering."

Joe exhaled sharply. "I know who UAE are. But you really think so? Seriously?" He scanned the nervous faces in the room. "What would UAE get out of the deal?"

Howard replied with two words.

"Your engine."

The room around them stopped and became devoid of noise, every pair of eyes turned to look at the two men in the corner of the room. Joe's last words spoken a little louder than he'd expected.

Howard grinned and looked back at the expectant faces. "New girlfriend." He said as way of deflection to the expectant crowd.

The room paused for a few seconds as it collectively digested the snippet of information then as one they returned to their hushed conversations.

Joe blushed slightly.

"I'm glad everyone thinks my personal life is of such interest." Howard joked. "And yes I'm serious. Think about it. Who's the Commercial Director. At UAE?"

"John McDonald."

"Right. He used to work here when it was McAllister Aeronautics. He left about seven years ago to take a senior sales role at UAE. Rumours are Thompson and McDonald remained close friends. Who would be the ideal person to negotiate a deal between UAE and GETAS?" Howard waited for the penny to drop.

"Are you saying Thompson engineered McDonald leaving so John could sow the seeds of a buy out?" Joe scratched his head somewhat unconvinced.

Howard nodded. "Basically, yes. Thompson gets an inflated pay off and John gets what he wants. A directorship."

"He's already a director." said Joe.

"Only in job title. This would give him an actual seat on the board."

"It's a stretch." Joe nervously chewed his bottom lip and adjusted his tie again.

"Ten quid says I'm right." He proffered a hand.

"You're on." Joe accepted Howards hand and shook it.

"Well, we'll soon find out." Howard pointed to the boardroom door. A grey-haired but impeccably dressed man entered the room closely followed by a second who was slightly overweight and balding with his shirt coming untucked at the front and his tie not straight in his collar. The second man was wearing a tailored three-piece suit that appeared to have been tailored for him when he was a stone or so lighter.

"John McDonald." whispered Joe, mouth open wide. "Christ he's let himself go a bit."

"Yeah, rumours are his wife left him, caught him in bed with his secretary. Looks like he's been having a little trouble looking after himself since. What do you think? Seventeen, eighteen stone."

The boardroom slowly became quiet as the last two men to enter the room took the two seats at the head of the large oval table, the remaining chairs quickly filled with a frenzy of excitement.

"Have to be honest." Howard grinned.

"Hmm, what?"

"I saw John in old man Thompson's office about an hour ago just after I got in."

"Twat!" Joe laughed.

"Right then." Adam Thompson stared in Joe's general

direction before continuing. "If we are all ready, then we'll get started." The grey haired man stroked his beard with his left hand as he opened a black note pad in front of him then took a sip from a glass of water. "As you all know I helped set up McAllister Aeronautics with Iain McAllister in nineteen sixty-eight. When Iain retired in eighty-four we rebranded as Guildford Engineering Technology and Aerodynamic Systems. Since then we've gone from strength to strength, increasing our market share and profitability year on year. But I'll be honest, I've taken this ship as far as I can and I feel that we need another hand at the wheel so to speak. I think it would be in the company's best interest to merge with a larger more forward thinking force. So to that end I approached UK Aeronautical Engineering with the basis of an offer. Over the past six months the lawyers have been thrashing things about and I believe what we have agreed is a good deal, a good deal for all of us.

"I still hold sixty percent of the stock in the company so technically I can force this through, however I thought it would be only fair to hear any thoughts and comments from you all before we sign anything. Some of you may know the man sat on my left." Adam gestured to his left. "This is John McDonald. Commercial Director at UAE. He worked at McAllister and GETAS during the rebranding and moved to UAE in ninety four. He will be looking after the merger to help ensure as smooth a transition as possible. On completion of the merger John will take up his role as Commercial Director of the engineering division and one of you will take up the role as Commercial Director of the aeronautical division."

How leaned back and grinned like a Cheshire cat. "Looks like you owe me a tenner."

"Umm." A voice broke the silence. "Err, how does this, um, will this affect us exactly?"

All eyes turned to Peter Jones.

"I was just wondering?"

"I'll let John explain what will be happening over the next three months, as I'm pretty sure all of you will have no qualms about the deal that has been brokered." Adam sat back in his chair and took another sip of water.

John thanked Adam before he addressed the room. "Over the next four weeks everyone will have a series of meetings with myself and HR to discuss how the transition will work, how it will affect your departments, projects, work load and ultimately your role within the organisation.

"The following four weeks will be a feasibility study on this building and whether we move everyone lock stock over to the UAE building across town or split the business in two having one division here and the other at the UAE building.

"The last four or five weeks we shall get everything moved. Offices, factory space, spares, servers, people, the lot and week thirteen will be an enforced shut down for both sites. All employees will get a weeks' paid holiday that should fall around Easter. The sixteen people in the room here will get their share options and be taken on a three-day team building exercise with the operational team leaders from UAE." John surveyed the room, waiting for the inevitable question, but who would be the one to ask it?

"Transition? You mean redundancy, right?"

And there it was. John smiled to himself. "Maybe. It is possible that there may be duplication of roles within the two companies that the best candidate will be selected and the other person would be offered another role or a redundancy payment. There will need to be a restructure. Look the merger will mean the creation of two divisions, an engineering and an aeronautical division. The two divisions will need manning, need managing by existing employees from both firms wherever possible. The projections we have looked at over the coming five years, should we merge, would mean that the work load of both divisions would increase by sixty-three percent and forty-two percent respectively. They are big numbers people."

"And if we want to take our share option now?" Another voice asked.

"You are contracted to give three to six months' notice

depending on your role. If you wish you may hand in your notice but that would mean foregoing the possibility of redundancy, should we even be considering it. As for your share option your contract states that." John looked down pulling a pair of glasses down off his forehead as he read. "should an employee with shares in GETAS resign after the prospect of a merger has been made, said merger be in progress and up to one year after completion of said merger the employee would forfeit eighty percent of the value of the shares they have in the company and said shares would be worth twenty pence in the pound." John looked up from the piece of paper in front of him. "Basically Mr Phillips, we have valued GETAS at one hundred and eight seven million pounds. Should you resign now your one and a half percent stake would reduce from two point eight million to just over half a million. So the choice is yours."

"Let's have a show of hands. All those in favour?" Adam Thompson raised his hand while John McDonald watched faces and reactions.

Howard and Joe raised their hands without hesitation, both men had clauses in their contracts relating to intellectual property that meant even if the whole deal went south they could walk with the designs of Joe's new engine and still be set up for life.

One by one other hands raised until all hands were up. Some happy but some feeling that they had no choice but to go with the flow and hope for the best.

"Look on the bright side Tristan. Howard said, hand still in the air. "At least one of us will have a job at the end of all of this. When they announce who will take over as commercial director of the aeronautical division." All heads swivelled to look at Howard. "Just saying." He concluded matter of factly.

A light seemed to switch on in everyone's head, one by one heads turned, looking from side to side, weighing each other up, trying to decide who that one person might be. Would it be them? Would it be someone that they got on with? Would it be someone who hated them, that wanted them out?

There was one man in the room, other than Adam Thompson and John McDonald who was not having those thoughts.

Howard Morris.

He had got wind of the deal almost four months ago and had negotiated a deal with John's boss. The Commercial Director's role was his. He had a copy of the contract in his jacket pocket already signed.

CHAPTER THREE

18:23hrs

Joe accelerated, jerked the steering wheel to the right and jumped into the outside lane in a small gap in front of a small Peugeot. A loud thud emanated from the back of the car. Joe looked into his rear-view mirror ignoring the sound. You snooze you lose he said in his head. The lane he'd just joined slowed and the car he'd been sat in front of in the middle lane under took him. That always happened to him. He sat in a lane and it moved the slowest, as soon as he joined another, that lane moved slowest.

Tuesday 05th April 2016

"Why did we drive?" Joe's foot twitched just above the accelerator pedal as he tried to massage some feeling back into his legs.

"It was your idea." Howard sounded as irritated as his friend sat next to him.

"If I suggest it again, shoot me." Joe cleared his throat. "We should have taken the train up last night. The A90 is never usually like this even on match day."

"You do know we're playing Celtic today?" Howards question was rhetorically and the two men knew it. It was Howards way of trying to be funny.

"You're not funny. You do know that don't you." Joe grinned.

Howard looked out of the passenger window trying to stifle a laugh. "Where are we meeting the Big Mac?"

"He said he'd meet us in the Legends Lounge for a few

drinks before we find our seats." Joe glanced at Howard a broad grin on his face. "And you'd better not call John Big Mac to his face. He is our boss after all." He shook his head and turned his attention back to the road taking the B960. He needed to remember where he was supposed to park. "Why did you ask that prick to come to the game with us today? You know how much I hate that fat smelly knob."

"Yes I know, you don't think I like him do you? But we do need to know how the negotiations are going with BAE and when he envisages that he'll want us to start the simulated and real time demonstrations. Besides we need to do it away from the office with a few beers in him. It'll loosen his lips." Howard took a breath. "Look we need to know how much time we have to get the inverter issue sorted. Hopefully we can get it sorted, that we won't have to tell anyone and there won't have been an inverter issue. If you know what I mean?"

"Fine. But did we have to do it here and ruin a good weekend away from the wife and err... what's the name of your current lady friend?" said Joe fishing.

Howard paused for a fraction of a second and glanced out of the corner of his eyes at Joe. "Lady friend? What lady friend?"

Joe chuckled. The split second pause and glance hadn't gone unnoticed. Besides Joe knew Howard almost as well as he knew himself and he could always tell when he was hiding something. "Oh come on Howard don't play coy with me. I know there's someone in your life at the moment. At that early stage of the relationship." Joe swung left onto Sandeman Road and right into Dens Park stadium carpark, the benefits of having parents working at the stadium. They never used their space on match day which meant he could.

Forty-five minutes later the two men were walking back towards Dens Park after having two quick pints in the Athletic Bar.

"So how long before we have to meet up with the Big Mac? Will he already be inside waiting for us?"

Howard checked his watch. "He should already be inside

waiting for us."

"Don't think I've forgotten about the conversation we started in the car. So tell me what is her name?" Joe asked. He looked down and brushed a fly off his dark navy football shirt. "How long have you been seeing each other? Where did you meet?" Joe looked up. "Well?"

Howard tried to deflect. He didn't want to answer any of those questions as he didn't want Joe to know what was going on. He thought he'd been so meticulous in covering his tracks and not saying anything that would give the game away about his new relationship. "How did you know? I've not said anything about any new ladies in my life." Howard didn't know what to say, he'd not prepared any cover stories as he'd not thought that he'd need them.

"Oh come on Howard I can read you like a book." It was nice to see Howard squirm for once. He was normally so cool and calm even under the most severe pressure. "Must be serious if you're reacting like this."

"Like what. I'm not acting like anything."

"You're all flustered and you're blushing." Joe nudged his friend in the ribs. "Come on. Dish the dirt." Independent

"No." Came the curt reply.

"Come on Howard. It's not like you not to kiss and tell."

"It's none of your business."

"Chill Howard. I'm just pulling your leg. If you don't want to talk about it, you don't have to. I'm just saying it's not like you. You're normally the first to brag about your conquests." Joe looked to his side. Howard wasn't there. Joe turned. His friend was stood several paces behind him. The look on Howards face was different than normal. Could it be? "Do you think this new lady of yours could be the one?"

Howard stumbled over his words as he tried to work out what to say, his face began to flush.

"You're in love!" The awe audible in Joe's voice. "I don't believe it. Howard Morris in love. Whatever next hey? You don't think Dundee could actually beat Celtic do you?"

Howard jumped at the opportunity not talk about his love life. It was complicated and he definitely didn't want Joe finding out any specifics as it would make the situation even more complicated. "Dundee beat Celtic, not a chance in hell. Dundee couldn't even get a draw against us, you're not in the same league."

"I think you're the deluded one. Celtic aren't having that good a run at the moment. You're 6th in the league, one place above us." Joe knew that Howard was doing whatever he could to keep the talk away from his personal life and Joe decided to leave it. In reality Howard wouldn't be able to keep it quiet for long anyway.

"Afternoon gentlemen." John McDonald appeared to Joe's right.

"John. I thought you'd be inside already." Said Howard as he shook the man's hand.

"Hi John, good journey up?" Asked Joe shaking the man's hand himself. Joe discreetly wiped his right hand on his jeans after he let go. That man just seemed to constantly sweat from everywhere. It was disgusting.

"Not bad, I flew up Friday night. It's so much easier than driving or coming up by train." John replied.

"Tell me about it." Howard shot a glance at his friend.

John turned and the three men strode off together towards Dens Park.

❖

Three hours later the three men stood together outside the Troll Inn on Arklay Street. John a little more unsteady on his feet that Joe and Howard. All three men had consumed an amount of alcohol that was in excess of what they would normally consume in a week in a vain macho effort to out drink and impress the other two.

Joe paused outside the front door hand resting on the handle. "Are we going in for one before we head home?"

"I hope so as our cars a mile away." Howard laughed, the

statement wasn't funny but the alcohol he'd consumed had gone to his head and all three men were feeling giddy.

John started to laugh, Joe shook his head and lead the way into the pub and on to the bar.

"Three pints of Tennets and three chasers." Joe recovered his wallet from his back pocket on the third attempt.

"So?" John scanned the small room, identified an empty table way from the bar, walked over and sat. John looked up as Howard walked over. "Why?"

"Why what?" Joe placed a tray with six drinks down on the table in between the two seated men. He sat and took a sip from his pint. "Why what?" he repeated.

"Why today?" John asked. "It was nice to come north of the border again and watch a decent football match for a change, and I know you guys do this quite often but why ask me?" John took a large mouthful of beer and watched Howard shift uncomfortably in his seat.

"Well, we err... thought it would be nice. We've been working together for ten years and apart from the obligatory company Christmas party we never socialise."

"Plus we had another motive." The words came out of Joe's mouth before he realised what he was saying.

Howard stepped in. "We wanted to get more involved with the negotiations, be there to answer any technical questions that get asked and we were hoping to sit in and watch you at work on the next round of BAE talks." Howard paused to take a drink. "How are they going by the way? Any closer to getting a signature on a contract?"

"God no. Terry, their Sub Contracts Procurement Manager, is a useless tool. He's insisting that lead time on manufacturing should be sixty weeks."

Howard spat out his drink chocking. "Sixty weeks to manufacture a jet engine for a fighter aircraft? On what planet is he living? Doesn't he know that it'll take almost double that, around one hundred and ten weeks and that's once we have the final specs agreed." He paused and took a gulp of his beer. "How's that going, are we going to have to do any redesigns so it fits in the fuselage?"

"Who knows, possibly. You know what? It might be a good idea if the two of you sit in with me on Thursday when BAE come in next. It'll be nice to have someone in the room who knows what their talking about." John laughed, "other than just me." He looked around the room again, stood slightly uncertainly and staggered off towards the gents.

Howard grinned at the retreating figure. "Fucking pretentious twat. Someone other than him that knows what they're talking about. He hasn't got a fucking clue what he's talking about."

"The problem is that he knows a little bit. And people that know a little are more dangerous than those that know nothing. A little information is worse than none at all. They try and fill in the gaps themselves and make all kinds of assumptions. Usually the wrong ones."

Howard gulped down the remainder of his pint. "It's time to get the hell out of dodge."

Joe shook his head. "No. We'll have to have another then we can head off." He finished his drink and stood. "Oh, looks like John beat us to the bar."

"I thought he was going to the gents."

"Obviously not. Looks like he's bought chasers."

"Here we go fellas, one for the road." John placed the drinks on the small table. "A wee dram to warm the cockles. Right, second time lucky on the gents and I expect my whiskey to still be there when I get back." John pointed lazily at his drink then staggered off for a second time in as many minutes.

Joe and Howard watched John this time to make sure that he actually made it into the gents before they started talking.

"Right then we have nothing to worry about. We have three days to sort out the invertor cosine and if we can't we'll have to see if we can stall the negotiations somehow now that we're going to be sitting in on Thursday." Howard took a deep breath. "Happy?"

"Yes I suppose so, but not with the football result. It'll be Nil nil. Our defence is solid, we proved that last month with a scoreless draw at Celtic Park but our attack lacks drive and finesse. I was really hoping that it'd be Dundee's day."

Howard raised his right eyebrow "Really?" He asked.

"You live in hope. Don't you?"

"What? About the football or the invertor cosine?"

"Both. If Dundee don't start scoring goals they'll stay on the foot of the table and get relegated back to the Championship, dad will be turning in his grave if he could see how his club's being run."

"You'd better hope St Johnstone beat Kilmarnock on Saturday so you've got a chance of catching them."

"St Johnston are chasing a top four finish and a Europa League place, they'll destroy Kilmarnock." Joe took a mouthful of the pint he didn't really want. His stomach already felt bloated and drinking another pint wouldn't help. "Are we still seeing your mum before we drive back to Guildford tomorrow?"

"Yes. I spoke to the home yesterday and they said she's been doing better over the past few weeks. Hopefully she'll remember who I am this time and not think that I'm my dad and spend ten minutes shouting at me and calling me all the names under the sun and then try and get into my pants." Howard shook his head. "That was disturbing."

"I'm sure it wasn't that bad." said Joe.

Howard gave his friend a long hard stare. "You weren't there. Believe me, it was."

A pregnant pause hung in the air, neither man know what to say next.

John appeared at the table apparently out of nowhere and solved that problem. "What are you two love birds talking about?" He asked.

CHAPTER FOUR

18:40hrs

Two miles to junction sixteen. Two miles left on the M25. The traffic seemed to have gotten a little heavier again now he was getting closer to the junction and exit from the motorway. Joe began to feel the weight of what he'd done bear down on his shoulders. Had it only been an hour or so ago since it happened? Had he really done the right thing? Questions started to flood his mind. He played the events of the past few months over in his mind. The events that had led to this point in time. Friday the twenty third of March two thousand and eighteen. He needed to try and make sense of what had happened. What had happened? Every time he tried to piece things together and answer his own questions it made no sense and elicited more questions. Lots of questions, none of which he seemed to have answers for. Answers, he desperately needed answers. Well, he'd have at least another seven or eight hours to mull things over and in that time, he'd hopefully come up with some.

Sunday 27th November 1988

It was early, the sun barely peaking over the grey buildings that lined the streets of the old Scottish town as Joe pushed the old grey steel framed door open and walked in to the British Transport Police Station on Union Street closely trailed by his parents. His best friend was there, sat next to his mother on two of the old grey plastic chairs bolted to the floor in the dull grey reception area. Bolted to the floor, why? Who'd want to steal such crappy old chairs? Margaret and Trevor Anderson walked over to Carol Gunn who raised out of her chair and three adults walked over to the opposite corner of the room where they began to talk in animated whispers, tears welled in Carol's eyes.

Joe sat next to his friend, both sixteen years old. They sat for a minute and silently stared forward into the dull grey space of the waiting room. Joe broke the silence between them noting that he and Howard were wearing the same light blue adidas tracksuit with the three dark blue stripes down the arms and legs.

"Nice tracksuit?"

"Mum's talking about changing her name." Howard replied, either oblivious to Joe's observation or choosing to ignore it. "She says this is the final straw, that she doesn't want to be associated with dad anymore."

"Is she?" Joe looked sideways at his friend. "Does she not like the name Carol?" He asked trying to take the sullen look from Howard's face.

Howard laughed. He couldn't contain himself. It was that or burst into tears. The laughter brought disapproving looks from the three parents on the other side of the room.

"Twat." Said Howard. "You'll get me into trouble. I mean her surname, she wants to change it back to her maiden name." A sigh. "If she does, I think I will too."

"Howard Morris has a certain ring to it don't you think? It could be worse." Joe's gaze moved down to his battered old trainers as he thought what to say next. This was new for the two of them, they never had trouble talking about anything. It got them into trouble continuously at school. "So what happened?"

Howard closed his eyes and sighed. The reality of what had happened had not sunk in. His mum and the police officer he'd spoken to had said he needed to articulate his feelings and get things out in order to be able to start dealing with things, help him grieve and ultimately help him move on. "What do you know?"

"Not much, mum and dad haven't told me anything, and they're always whispering." He motioned to the whispering parents in the corner. "so I've not overheard much either."

"Dad's dead." Howard blurted it out a little louder than he had wanted too which brought more scowls from his mum. "The police say they found him hanging close to the south end of the Tay Rail Bridge over the river." He stared at his mum for a long moment wondering how she would act over the coming weeks, he didn't know so there was no real point speculating. He sighed, took a deep breath and continued. "Mum and dad had a fight again last night about dad's drinking and the fact that he's not helping out with the bills, that he hasn't got a job and that he's not looking for one or will never get one if he does start looking because of his drinking. It started as most Saturday nights have started over the past year or more." Howard's breathing started to come faster, became more shallow as he tried to compose and settle himself. "Then dad snapped, out of nowhere he just snapped. Normally he'd grumble and mumble and then skulk off down the pub but not yesterday. Yesterday he snapped. He lashed out and hit my mum, threw her half way across the lounge. He stood over her shouting, blaming her for him hitting her, said she'd driven him to it. Then he just left. Calm as you like, just walked out the front door. Mum sent me to my room and spent the rest of the evening crying. This morning we got up and had breakfast mostly in silence then mum told me that dad had gone away for a few weeks with the possibility of work. I knew it wasn't true and when the police arrived at the door they just confirmed it." Howard rubbed his eyes trying to remove the stinging behind them. What he hadn't told Joe was that he had spent most of the night awake, crying. Howard hadn't really known why he had cried, he wasn't sad just angry, very angry.

Joe looked over at Howard's mum and noticed the bruise around her left eye. He hadn't noticed it before, but the makeup Carol had applied hadn't quite covered all of the bruise, it was obvious unless you knew what you were looking for.

"About an hour ago we got a visit from two officers and we came here."

"Mum said your dad hasn't been well for the past year or so since he lost his job." Joe's sentence was as much a question as a statement.

"Yeah, my mum said he was an anabolic or something."

Joe scrunched his face up thinking. "Anabolic? Do you mean alcoholic?"

"Yeah that's it. Alcoholic." Howard cleared his throat and continued. "All he did all day was drink, shout and sleep. Mum spent most of the time crying and trying to hide it from me. She thinks I'm stupid."

"I'm sure she was trying to protect you."

Howard looked over at his mum who were stood facing him, a blank look in her eyes. Awkward smiles were exchanged. "He's not even cold yet." He said through gritted teeth.

Carol walked over to the two sixteen-year-old boys. She stood then crouched in front of her seated son. She sniffled and fought back tears. "Howie, I've spoken to Trevor and Margaret and they've agreed that you can stay with them for a while, a few days at most, just until I get things sorted out. Is that ok with you little man?" A forced smile creeped across her face and she place a hand on Howard's shoulder.

Howard reciprocated with a forced smile of his own and nodded. He hated it when his mum called him Howie or little man, like he was five. He leaned forward and hugged his mum, holding her tight. "I want to be there with you mum. You need me there with you. I can help, I'm not five anymore."

"No." Carol's reply was a little sharper than she had wanted but she felt cold and devoid of emotions, her selfish, self-centred and now dead husband had seen to that. She pulled herself back and looked into her sons' eyes. "You're better off out of the house for a week or so, away from all the fuss as I sort things out. I need to work out what's what, what's going to happen next and where we go after this." Carol stood, nodded to herself and took a deep breath. "You'll go with Mr and Mrs Anderson. The police need me to stay a little longer and answer some more questions. I'll drop your things off later when I'm done here. Ok?"

"Ok." What else could Howard say? His voice was flat and emotionless. In that moment Howard felt like he had lost both his father and mother. He felt lost and alone. He wanted, no, he needed to be with his mum at this difficult time. His dad was dead and his mum didn't want him around. I want to go home with you, Howard screamed in his head. He pushed his emotions deep down inside forcing the tears back drinking in the grey surroundings of the police waiting room that matched his growing mood. "Ok." Howard repeated. "Mum, I... I..." he knew it was pointless to argue. "I love you." Howard flung his arms around his mum and hugged her tightly not wanting to let go. Reluctantly he released his grip looked at his mum for a second and turned towards the door as he followed Joe outside.

"Thanks Margaret, Trevor." Called Carol as she forced another smile. She watched as her son left the police station reception area then sat and started to silently cry into her hands as she waited to be called again for further questioning.

CHAPTER FIVE

19:30hrs

Harriet's name popped up on the screen of Joe's phone that was sat in the phone holder in the window lighting up the dark cabin of his car. He pressed a button on the steering wheel to answer the call.

"Hi darling. Where are you?" Harriet's voice echoed around the interior of the car.

"I finished work early so I've decided to head north tonight." Joe could barely conceal his feelings of hatred and betrayal for his wife. His voice sounded sharp and terse.

"Are you ok?"

Joe couldn't decide if it was concern dripping from Harriet's voice or contempt and for the first time he realised that he didn't actually care.

"Fine. Just traffic is bad." Replied Joe paying attention to the road in front of him and not the voice on the other end of the line.

"What's your ETA?"

"Early hours. I'll drop you a message when I arrive so you know I'm safe. Ok?"

"Ok." Harriet replied.

Joe wasn't sure if it was he or Harriet who ended the call; all he knew was that it ended and again he didn't care. This weekend was going to be difficult for a lot of reasons but mainly because he was going to have to play happy families with his wife and his mum.

He was hoping to see Harriet this evening and present the information he had on her in the same way he had with Howard.

Revelling her affair with Howard and then giving her the weekend to move out while he visited his mum ang gave her the good news. Joe was also hoping to have some time to think about his future about what he was going to do next. He wasn't sure if he could continue working at GETAS in light of what happened less than three hours earlier and if Howard decided to stay. He needed to think about his options. The engine designs he was working on were kept in a secure database on a none networked server so if he wanted to take them with him, wherever he decided to go, he'd have to go back in and access all the data from his terminal. And that wouldn't be easy. With all the safety protocols in place the IT team would detect such a large download of data.

Joe took a deep breath. So much to consider. Well, he thought, now was as good a time as any.

Wednesday 25th March 2015

Harriet stood in yet another food court of yet another motorway service station paying for yet another bland meal. This time it was Beaconsfield about eight miles east of High Wycombe. She walked, tray in hand, through the food court and out to find a small table by the small lake behind the main building. She sat in her dark blue pin striped suit, pale pink blouse and blue and brown brogues beneath a glowing orange heating lamp. That seemed to be the story of her life now, jumping from one dull depressive moment to the next. That feeling of being surrounded by people but at the same time being totally alone. Seemingly reaching out for something, getting close and never able to take hold of what she needed.

Harriet knew she should be happier than she was. She had started her new job on Monday as the Director of UK Sales. She was meeting the young man that she had helped hire to take over her old sales area, everything south of Gloucester to Colchester. She would continue to dip her toe in the proverbial waters from time to time but her travelling would be more extensive as she managed her new team. Harriet checked her watch. She had about forty-five minutes before Shontayne arrived and a further fifteen before they had to leave for their meeting at John Radcliffe Hospital in Oxford.

Harriet sat at her small table watching the people in the seating area going about their little lives making whatever difference in the world that they did, oblivious to the world around them, of the wants and desires of those that passed them by and bumped them. Paying little attention to anyone or anything other than themselves, consumed by themselves. Did their lives have any real meaning? Did hers? The philosophical ramblings in her head had started just over thirteen years ago after her miscarriage in two thousand and four. Her and Joe had been trying for a baby since two thousand and two and apart from that one time with the miscarriage they had been unsuccessful.

Their sex life had become more and more regular, less spontaneous and increasingly monotonous, pre-planned to coincide with her ovulating. They were going through the motions and it was getting her down, Joe was becoming distant, working longer hours and the spark had gone from their relationship. She had tried to get it back and she knew Joe was trying but they just didn't seem to have what they once had. Harriet craved the attention, the affection and the love they'd once had. Was it gone? Would it ever return? Nine months ago, she had run into Howard's arms and for the briefest of moments she had felt alive, desired and dare she say, loved. But then the guilt of her actions had hit her like a speeding car hitting a wall. Harriet had avoided Howard as much as she could. She had tried to ensure Joe was with her whenever he was there. She had tried to act natural, nonchalant and relaxed but inside she had been anything but.

"Mrs Anderson."

The voice startled Harriet and ripped her from her thoughts and she looked up into the eyes of the young twenty-seven-year-old man stood to her left. His thin five foot ten inch frame cast a dull grey shadow on the table at which she sat. She looked back at her empty plate in front of her, had she eaten her meal already? Obviously otherwise her plate wouldn't be empty. She drained her mug of coffee and stood extending her hand.

"Mr Vaughn."

"Call me Shonts, please. All my friends do." Came the slightly nervous reply.

"Nervous Mr Vaughn?" Harriet asked with a grin on her face. She watched Shontayne's face as he stood in front of her and tentatively took her hand. His whole demeanour reminded her of her husband when they first met and she had to admit that it kind of turned her on. Was that why she had decided to give him the job over the other prospective candidates? If it was, it was a little late to change her mind now. She'd have to give him a few months to see how he got on and then complete his probationary assessment to see if he was actually suited to the role he had. Shontayne's touch was delicate, his hand soft yet his grip was firm and reassuring. Harriet's heart started to beat slightly faster and she felt herself begin to flush. This was an unexpected twist. Their touch lingered longer than it should, neither one seemingly wanting it to end. Harriet continued to watched the face in front of her trying desperately to read what was going on behind his eyes. She noticed his right eyebrow raise slightly, the corner of his mouth twitched before a broad grin spread across his face. Their eyes locked on one another's. Words that needed to be said remained in their heads and in their throats, trying to push forwards, to be released but inexplicably locked behind self-built facades.

She wasn't sure if she made the first move or if it was Shontayne but their hands locked, fingers entwined as they walked slowly into the service station, through the food court and they disappeared into the disabled toilets.

Fifteen minutes later Shontayne emerged from behind the grey door, hair dishevelled and flies still undone. He ambled slowly to over to the Costa Coffee shop playing with his hair in a vain attempt to make it look presentable.

Several minutes later Harriet emerged from behind the same door looking as fresh as when she walked in. Well, thought Harriet to herself as she followed Shontayne to the coffee bar, that could complicate things a little. She knew why she had done that, for the attention and those few moments of gratification that it had brought her. But she felt guilty, for betraying her husband, yet again. There was something else though. A second layer of guilt. Guilt she had not experienced before. Guilt for another, for betraying Howard. She had only spent that one night with him, had spend the last nine months trying to avoid him but she suddenly yearned for him, for his touch, for his gentle caress. She realised in that moment that she had feelings for her husbands' best friend. Realised that he gave her something that neither this young man that she was now looking at nor her husband could give her. Affection. But it was more than that. He knew what she wanted. Knew when she wanted it. Listened to her when she needed to be listened to. Talked to her like a human being. He didn't patronise her, or belittle her. Didn't bully or degrade her, didn't dismiss what she said because she was a woman. She felt empowered around him. Feelings that she'd once felt from Joe, that she still craved from him but feared that she'd never get again.

Her life was a mess. She could handle Shonts, he was a young man and would put a proverbial notch on his bed post, potentially bragging about it to his friends. Harriet breathed through fingers held over her mouth as she walked forwards thinking. She needed to sort herself out, decide what she wanted from life, stop drifting along and playing games with everyone's feelings. She loved her husband but her feelings for Howard complicated things. Did she love her husband enough to try and make the marriage work or was it Howard she wanted to be with? She needed to make a decision, then stick with that decision, work at making whatever she decided, a success, and try not to mess her future up. She always seemed to do this. Get involved in a serious relationship and then try her hardest to mess it up. She thought she had gotten over it with Joe but here she was again. If she did stay with Joe she needed to convince him that they should move away from Guildford. Away from Howard as she couldn't trust herself not to jump back into his arms should things get difficult again. The big question was, would

Joe move? She knew if she asked Howard he'd have his notice on his boss's desk five minutes after she'd ask him, have his flat on the market five minutes later and be parked outside her house ready to take her wherever she wanted to go five minutes after that.

"What do you want?"

Shontayne's voice cut through the buzz of the food court and pulled Harriet from her thoughts.

"Flat White." Harriet said looking up. "Please." She added with a wavering smile.

Shontayne lead Harriet out into the car park and looked around at the multitude of cars parked in neat little rows like a battalion of soldiers on parade. Harriet pointed to the right as she walked round her new Sales Manager leading him to her company car. "I assume we're taking mine."

"Um, yes?" The questions formed in Shontayne's throat at the same time that it formed in his head. He didn't mean to ask the question but he felt giddy around this strong woman. She excited him, aroused his senses and his sensibility. He wanted to impress her and hoped he'd live up to her expectations of him, whatever they may be. "It makes sense to take one car. Which one's yours?"

Harriet pointed again. "The blue beamer."

"Nice." Shontayne looked over the car coming up in front of him. "A 520i M Sport in Phytonic Blue with twenty-inch alloys."

Harriet looked sideways at the man stood next to her, he suddenly looked so young, drooling over cars, his hair still ruffled from their foray but his shirt, tie, suit and shoes impeccable not like the old perverts she had been having meetings with for the past twenty years. NHS executives leaching over her, spending all their time staring at her breasts, perving and having inappropriate thoughts. She could see it in their eyes. At first, she had loathed it but after a while she had decided to enjoy the attention, use it to her advantage and play their games, plus, it had done wonders for her sales figures. Now she was passing her area to this young man. Harriet didn't think that Mr Vaughn would have any issues, this was still a men's game despite the increasing number of women executives and he had the personality to fit right in. A youthful arrogance that the people he would be meeting would see in themselves so many years before. They would relate to him, wish to still be a young as him, tell misogynistic jokes but he'd get the business and make his sales.

"Shall we?" Harriet asked and forced yet another smile across her face. The forced smile broadened as she watched Shontayne round the car to the passenger seat.

"Something funny Harriet?" He asked over the roof of the metallic blue car that separated them.

"What? Oh, err no Shonts." Harriet opened her door. She had noticed that his flies were still open. She had forty-five minutes or so to decide whether she would tell him or not before they got to their meeting, that was if he didn't notice himself before they arrived.

CHAPTER SIX

20:22hrs

"Life is precocious in a most peculiar way, Sister psychosis don't got a lot to say, she go let it out, she go get it in, she go let it out." Joe realised that he was singing. How long had he been doing that? Well it was a good sign wasn't it? At least it meant he was relaxed. Relaxed might be a bit of a stretch. He was relatively calm given the situation that he found himself in, a situation that he couldn't have predicted and wish he wasn't in. His eyes darting this way and that looking for something but not sure what. His hands gripping the steering wheel tightly in an effort to look normal, to drive smoothly. He needed to actually relax, his movements were jerky and erratic. Feel the music and let it flow through him, use it. He was glad Oasis was playing and not one of Harri's Slipknot CD's. He chuckled under his breath. Imagine trying to stay relaxed and driving to that.

Friday 01st May 1992

Harriet MacIntosh walked into the kitchen taking small steady steps, her left hand sliding slowly across the wall in an effort to steady herself and not to fall over. Her makeup from the night before still half applied but smudged across her face.

James MacIntosh stood by the sink, back to his sister, staring out of the window at the already bright morning wearing nothing but a pair of jeans, the soles of his bare feet enjoying the feel of the cool tiled floor, hands wrapped around a warm coffee mug his palms enjoying the contrast in temperatures. "Morning sis." He said over his shoulder as he inhaled the nutty aroma emanating from the hot brown liquid in his mug.

"Do you have to make so much noise?" Harriet's voice was quiet and hoarse. Her head was a little foggy from the heavy drinking of the night before. How was her brother ok? She had seen him consume at least as much alcohol as she had.

"There's fresh coffee in the pot." James continued to stare out of the window past the fence at the bottom of the garden to the plethora of trees and hills that filled the skyline beyond. "And the noise was mum and dad leaving for work."

"I though you were in Wales at the Valley." Harriet continued her tentative journey through the kitchen heading straight for the coffee machine and caught sight of her reflec tion in the oven door and sighed. God, she looked as bad as she felt. Her makeup was a state and her hair a mess. It looked like she had been sat in her boyfriend Simon's soft top GTI after he'd raced to Lincoln. If that had been the reason for her looking the way she did she wouldn't feel half as bad as she did right now. Harriet adjusted the strap on her white vest top and reached for a mug.

"I completed my flight training on the Hawk Wednesday and start my flight training on the Tornado a week Monday, so I've taken some leave to come home and see my family. I called last week and told you I'd be home, don't you remember?"

Harriet ignored the barbed question with one of her own. "When did you get back?"

"About nine o'clock last night. Don't you remember, I joined you in the six bells at about half past? Gosh your memory is getting bad." James laughed to himself and drained his mug. He finally turned to face his sister and took the three steps to the side counter poured his sister a coffee and refilled his mug.

Harriet took a cautious sip of the hot coffee in her cup and scratched her head symbolically trying to reawaken memories that she knew she'd probably never get back. Start from the start and it might come back to her. "Jane and I went into the Six Bells about four celebrating finishing our last A level exams. We started playing pool but it gets a bit fuzzy around seven, eight o'clock."

James placed his mug on the side next to the sink, he needed to go for a run, stay in a routine he had spent the last two years getting into. If he didn't go for one this morning he knew he'd slip into the *"I'll do it tomorrow"* routine, where he'd say to himself that he'd run tomorrow but tomorrow would come and he'd say he'd run tomorrow and so on and so on. James checked his watch, seven-twenty. "So, what happened to old lover boy Simon?"

"What do you mean?" Harriet asked perplexed.

"Well, when I last spoke to you, you and he were, how did you put it? Oh yeah, tight. But last night no Simon and you spent a lot of time trying to find Carl Parkin's tonsils."

Harriet almost choked on her coffee, she wiped the dribbles of coffee from the corners of her mouth. "Carl Parkin!" She coughed. "You're joking? Parky!" Harriet felt physically sick. "Oh God no, that guy's a creep. He's fat and ugly and about four foot tall."

"He's five six and he's not fat." James stared at his sister with his dark brown eyes. Sometimes she could be a horrible person.

"What was he doing there? He never goes to the Six Bells, not since he split up with Emma."

James turned back to stare out of the kitchen window and slowly shook his head. "I called Parky to arrange to meet me at the Six Bells. He got there just after me, we'd barely finished our first pint and you were all over him like a rash. Around eleven I caught him trying to convince you to go home with him, which, had I not stepped in would probably have happened. You didn't look like you were in any sort of state to be going off with him so, I dragged you home and threw you into bed." James shrugged. "I assumed that you and Simon had split up and that you and Carl were an item, until I got a call about twenty minutes after I got you home." James scratched the back of his head. "Carl was apologising for what he'd done, begged me to say sorry to you and not to say anything to Simon as he didn't want to get his head kicked in." James saw the horrified face of his sister reflected in the kitchen window. “So?” He asked, voice still calm. “What the fuck is going on with you?” James paused. “And I want an abridged version as I’m going for a run in five minutes.”

“Simon and I are fine, at least I hope we still are. He has an exam this morning and was studying last night. My last exam was yesterday so I was celebrating. I got drunk, Carl was there and he’s been trying to get me to go out with him for years and I…” What? What had she done? Why? Why had she done it? Two good questions. Two questions she had no answers to. “I don’t know.” She continued, she truly didn’t. “I was drunk. I can’t remember what I was thinking and why I don’t know why I did what I did.” Shit she thought. “What have I done?” Harriet hung her head in shame. What if Simon found out? Would he still want to be with her? Could he ever trust her? Could she ever trust herself ever again? Her head filled with questions she could not begin to answer. “What if Simon finds out?”

“If?” Asked James. The question was rhetorical. “There is no if. Hopton’s too small a village, everyone knows everyone, and word gets around. It gets around fast. I give it a day, two at the most before someone says something.”

“But what do I tell Simon?”

“The truth.” Two words, that’s all James really needed to say but he continued anyway. If felt that Harriet needed more. “Don’t blame Carl. This was your doing and you need to take responsibility for your actions.” James walked out of the kitchen stopping to give his little sister a hug and a kiss on his forehead. “It’ll be alright. Simon will forgive you or he won’t but the world will keep turning and life will go on.” James walked out of the kitchen to go get ready for his run. “Have a good one sis’,” he called over his shoulder, “and do the right thing.”

The right thing. What did that even mean? Harriet needed a shower but she also needed to make some calls. She supposed Simon would be a good start but he had an exam. Maybe she’d meet him at school outside the exam hall, they could go for a drink and talk about what had happened the night before. Her head was beginning to clear and she walked around her parent's kitchen considering what she wanted for breakfast. Toast would be the best option and a glass of water. Harriet spotted what looked like a phone on the kitchen counter. What was that? A mobile? It looked like the new Nokia 101. Was that James'? Harriet walked to the bottom of the stairs. "James!" Called Harriet up the stairs. "Is this yours?"

"Is what mine?" James' voice proceeded him as he jogged down the stairs in his shorts, t-shirt and running shoes. "Oh that, yes"

Harriet waved the large handset from side to side. "Can I use it?"

"No. Do you know how much it costs to make a call from that. It's for emergencies."

"Like arranging to go for a drink with Parky."

"Funny, put the phone down and use the land line." James continued to stretch. "I'm going to go for a run, put down the phone." He repeated then left the house.

Harriet thought about it for several seconds then placed the phone gently down on the surface. She walked into the hall and picked up the receiver of the home phone and dialled her best friend Claire Robertson. "Hi Claire."

"Hi slut." Claire laughed. "What were you thinking?" The question came around chuckles. "To cheat on Simon with Carl Parkin of all people. Why?" She asked again. "You can be so stupid at times. So stupid."

"What's that supposed to mean?" Harriet was not in the mood for this. What she needed right now was some support and help, not scorn and dissention especially from her best friend. "Come on, there's no need for that."

Claire continued to laugh. "What? It's not as if you haven't done this sort of thing before. Come on girl, you've got form." Claire stopped laughing, her voice became serious and stern. "I love you girl, but you have to start taking responsibility for your actions. Remember Timmy Jones, Bobby Lemke, Harry Clarke, need I go on? You were dating all of them and cheated on all of them. Why do you do it Harri, why? Do you enjoy the pain you inflict on others? Or is it darker than that, self-inflicted pain and distress you enjoy? I just don't understand you at times."

"It was the drink, no other reason or dark meanings behind it. I drank too much, that's it." Harriet's voice sounded agitated.

"What will you do?" Claire asked. "Do you want me to come over?"

"No, fuck it, I'll come over to you. It's on the way to school. I'll speak to Simon after his exam. Besides, I need a shower." Harriet slowly replaced the receiver in its cradle and stood looking down at the phone for several minutes. No thoughts entered her head during this time. She just stood breathing slowly. She was pulled out of her black hole of a head by the sound of a dog barking outside, her eyes darted around the room in which she stood, almost alien to her. Was this really her home, was this where she wanted to be? The simple answer was no. She wanted to be as far away from this place as possible. In four months, she would be at university in Guildford, one hundred and eighty miles away from this inbred shithole she had called home. A shithole she hoped she'd never have to come back to.

CHAPTER SEVEN

20:45hrs

His hands ached. He was still gripping the steering wheel too tightly, but Joe was angry. His thoughts over the past fifteen minutes had drifted on to the night he'd taken Harriet out for a meal, a romantic night out just the two of them. The night he'd asked the question that had been on his mind for months before. Was Harriet having an affair? She had reacted badly as he'd expected, shouting, asking him how could he even think that she would, but then she had paused and calmly taken a sip of her wine before she'd over reacted again and stormed off. It had been at that point he'd known, known for sure. His grip tightened again.

Relax Joe. Relax. After tonight he knew it didn't matter anymore as it could never happen again.

Joe passed junction eight for the A40. Oxford. It had been almost ten years since he'd last been to oxford. Harriet and he had gone for their tenth wedding anniversary back in 2009 when things had still been good between them. A city so close to them that neither had visited until that point and one Joe had not visited since.

They'd stayed in a little guesthouse in Woodstock and visited Blenheim Palace. The thoughts distracted Joe temporarily from his journey and allowed him a few moments of peace. The hum of the engine and the occasional thump elicited by a pot hole his only companion.

Saturday 23rd September 2017

"Harri are you ready?" Joe shouted upstairs. He checked his watch again. It was twenty to seven. Why did she do this?

Leave everything to the last minute. Their table reservation was at half past and with the walk into town taking about twenty minutes they would be hard pressed to have time for a drink before the meal. Joe began to pace backwards and forwards then called upstairs again. "How long will you be?" Nothing. "Are you nearly ready?"

"Nearly darling." Came the reply.

Nearly, what that really meant was she'd be at least another ten to fifteen minutes. Joe exhaled and rolled his eyes. Sod it. He stormed into the kitchen, opened the fridge and grabbed a beer. Breaking the seal, he took two large gulps then belched loudly. Joe hated feeling like this. Unimportant in his relationship. He had planned the evening perfectly, told Harriet when she needed to be ready, what time they needed to leave the house, where they would be going for a pre-meal drink, when they would be eating and she just seemed to ignore everything, throw his plans out of the window and do whatever she wanted. She always did what she wanted. He'd known that since the moment they'd met and had found it delightful and quirky, it hadn't bothered him, but recently he had begun to resent it. It wound him up and drove him crazy. Joe was sure Harriet wasn't aware just how much it annoyed him as he always acted relaxed, nonchalant and unflustered around her.

Joe checked his watch again.

Quarter to Seven.

He swore under his breath through gritted teeth. Joe gulped down the rest of his beer. He wished she'd be ready on time. Just once. He'd tried telling her they needed to leave half an hour, an hour before they actually did but she was still always late. He grabbed another beer from the fridge and trudged into the lounge, sat feet on the coffee table in front of him. Singing drifted down the stairs. A sure sign Harriet was relaxed and in no rush to be ready. Joe continued to mutter and seethe under his breath resigning himself to the fact that they'd not be leaving the house before seven which meant they'd have to rush and wouldn't have time for a drink before the meal.

The TV flickered to life and Joe sat changing channels, scrolling up from one to the next not registering what was on. Random images appeared and as quickly disappeared.

A third beer followed his second. Joe was contemplating a fourth when a strange feeling washed over him causing him to switch off the TV and he turned in his chair to look over his shoulder. Harriet had appeared in the lounge doorway. He gazed at the beautiful woman standing behind him. The little black dress hugged her slender curvaceous figure in all the right places. Despite everything that he was feeling, everything that was happening between them he still felt an overwhelming sensation of love for his wife whenever he saw her.

"Feet."

And just like that the moment was lost.

Joe exhaled sharply, stood and checked his watch. Almost ten past seven. "Are you ready? We're going to have to get a move on if we're going to get to the restaurant for half past."

The doorbell rang. Harriet opened the front door and nodded at the man standing there. She turned and faced Joe. "I called a cab an hour and a half ago." With that she dropped her small handbag over her shoulder and followed the taxi driver to his cab.

Joe hustled out of the house, locked the door and rushed to the open door of the taxi waiting at the end of the drive.

"The Ashai?" Asked the driver by way of confirmation of his fare.

"Yes please." Harriet cooed sweetly.

"Why didn't you tell me that you'd booked a cab?" Joe asked as the taxi pulled away.

"And spoil all the fun." Harriet smiled at her husband then switched her attention to the houses and trees flowing past the window of the car.

Spoil the fun?! Spoil the fun! What fun? Where is the fun in keeping secrets and winding people up, people they were supposed to love? Joe began to fume again. Secrets. He wanted to confront her there and then. But it wasn't the right time, but then, when was the right time? If he did confront her and he was wrong she would get offended, over react and start shouting. If he confronted her and he was right she would fain offence, then over react and start shouting. Either way it would be an unpleasant and stressful conversation, one that he didn't particularly want to have but knew he couldn't avoid for much longer.

The taxi ride took just over five minutes to reach the restaurant at which point the couple paid, exited the taxi and walked hand in hand across the road to the Ashai.

They entered the restaurant, waited less than a minute and were shown to their table, a small intermate table for two in the corner of the room.

"This is nice."

Joe couldn't tell if Harriet was being sincere or not, he seemed to have lost his connection he had with her. The connection they'd had since the day they'd met. A sadness gripped him and he forced a smile trying to look happy and interested in the small talk that begun.

"Is everything alright darling?" The soft smile on Harriet's face was replaced by a look of concern, she reached forward and took Joe's hand in hers. "Joe?"

Joe said nothing and continued to stare blankly at the woman sat opposite him. The woman that he was losing, that he was pushing away, an involuntary defence mechanism in a desperate attempt to reduce the pain he was feeling. Was he making the situation worse with his actions?

Probably.

Did he care?

No.

No? Who was he kidding, of course he cared, he was losing the woman he loved, the woman he'd cared for, for over twenty years.

"Joe. What's wrong? You know you can talk to me about anything." Harriet said.

"Can I?" came the questioning reply.

"Of course you can. When have we ever not been able

to talk about anything? To sort things out." Harriet's voice was soft, her gaze loving. "We always talk."

"We do." Joe conceded.

"Is it work? Harriet paused as a waiter brought their drinks to the table and took their food order. Harriet watched the waiter walk away and continued from where she'd left off. "Is it about the new MoD contract for the Mark III engine you're working on?"

Joe looked quizzically at his wife.

"I know if the tests go well at the start of next month then you're about six months away from signing a multi-billion-pound contract and you and Howard will get made for life. It's what you and Howard have been working on since university."

"It is..." Joe's quizzical look intensified.

Harriet could see her husband's mood darken. "Talk to me Joe, talk to me. What's on your mind? If you don't talk to me I can't help."

"How? How do you know about that? I haven't told you what I'm working on. I was planning on telling you tonight. It was going to be a surprise. That was the reason behind tonight." Joe lied but he wanted to find out what Harriet was talking about and if he was being honest with himself he wanted to see her squirm.

"Howard let it slip last week when I saw him." Harriet's words stumbled out of her mouth and her palms became clammy in an instance.

"Last week?" Asked Joe. "You never mentioned that you'd seen Howard." Joe's brow furrowed.

Harriet suddenly became defensive. "I don't have to tell you every time I see someone, besides Howard told me not to say anything as he knew you wanted to tell me. He let it slip and then made me promise not to say anything but I'm worried about you."

Joe looked at his wife. The thoughts in his head were all over the place. Was she telling the truth or was she lying? Was it all in his head? There was only one way to find out, he has to ask her the question. He had to ask his wife if she was having an affair, an affair with his best friend and see how she reacted. He really hoped it wasn't true.

"Joe I'm worried."

"Are you? Are you really? Or are you just trying to cover up your improprieties with feigned concern or me?" Joe's anger boiled up inside him and spilled out in his words.

"What's that supposed to mean? Improprieties? What improprieties? What are you talking about?" Harriet leaned forward scowling at her husband.

"You know exactly what I'm talking about." Contempt dripped from Joe's voice. "You and Howard."

"What about me and Howard?" Harriet's voice seemed to raise almost an octave as she spoke.

"Oh! come on, I'm not stupid. I've seen the way you look at each other. The way you pretend not to be interested whenever I talk about him. I hear the excitement in your voice when you talk about him." He caught his breath. "I've seen the text messages you send each other, all flirtatious. The clandestine meetings that you never seem to tell me about."

"You're being ridiculous." Harriet spat the words out.

"Am I?" Joe sat back in his chair staring forward into Harriet's eyes.

"Yes you're imagining things that aren't there." Harriet's eyes glanced down at her phone on the table next to her drink. She wanted to down the rum and coke but that would make her look guilty. Besides Harriet wasn't sure she would be able to keep hold of the glass, her hands were that sweaty.

Joe saw Harriet's gaze drop and in that split second he knew he was right. He knew his fears had been realised. Harriet and Howard were having an affair. But how long had it been going on for? When had it started? Why had it started? So many unanswered questions jumped around Joe's head.

The couple sat staring at each other, neither one wanting to continue the conversation for fear of where it might lead.

Joe reached forward in an attempt to grab Harriet's phone

but she was too fast for him, whipping it off the table and into her lap.

"Really?" Asked Harriet, head tilted to one side.

"So, what are you hiding." Joe brushed the whiskers of his close cropped beard as he leaned back in his chair. He looked at his wife and took a sip from his drink.

"Nothing."

"So let me have the phone." Joe extended his left hand out across the table.

"Why?"

"If you have nothing to hide then why won't you let me have your phone?" Joe asked.

Harriet scooped up her hand bag from off the back of her chair and deposited the phone inside. "No."

"Tell me the truth, what's going on between the two of you?"

"Nothing." Harriet protested. She tried to covertly move her hand bag further away from Joe.

"Tell me, I know. I'm not stupid." Joe took another sip of his drink his throat had become dry. "I just want to hear it from you. Just tell me, admit it."

"Admit what? That I bumped into Howard a few times and forgot to tell you, it's no big deal. Ha! I'd say the two of you have been bumping into each other, a lot. I think you're having the affair, how long has that been going on for hey?"

"An affair?" Joe asked. "Where did that come from? I never said anything about an affair." He stared intensely into Harriet's eyes. And in that second he knew it all. "I just want to hear you say it." His voice now overly calm and quiet.

"You're accusing me of having an affair." Harriet's mind raced. How? She had been so careful. She couldn't admit to it, not here, not now. "How dare you!" She stood. Grabbed her scarf and scooped up her handbag. "How dare you!" And with that she stormed out of the restaurant.

Joe screwed up his eyes, fists clenched on the table exasperated. Why had he pushed it? Why had he asked her those questions? Guilt washed over him for a moment before it turned to rage.

He'd been right. She had been having, was probably still having an affair with his best friend.

Should he go after Harriet?

No.

He needed time to process the information and decide what he should do next.

CHAPTER EIGHT

21:20hrs

Joe pulled to the left then followed as the slip road swung to the right, the M40 becoming, for him, the 42 and in another thirteen miles it would become the M6 where he would skim across the north of Birmingham before turning north again. Joe liked Birmingham. He had gone there for his stag weekend which Howard and Dave had organised.

He and Howard had met Dave at Guildford Uni where he had studied Business Management. Dave often told them that his parents had not been happy that he had 'thrown it all away' to run a pub in Guildford after graduation. The fact that it was thriving when so many in recent years had failed seemed to be irrelevant.

Friday 11th June 1999

"Back in Gods own country." Dave exclaimed as they all clambered off the train and onto the platform at Birmingham New Street station.

"I thought that was Yorkshire." Said Joe.

"I thought it was Israel." Said Howard.

"Very funny." Said Dave as he inhaled deeply, "Back home." He turned to face his companions. "You guys are going to enjoy the weekend we have planned for you." Dave double checked the time. "Right guys we need to get checked in to the Premier Inn, it's just outside the station. You've got an hour to get ready then we're booked into the steakhouse restaurant at seven. I suggest we get checked in and meet in the bar after we've dropped out bags in our rooms and freshened up. Ok?"

A chorus of yeses came back from the seven other men stood on the platform with Dave before they headed off the platform towards the exit and the hotel.

As they walked out of the station Howard looked for Joe. His best friend and soon to be groom seemed to have disappeared.

"Howard." Called Joe making his friend jump. "Looking for anything in particular?"

"Yes as it happens. You. I've just had a text from Trevor. He and your Uncle Jim arrived about forty minutes ago and are already in the bar waiting for us."

"Why did you have to invite my dad and uncle, they're just going to spend the whole weekend embarrassing me." Joe was not happy.

"They won't." Howard said. "They're here tonight, they're joining us for the go carting in the morning and paintballing in the afternoon, which they've paid for by the way, and then they're heading home. Your dad's got to be at Tannadice Park first thing Sunday morning. He did tell me why but to be honest I wasn't listening so I can't tell you why."

"I know, but still."

"Look Joe, you're getting married in two weeks, we're here for your stag do and I thought it was only right to ask your dad and uncle, I never actually expected them to say yes."

"Still." Joe's annoyance was obvious in his voice, not that he could change things now. He'd just have to make the best of it.

"Look mate, it is what it is, plus with ten we have the track to ourselves in the morning and don't have to have anyone else join our group for the paintballing in the afternoon."

"Fine, but why didn't you ask the two Peter's from accounts. I'm sure they'd have come if you'd asked them."

Howard shook his head. "I'm sure they would have but Dave and I discussed it and had Ant and Dec come then most of the other guys wouldn't have."

"Ant and Dec?"

"Yes Ant and Dec. Peter Jones, PJ." Said Dave over Joe's ear. "And Peter Duncan. Hence PJ and Duncan, and…"

"Ant and Dec." Finished Howard.

"Do they know you call them that?" Asked Joe. "I bet they wouldn't be happy."

"Happy. They started it when they moved in together last year and change the name of the house from Dunromin to Byker Grove. Pair of twits." Dave concluded.

"Must be a gay thing wanting to give everything and everyone stupid names." Said Howard.

"Gay? The two Peter's are gay? I thought them moving in together was a house share so they could afford the bills." Said Joe, his voice steeped in disbelief.

"They're sharing a little more than the bills if you know what I mean." Howards voice was steeped in sarcasm as he jabbed Joe in the ribs.

"That's not funny." Said Dave. "And seriously Joe, you didn't know? They're always holding hands when they're in the pub."

"No. I never suspected, and I can't say I noticed." Joe paused to take stock of the revelation about the two Peter's, Ant and Dec. "Hold on a minute, you're telling me that the rest of the guys wouldn't have come if the Peter's had, because they're gay?"

"No that's not the reason." Dave replied as the three men followed the rest of their companions off Lower Temple Street on to Temple Street. "It's because Ant becomes a massive flirt when he's drunk and tries to have sex with everyone claiming they're closet homosexuals. And Dec gets super aggressive, especially with anyone Ant flirts with and wants to start fights all the time. It gets very messy very quickly." Dave looked sideways at Joe. "But seriously, you never noticed?"

"Dave mate." Howard grinned. "He didn't know they were gay so how would he have noticed any of that?"

"True."

"Oh." Joe paused for a few seconds. "So that's why they always sing let's get ready to rumble whenever they enter a room."

Realisation finally dawning on him.

Howard and Dave burst out laughing both thinking the same thing. For such an intelligent man Joe could be really slow on the uptake at times.

Dave lead the group out of the Dragon Inn and they headed down the street to the Old Fox. Dave was having the time of his life visiting all the pubs he'd frequented in his youth. Joe had to admit that he was enjoying himself too. Maybe it was the company, maybe the copious amounts of alcohol he'd consumed in the past four hours. He knew Howard was not happy. His best friend was not happy that Dave had beaten him into second place at the mornings go-carting. Then to make matters worse he'd picked up a black eye at the afternoons paintballing and had blamed Dave for that too. Howard was convinced Dave had shot him in the safe area as revenge for beating his team in the capture the flag game. Dave swore it wasn't him, Howard didn't believe him and Joe didn't know what the truth was. Regardless of what the truth was it was safe to say Dave wasn't Howard's favourite person at the moment. It was causing tension in the group that was threatening to ruin what had been to this point, a good day.

Joe suspected that the main reason Howard was upset about the black eye was that it was seriously cramping his ability to pull. Howard hadn't yet, something he always seemed to do on a night out. Joe thought the fact that Howard was acting pretentious and grumpy was more of an issue than his black eye.

Joe laughed half-heartedly at the not very funny joke told by one of the guys and followed Dave into the Old Fox.

Ian was already returning from the bar with a tray of shot glasses in each hand. Adrian and Mike were behind him each carrying four pints of larger. The drinks landed on a table and Ian began rubbing his hands together.

"Right lads. We're at the point of the evening where it's time for some drinking games."

A cheer emanated from the group and all differences were

forgotten for the moment at least.

❖

Joe's fingers gripped the back of the toilet seat that sat atop the white hotel toilet. His stomach churned and he heaved again but had already emptied the contents of his stomach almost an hour earlier. Joe pushed himself up off the floor and stood unsteadily staring into the large obligatory bathroom mirror of the hotel room. He looked pale, blood shot eyes stared back at him.

Joe licked his lips and immediately regretted it, the acidic taste of his vomit still fresh. He splashed water from the bathroom tap onto his face and in to his mouth before pouring himself a glass of water. He swilled the water round his mouth for a few seconds then spat it back into the sink and washed it away. He drained the small glass of water and poured a second.

Joe left the bathroom, the toilet flushing behind him. Pulled the door almost to and left the light on to give his blurry eyes something to see by in the dark unlit hotel bedroom. He passed the prone snoring body of Howard and stumbled round the edge of his bed stubbing his toe on the way and swore under his breath trying not to wake his friend. Then he giggled to himself, Howard was not waking up anytime soon. Joe sat down heavily, swung his legs up and laid himself back down into bed. He desperately needed to sleep. They were meeting in the restaurant at eight thirty for breakfast as their train home left at ten. Fortunately, the station was only about a five-minute walk away from the hotel.

As Joe lay there, head slightly spinning, eyes seeing dark shapes swimming before them, he drifted off to sleep and marvelled off handily at just how much he and everyone else had actually drunk that night, surprised that he didn't feel a lot worse than he did.

CHAPTER NINE

21:28hrs

Joe took the slip road to join the M6 almost on autopilot, not really registering where he was, he just seemed to know. It was a good thing really as he was not paying attention to anything outside, his mind was wandering all over the place. His thoughts jumped from his childhood to his wedding to the incident this afternoon that had put him where he was now and everywhere in between.

Tuesday 06th March 2018

Harriet rolled over on to her back half asleep and licked her dry lips with a tongue that was twice as dry. A sleepy right arm reached across her naked chest searching for the glass of water she'd left on the bedside table. She knew it was there somewhere. Her hand searched clumsily in the gloomy morning light her eyes half closed and foggy. The back of her hand touched something cold and her reflexes jerked her arm. She heard a clink and felt water cover her hand. Well there goes her water.

The gravelly voice of a man not fully awake whispered to her. "Do you want mine?"

Harriet rolled back over on to her right side, kissed the man next to her, took the proffered glass and sipped frantically at the tepid liquid. She hated hotel tap water at the best of times but first thing in the morning it tasted worse than ever, stale, overly chlorinated and old. Water shouldn't be able to taste old but it did. She chided herself for not buying a bottle of water the day before. Harriet drained the glass and placed it on the side in the pool of water she'd spilt there a minute before. A body snuggled in close behind her, she felt his naked flesh press close to hers making her feel warm and safe. She smiled, a smile that the man behind her couldn't see but felt with the tightened grip around his muscular arm that was swathed across her shoulder.

"What time do you have to leave?" The gravelly voice was close to her ear.

Harriet felt teeth lightly nibble her ear.

"Stop that." Harriet wriggled free of the hands that appeared to be all over her and sat up on the edge of the bed rubbing her neck. "I need a shower." She looked at the digital clock next to the bed. Six-thirty. "Ninety minutes. I need to be out of here in about ninety minutes."

Harriet stood, the Egyptian cotton sheets slid seductively off her naked body eliciting a sharp exhale from the man behind her, a hand reached out tracing the curve of her hip but not connecting. Harriet felt the subtle movement in the air behind her on her skin and felt the hairs on the back of her neck raise, sending an excited chill running down her back. She closed her eyes remembering the night before. No. She didn't have time to mess about again, she needed a shower and to get to her meeting at St Thomas' Hospital at nine. The walk would take her about forty minutes or so from the hotel in Mayfair through Green Park, St James' Park and over Westminster Bridge. She wanted to walk, to clear her head, get her thoughts in order, be sharp and focused, be ready for her meeting.

"You're going to have breakfast before you go? Right?" The question asked was rhetorical as they both knew Harriet would have a croissant and a coffee before she left as was her weekday routine.

Harriet walked round the bed, the room felt fresh but warm as she headed into the en-suite and quickly climbed into the shower. The hot water hit her skin but she suddenly felt dirty, unclean. Harriet swore under her breath.

"Are you ok?"

Obviously not as under her breath as she thought.

"Harri?" The voice called from the bedroom and for a moment she heard her husband's voice through the partially closed door.

"I'm fine." She lied. "Water was just a bit cold."

But it wasn't her husband in the next room.

It was his best friend.

Again.

Since that night in June, two thousand fourteen, their meetings had become more frequent. Nothing had happened for over eight months then she'd gotten drunk, Joe had been in Dundee visiting his mum, she had a conference that she couldn't get out of and had planned to travel up to meet him on the Saturday. She had bumped in to Howard at the hotel bar she'd been staying at on the Wednesday night and knew it had not been a coincidence. Why else would Howard be in London at the same time as she had been. In the months after that first liaison Harriet had made a concerted effort to avoid Howard wherever possible and when she couldn't avoid him she made sure Joe was there with her. But not that night. She had been out with work colleagues and Howard had deliberately gone to the hotel to see her knowing that Joe wasn't going to be with her. He had waited until around ten when she and her colleagues had drunk a lot of alcohol and he had taken advantage of her.

No that wasn't true. Why lie to herself? She had wanted him as much as he had wanted her. She craved the excitement, the attention, a break from the monotony that her marriage had slipped into, for something... more. Harriet wondered if Joe was seeing someone else also. No, Harriet doubted that was the case and to be honest she was just trying to justify her own actions.

The last twelve months since that evening had seen their rendezvous become more frequent and more intense. The lies she had told her husband had become more elaborate and far fetched but he didn't seem to notice or care. She barely hid her deceit, subconsciously hoping that she'd get caught and she could end this, this, whatever this was once and for all.

Harriet realised she was scrubbing her skin hard with the shower scrunchie or puff ball, whatever it was called. However hard she tried she knew she wasn't going to wash the feelings away, the feelings of disgust she had for herself and betrayal and guilt she felt for her husband.

She felt hands on her skin from behind. The cold hands of Howard moving up her back and her feelings slipped away like the water cascading down the plug hole.

Last night had been a blur of frantic and passionate love making. The last year had passed so fast. Her feelings for Howard had spiralled form lust to love. Love. She loved him. She still loved her husband but she had feelings for the man with her now. How was that possible? Loving two men at the same time.

Harriet rinsed the soap off her and squeezed passed Howard kissing him as she did. Now was not the time, she wanted to look her best for her meeting and needed as much time as she could get if she wanted to have breakfast before she left.

❖

The two of them sat in silence passing glances at each other over the table, taking sips from their coffee and tentatively prodding at their breakfasts, Howard at his eggs benedict and Harriet with her croissant. Something hung in the air like a bad smell, both knew it was there but neither seemed to want to point it out, say the first words, make the first move. After the shower they had not said a word, getting ready in silence. They had packed up their things then moved down the restaurant, foregoing their usual intimate morning before they made their separate ways out in to the world. The awkward silence broken by the crashing sound of a tray being dropped.

Howard laughed. "Sack the juggler." He laughed again.

Harriet's head dropped and her shoulders jiggled up and down. Her head came back up shaking slowly from side to side. "You're such a child."

"And that's why you love me."

"I need time to get my head straight. Figure out what it is we're doing, aside from the obvious and betraying Joe." She took another sip of her coffee. "Why does someone always get hurt?"

Howard could barely believe what he was hearing. Did she mean it? "Are you going to tell Joe about us?" This was big. His dreams had come true. The moment he'd been waiting for, for over twenty years had finally happened. Howard knew that Joe would never forgive him. That the friendship they had forged over the last thirty years would be destroyed in a way that there was no coming back from. But did it matter in the grand scheme of things? Howard noticed a pause but didn't dare say a word for fear of losing the moment, of having Harriet changing her mind. He was not sure how long he had been doing it but he was holding his breath, food sat half-chewed in his mouth.

The moment seemed to stretched on in to eternity as Howard and Harriet looked in to each other's eyes.

A grin spread across Harriet's face. "Are you holding your breath?"

Howard spluttered and brought his hand up in front of his face in a vain effort to stop himself spraying his half-chewed food across the table in front of him.

Harriet realised that Howard was waiting for her answer and she felt a little guilty for apparently leaving him hanging. "Joe and I are going to Dundee this weekend to see his mum. I'm up in Glasgow Friday for a conference and am meeting Joe in Dundee Saturday around lunch time. I'll talk to him Sunday evening when we get back."

"Why leave it until Sunday?" Howard was genuinely perplexed.

"Because unlike you I don't want to give my partner bad news by text." Harriet looked over the rim of her coffee cup at the scowl on Howards face. "What?" She asked before she took a sip. "It's not like it's not true." She took another sip from her cup. "I'm not going to see Joe until Saturday and he deserves to be told in person. Plus, I'd rather not do it anywhere near his mother. I know she's not my biggest fan and she'll blame me not you for all of this."

"As if I'm to blame for falling in love with you and deliberately sabotaging any relationship that was going anywhere for the past twenty years." Howard was suddenly relaxed again. He could finally see the proverbial wood. Howard's demeanour returned to its usual confident extroverted self. Howard took a large mouthful of his eggs and realised that his future looked brighter than it had ever done before.

Harriet swore quietly, but just loud enough to be heard by Howard who was sat not three feet away from her causing him to sit back and look hastily around the room.

"What's up?" Howard asked.

"I need to leave. My meeting starts in an hour. The walk to St Thomas' Hospital is only about forty minutes but the old building is a rabbit warren and I always get lost. I need to be going."

The couple stood together and Howard leaned over to kiss Harriet. "I'll sort out the bill." He said kissing her again. "You get to your meeting"

"Are you sure? It is my turn." Harriet hesitated. She didn't know why, but Harriet suddenly felt a little cheap despite the cost of the hotel room they had stayed in. Howard offering to pay for the room somehow made her feel like a prostitute, all be it a high-class prostitute, plying her trade. Every now and again Howard still managed to say something that objectified the time they spent together.

"Yes, I'm sure. It's the least I can do for making me the happiest man alive."

Harriet blushed, but then he said something that made her feel loved and desired. She scurried away collecting her small wheeled suitcase that she'd left in the reception area. Howard could be a little over the top with his adulation for her and it embarrassed her how soppy he was around her. Joe was not like that. He was about as romantic as a sixteen-year-old boy trying to get into his girlfriend's pants for the first time. Clumsy and awkward, but that was one of the things that had attracted her to Joe in the first place. As Harriet exited the Connaught Hotel through its arched doorway and headed on to Carlos Place under the wrought iron canopy she suddenly had second thoughts. Was this the right decision to be making? Did she really want to try and forge a new relationship with Howard? Could she bring herself to leave the man she had been married to for twenty years? Joe had done nothing wrong aside from becoming a bit stale and predictable but if she was being honest with herself Joe could probably say the same about her. Neither of them was making an effort. Both were going through the motions and pretending to be happy.

Harriet crossed the road onto Mount Street and paused to peer into the window of Carolina Herrera. If she had time, she would pop back and have a proper look in. She had said that the last three times she had stayed at the Connaught with Howard and each time she had forgotten to go back after her meetings.

CHAPTER TEN

21:35hrs

Joe was expecting a lot more traffic than he was experiencing especially for a Friday night. There had been the usual traffic on the M25 and it'd been heavy on the M40 round Oxford but since he'd hit the M6 it'd been comparatively clear and unusually quiet. It was as if everyone knew what he'd done and they wanted to keep out of his way. Maybe they believed what he'd done and what he was doing was right and wanted to give him a clear run home. Joe snorted at the stupid thought.

Friday 10th August 1984

"Come home before it gets dark." Howard's mum wiped her hands on her apron and called after the two boys as they ran down the street and disappeared around a corner as they headed towards the park. "Before it gets dark." She shouted again this time at an empty street knowing full well that they would hear her but take no heed of her words as she checked her watch. Six thirty-two. Before it got dark, that could be another four hours. She looked up the street, where was Jack? The move from Glasgow was supposed to have been a second chance for their marriage and a fresh start for them all but he seemed to spend more and more time either at work making those damned computers or down the pub spending the money he made from the overtime he was supposed to bring home. She had already started to regret moving away from all of her family and friends in what was seeming like a futile attempt to save a marriage that only one of them seemed to be making any effort to save. A marriage that deep down she knew was most probably already dead.

The two young boys ran the four hundred meters to the end of Sandeman Street and slowed as they crossed onto the large grassed area.

"How's are things at home Morph?" Joe laughed.

"Shit. All mum does is shout, all dad does is drink. And don't call me Morph, you know I hate it when you do that." Replied Howard.

"Yeah but with that tan of yours you look so much like Morph." Joe laughed again. "And shit, that's fucked up language for a twelve-year-old."

Howard slapped his bare thigh below his shorts and started laughing as well. "Look you're just jealous that I got to go Benidorm and you spent two weeks walking along the north coast of Scotland."

The laughter subsided and the two boys walked in silence for several minutes, kicking at piles of cut grass and small stones that were dotted about the large park as Joe waited patiently for Howard to start talking again.

"The worst thing about it is that my parents think I don't know what's going on. They think that I don't hear the arguments or notice that dad's never at home and when he is, all he does is drink. Mum spends all of her time shouting or crying. I hate it. I wish they'd just split up. I hate them. I hate them both!"

"Is it really that bad?"

"Worse!" Howard was visibly upset.

Joe looked at his friend. "I'm here for you, I'll never leave you." The words just came out, from where he didn't know but in that moment he knew he meant them. "Friends for life. Best friends for life."

"Best friends for life." Howard had only known Joe for a little over a year, since he'd moved from Glasgow but in that time the two boys had developed a bond that they both believed would last the tests of time. Joe was and would always be his best friend. "What do I do about it? They won't listen to me. Whenever I say anything dad just tells me to shut up and go to my room calling me a stupid child and mum ignores me or tells me that I don't understand, that I'm too young." Howard lazily threw a stone into the space in front of him.

"Careful you might hit someone." Joe tried to defuse the tension that he sensed in his best friend.

CHAPTER ELEVEN

21:42hrs

Joe's breathing had slowed somewhat. He had been driving for over four hours and still had another six hours or so ahead of him. A coffee. Joe needed a coffee. Hilton Park Services was still another five minutes away. The adrenaline that had been fuelling him since he had left Guildford was all but spent.

Tuesday 12th November 2013

"Coffee's on sweetie, I'm just off for a shower." The coffee machine started to percolate, bubble and crackle behind him as he walked out of the kitchen hands stuffed in the pockets of his dark blue dressing gown.

Harriet watched her husband walk out of the kitchen and head towards the stairs. They'd been married for nearly fifteen years and it still amazed her that every morning he followed the same little routine regardless of if it was a weekday or a weekend. It had been one of the first things that she had noticed about him when they had first met, his almost robotic regimented schedule. She had found it quirky and cute and if she was being honest with herself she still did. Her thoughts began to drift back to that day on the university campus when they had spent their first night together and she had watched him in the morning following a set of seemingly invisible instructions. He got up, put coffee on, went to the loo, showered, shaved and dressed in a little over twenty minutes. Just enough time for the coffee to finish percolating. He'd then sit down have his coffee and read the paper before eating breakfast.

Harriet jumped slightly. The phone next to her began to ring startling her out of her daydream. She wondered who could be calling at this time of the day. Six thirty was such an unsociable time for a call. It was most probably Joes mum, she always seemed to call at the most inconvenient time possible or stupidly early in the morning. Well she wasn't going to find out who it was by standing around listening to the phone ring. Harriet lifted the receiver. "Anderson residence."

"Is that the sexy lady of the house?" Howard's voice crackled from the other end of the line.

Harriet giggled. "You know Mr Morris my husband would have a heart attack if he knew you spoke to me like that."

"Really? You should hear what he says about you."

"Should I now?"

"Well." Howard paused. "Probably not."

Harriet waited a few seconds for Howard to continue but it became obvious quite quickly he was not going to say anything more on the matter. "Well?" She said. "Why exactly have you called at this ungodly hour? You do know it's half past six in the morning?" Her question was rhetorical.

"Yes I'm fully aware of the time and believe me I wish I was still in bed. I need to talk to Joe. Is he available?"

"Sorry. He's just headed up to the shower."

"Ok tell him I'll be there to pick him up at seven not half eight as originally planned. Tell him the MOD have called the meeting forward to ten and we still have a lot to prep if we're going to be ready for them."

Harriet noticed that Howard's voice had become emotionless as it seemed to do whenever they spoke for more than a minute or two. She was never sure why. He seemed to like her and Joe always said that he was happy that she and Joe were together but...

"I'll pass on the message and make sure he's ready when you arrive."

"You'd better be dressed when I get there, otherwise I

can't guarantee I'll be able to control myself."

Harriet giggled again and hung up. He was saying the words but there was not cheekiness in his voice as she would have expected had any other of Joe's friends said them. It felt like he was flirting with her. She shook off the thought. Joe wouldn't be happy, he'd struggle to get time for his coffee. Oh well, she'd better break the good news to her husband and start to get ready herself. Joe should just be getting out of the shower just about now. Harriet ran up the stairs and into the bathroom where Joe stood naked before her, oblivious to her presence. Soap covered his body and hair. Despite his slightly round belly she couldn't help but find the man in front of her sexy as hell. The dressing gown slipped off her shoulders as she stepped into the shower with her husband. Five minutes wouldn't hurt, would it?

❖

Joe rushed downstairs half an hour later, his tie loose around his neck and his suit jacket on one shoulder as the doorbell rang for a second time. He reached the front door frantically pulling his jacket on to his right arm, took a deep breath before opening the door to his friend and work colleague.

"In a rush Joe?" Howard smiled as his friend turned to grab his brief case and shoes. He caught site of Harriet at the top of the stairs partially dressed, wet hair draped over a bare shoulder.

"Don't forget your coffee Joey." Harriet called down "I love you." And she disappeared from view.

Joe sighed, rushed back in to the kitchen and returned with two small thermos flasks in his hands. "A new Columbian blend. Picked it up yesterday." Joe offered one of the flasks to Howard. "I think you'll like it."

Howard's gaze moved from the top of the stairs to the proffered thermos in Joe's hand. "Hmm? What? Oh, err yes, thanks Joey."

"Don't you start. You know how much I hate being called Joey."

Howard looked at his watch. Almost five past seven. He hoped the traffic would be light and they'd be in the office by half past.

"What time will John be in?" Joe asked as he closed the door and followed Howard towards his car.

"Big Mac? About half eight I think. The meetings now at ten so it should give us time to do the preliminaries, go over everything when Big Mac arrives and be ready for the MOD team."

"Ok and you'd better be careful not to call John that to his face."

Howard snorted. "The guys like a big mac. Cheap, fat, greasy and always leaves a bad taste in your mouth whenever you're with him."

"Maybe so but he is still the Commercial Director, our boss and we have annual reviews in less than a month."

"So? I've already written mine and emailed it to Big Mac last Friday. Besides this deal, if it goes to plan, will set us up for the next twenty years. The new prototype jet engine is thirty percent more efficient and gives twenty percent more thrust and power than anything else out there. The Americans, Russians, Chinese and French have nothing remotely as good as it. It's a game changer. Especially if we can get the new polycarbonate composite for the fuselage to stop expanding under extreme G's. It'll reduce weight and drag, increase structural strength and increase the power and efficiency of the aircraft by a further fifteen to twenty percent. Don't forget that all Big Mac has done is opened negotiations with the MOD. And he wouldn't have a deal to open if it wasn't for us. You know it and he knows it. Why do you think he's being so nice to us? Without us he has nothing' Look at it this way, he's a glorified salesman riding on the back of the deal he helped broker back in two thousand and two between Adam Thompson and UK Aeronautical Engineering when Adam sold GETAS and us for about a quarter of what it was actually worth."

"Don't forget he also screwed you over. You were supposed to be the new the Commercial Director for the whole of UK Aeronautical Engineering and not just for the division." Joe was as bitter about that as Howard was as neither man was able to move Joe's engine forward at the pace it should have been. They were still trying to sell the Mark 4 and Joe was already half way through his designs for the Anderson Mark 5. Even Howard was not aware of the work he'd been doing, all of it off the UK Aeronautical Engineering servers. He'd set himself up a server at home and been working on the new engine design for about three years. He had already solved the issues with the polycarbonate composite and made further modifications to reduce weight and increase performance by a further ten to fifteen percent. This was going to be his, all his. He just needed to find a way to get it to the market so he realised all of the profit and recognition without Big Mac or Howard taking credit for work that wasn't actually theirs.

"Yes." Said Howard. "I remember. Don't you worry, he'll get his sooner than you think. I have a few cards left up my sleeve for Big Mac."

The two men climbed into Joe's Saab 93 convertible, the engine roaring into life as Howard pulled away from the house. Joe sat in silence for a few minutes thinking about the work he and Howard had completed over twenty or so hard years. It had started as a joint thesis as part of their degrees in aerodynamics and aircraft structures at the University of Surrey. They'd carried it on through their PHDs where they'd both obtained first class with honours, filing over six hundred patents along the way. It had paved the way for their jobs with McAllister Aeronautics, for the development of the Mark 2, Mark 3 and the Anderson Mark 4 engines. And if the deal with the MOD was signed today and went even half as well as everyone expected it would make the two men multimillionaires over the next ten years in licencing and bonuses.

Joe looked over at his friend in the driver's seat beside him. He knew that he had done about seventy percent of the technical work, solving the seemingly impossible equations and making the design work but Howard had been invaluable in his own right. Howard had pushed Joe to levels that even he hadn't thought possible coming up with concepts and pushing the boundaries of what was thought to be possible. Howard had picked Joe up when he was down and he couldn't see the wood for the trees. Howard had translated Joe's thoughts and workings into language that the lecturers and then their employees could understand; almost dumbed it down for everyone else. This had a twofold benefit in that it made it easier for people to understand the basics but harder to steal the idea, plagiarise his work and outright copy things. Howard had made himself and Joe indispensable. On top of that Howard was a businessman with nerves of steel, the charmer, so confident and outgoing. It was Howard who had negotiated the contract with McAllister that paid them both salaries in excess of anything anyone coming out of university could normally expect and it had clauses and sub clauses pertaining to licencing fees the use of their patents and percentage deals all of which Joe had not even contemplated when thinking about a job. He'd just left it to Howard knowing full well his friend had looked out for them both.

He did however take some satisfaction in the fact that he, and not Howard had won the heart of Harriet. Joe was never quite sure why she had chosen him over Howard but to be honest he didn't care, he was just happy that she had. They had been married fifteen years, been in their new house together nine years and together for twenty-one years and were still passionately in love. Howard on the other hand seemed to jump from one beautiful young lady to the next still living the life of a single man never seeming to want to settle down. Joe hoped that Howard would someday soon find the right woman for him, settle down and be happy. It never occurred to him that Howard might actually be happy with the life he had.

"So?" Joe started. "How are you going to play this today?"

"Simple." Howard said. "I'll do most of the talking, you'll be there to answer any overly technical questions and dazzle them with science. Remember big words and lots of numbers.

Once that's done Big Mac discusses the contract and you and I go to lunch very happy and very rich men." Howard saw the nervous look on Joe's face. "There's nothing to be nervous about. We have it in our contracts that any deal UK Aeronautical Engineering signs which involves any part of our, and by our I mean your, Anderson Mark 4 engine in part or in full, in its original or any developed state makes us each 10% of that deal until the day we retire." He paused to let the statement sink in. "There's some big numbers, *big* numbers."

"You're right but you don't realise that it's going to be at least three years, possibly five before we see any of that. You know what the MOD can be like."

"You're right, but what you don't realise is I negotiated a two hundred thousand signing bonus and a twenty-five thousand a year annual bonus until the final contract is completed, for each of us." Howard laughed. "Didn't know that now did you Joe?"

"When did you agree that, and when were you going to tell me?"

"When I negotiated our contracts with GETAS, and I had them carried over when UK Aerodynamic Systems bought them out and oh," Howard shrugged "today."

CHAPTER TWELVE

21:47hrs

Joe indicated left and took the exit to Hilton Park Services. He was ready for a break. With the traffic on the M25 and on the M40 around Oxford what should have taken around two and a half hours had taken over four. Joe glanced at the digital clock on his dashboard. Nine forty-seven. He had a further three hundred and fifty miles to go and with any luck he should complete his journey sometime around four in the morning.

Thursday 14th April 2016

Beep Beep Beep.

Beep Beep Beep.

The alarm by the side of the bed fell silent.

Harriet slung her legs out of the bed and sat up. Four in the morning! Why had she agreed to this business trip? Oh yeah. It was the post meeting rendezvous that had tipped her hand in the end. She glanced back at her husband still dozing on the bed behind her. She loved Joe but in the past two years she'd begun to feel more and more alone. He worked all hours on that god forsaken engine of his, leaving her to fend for herself. If she had pursued her dreams when she had left university maybe she would feel fulfilled and not have a giant emotional hole inside her. But she had put her life on hold to support Joe and gotten a sales job. Twenty-one years later she was a Director of UK Sales for one of the largest pharmaceutical companies in the UK. It was a job she was good at, really good at but not one she particularly enjoyed if she was being honest. She had to mostly deal with men in their late forties and early fifties, men that spent most of their time perving over her and making inappropriate comments. The industry was dominated by men in senior positions. Institutionalised sexism was rife. Harriet had discussed this with Joe, Howard and some of her work colleagues, discussed ways of changing things but everything she tried seemed to fail to bring the changes she so badly desired.

Harriet hustled into the bathroom, dropped her nightdress and slipped into the shower.

Thirty minutes later she was showered, dressed, make up on, coffee in her travel mug, car keys in her hand walking out the front door of her house ready for the three-and-a-half-hour drive to the Royal Devon and Exeter Hospital. Harriet just wished she'd driven over to Exeter last night or arranged the meeting for a reasonable hour of the day.

❖

Harriet walked out the main entrance of Truro hospital and headed for her car. Her meeting had taken the best part of four hours, four hours. All that time trapped in a room being leered at and having inappropriate comments thrown in her direction. They hadn't even tried to be subtle, just overtly sexist and misogynistic. She hated the pharmaceutical industry. Hated it with a passion. That was in spite of just landing a substantial deal that would land her a tidy little bonus and push her over her annual sales target in less than four months. She walked to the carpark to her car and lit a cigarette. If Joe could see her now he wouldn't be happy but every now and then she just needed to smoke, to feel dirty from the cigarette smoke caressing her lungs and not from being objectified. For feeling like she had to flirt with a bunch of dirty old men. Harriet needed a shower. She had a two-hour drive to Truro in front of her where she could check into her hotel, the second is as many days, shower, eat some dinner and prepare for her meeting in the morning at Treliske Hospital. At least she'd have some company tonight. Someone to hold her and to show her some attention. Attention she so desperately craved. With any luck she'd be checking in by four, showered and eaten by six, a few hours to relax before her friend who she was expecting at eight arrived. It would also give her time to call Joe at about seven before he went down to the pub. Joe was such a creature of habit. Whenever she went away he always went to the pub with friends.

The drive to Truro was dull, uneventful and surprisingly fast. She had to wait in reception for over half an hour before the jobsworth on front desk would issue her with a room key, something about company policy and not allowing guests to check in before four pm.

The shower, her second of the day was cramped in the small en-suite but did its job to make her feel clean again.

Dinner in the hotel restaurant was as dull as the drive to it. The steak she ordered rare was almost well done, there was no point complaining as they would just over cook her another one. She knew this as she'd complained the last time and had a steak even more over cooked than the first. Harriet hoped that one day she would get what she ordered, a rare steak, in reality she knew it was very unlikely to happen.

By quarter past seven Harriet was back in her room on the phone listening to her husband drone on about the latest development he'd made on that fucking engine of his.

By quarter to eight she felt like she had said about ten words, when Joe was on one he would prattle on incessantly without listening to anything she had to say. In all honesty Harriet had switched off about five minutes into the conversation the occasional yes or ok interjected into Joe's torrent of words, her mind drifting off to what might happen later that evening.

Knock, knock.

Harriet was jolted back into the room.

"Room service." Came the voice from the other side of the room door.

"What was that?" Joe's voice sounded surprised by the interruption from the other end of the line.

"Err, room service." Harriet was as surprised as Joe, she hadn't ordered anything from room service. Had she?

"Oh ok, well I'd better let you go then. I'm off down the Dog and Duck with guys shortly anyway." Joe coughed lightly. "Love you Harri."

"What? Oh, yes. I love you too Joe." Harriet ended the call, plugged her mobile phone in to her charger and put it down on the bedside table next to the oversized bed she was sat on. She made her way to the door and peered through the spy hole onto the back of a man's head. She recognised that profile...

He was early.

CHAPTER THIRTEEN

21:52hrs

Joe washed his hands concentrating on the water and soap foaming on his fingers, thoughts spinning around his head. Was he doing the right thing? Would he get away with what he'd done? Would anyone forgive him when they found out? Could anyone forgive him? Did he care if they didn't? These were not constructive thoughts. He had about another six hours to go, with stops, in front of him. A coffee. He needed a coffee. Joe dried his hands and walked to the nearest coffee shop. Paranoia suddenly hit him. As he walked every pair of eyes in the place seemed to be staring at him. They knew, they all knew. His palms started to sweat and his breathing quickened.

"Sir?" A pause. "Sir, what can I get you?"

Joe looked around. He was at the front of the queue. He looked around again, everyone was ignoring him except the Barista who had a tired impatient look on her face. Up until recently Joe was sure Howard would have been better in this situation. He had always been better under pressure, but Joe knew that there was no way Howard could have been here, not now. Joe glanced quickly at his car through the large glass window in front of him, his gaze focusing in the back and he smiled to himself, his calm gradually returning.

"Sir?" Impatience resonating towards him.

"Yes, sorry it's been one of those days. I'll have a flat white, please. No sugar, thank you." Joe grinned at the young lady wearing the horrible brown franchised polo shirt. She squawked a price at him took the proffered five-pound note and moments later dropped some change in Joe's outstretched hand.

"Thanks." Joe moved down to the end of the counter and looked forward again through the window to his car sat amidst a sea of dull family cars and business saloons in the dimly lit carpark.

Where were they all going? He could guarantee that no one else had in their cars what he had in his. No one.

Saturday 26th September 2008

"Easy your end. Up a bit. Ok. To me. Right we're in at the bottom."

Joe walked down the drive and left the glazers fitting the glass in his front window behind him. It was almost one and there was no sign of Harriet anywhere. She'd nipped to the shops at ten thirty to get some milk and bread and a large pizza for lunch. The supermarket was only fifteen minutes down the road. Joe's stomach growled.

Where was she?

He had tried calling her on her mobile twice, both times it had gone straight to voicemail so he'd sent her a text, and another and a third.

He checked his phone. Still no reply.

Where was she?

He was starting to get angry. A combination of hunger and worry.

A car horn sounded startling Joe, he turned to see Harriet's maroon Ford Focus heading down the road. She braked late as she always did and swung onto the drive way narrowly missing Joe and stopped close to the glazers van parked in front of the garages to the right of the house.

"I forgot the glazers were coming today." Harriet jumped out of her car looking excited and walked to meet her husband's car door left open behind her. On reaching Joe she slipped her right hand round the back of his head pulled him hard towards her and kissed him, passionately.

"Guess what?" she asked.

Joe hated guessing games at the best of times and his current mood did not help the situation at all. "What?" he replied.

"No, you've got to guess."

"I've no idea." Joe thought and blurted out the first thing that popped into his head. "You bumped into Mark Butcher in Sainsbury's."

"What, who? err no." She stared at her husband jumping around like an excited child. "Guess."

Again Joe racked his brain and shook his head, it could be anything. "It could be anything." Joe fought to keep the sound of annoyance from his voice but doubted whether Harriet would actually notice in her current excited state. He hated the way she always wanted him to guess something, what she was thinking, what she had done, who she had seen, what she wanted. It was always something totally random and uninteresting. "I don't know."

"I bought a scratch card." Harriet could hardly contain her excitement. "And I've won ten grand. I've no idea why I bought it. I mean I never buy scratch cards or play the lottery but I just felt lucky so I bought one totally random like and hey presto. Isn't that amazing?"

"Well yes I suppose but why did it take so long to buy a loaf of bread and milk?" Joe sounded grumpy. He began to walk towards the house.

"Oh yes," Harriet followed her husband, her excitement hadn't waned, "well I bumped into Howard and we had a coffee."

"So why didn't you call me?" Joe's mood hadn't lightened at all.

"I left my phone in the car and was so excited by the win on the scratch card that it just didn't occur to me." Harriet tilted her head and looked up at Joe. "I'm sorry." She said and extended her arms towards him.

Joe looked into Harriet's beautiful eyes and let her hug him. He kissed her head and felt a warm glow rise within him. No matter how bad he felt, how annoyed he was a hug from Harriet seemed to always make everything better.

Harriet looked up into Joe's big brown puppy dog eyes, kissed him and walked away into the house to make lunch, a cheeky grin on her face.

Joe watched the back of the woman he loved disappear through the front door. As much as he loved his wife she really knew how to push his buttons. She didn't think to call him. Joe wished he hadn't stopped smoking. It had been six days since Harriet and he had stopped. She seemed to be happier and more alive over the past week, while Joe just felt constantly angry craving the nicotine he could no longer have.

Just one.

That's all he wanted.

Just one last one.

CHAPTER FOURTEEN

22:14hrs

Joe stood, pushing the chair he'd been sat on backwards with the annoying scraping squeaking sound of the rubber tipped feet dragging on the food court floor. He sighed, replaced the chair under the small table, throw the empty coffee cup into the nearest bin and started for the exit. His legs felt leaden as he trudged over the food court floor, his feet gripping the sticky floor. He'd left Guildford almost five hours before and the weight of the drive still ahead of him weighed heavily on his shoulders. Was he doing the right thing? He'd asked himself that very same question as he'd pulled out of the UK Aerodynamic Systems carpark just before half past five. He didn't have the answer then and didn't have the answer now. All he knew was that he was committed and that he couldn't turn back.

Wednesday 21st October 1992

Joe walked across the car park towards his car; an old beat up beige Fiesta. He should have put a coat on this morning before he'd left the house, but like most mornings he'd gotten up late trying to grab a few extra minutes in bed after yet another late-night studying. If he was being honest with himself, he couldn't remember where his coat was. He hadn't seen it since last Saturday when Howard had driven him and Dave to watch Woking play Northwich Victoria. Woking had won one nil in what had been a scrappy game but the atmosphere in the ground had been good and Dave had suggested they go to the Gateshead game next month. It would mean Dave would have to watch his beloved Tyne-siders from the wrong end of the ground but none of them were overly fussed with that.

Joe had asked why Dave loved Northwich so much when he was from London. Apparently, his uncle used to take him to non-league football matches as a child and he'd just liked their green kit. It was as simple as that and he'd followed them ever since.

Maybe he'd left his coat in Howard's beat up old Golf. He'd have to check in there tonight before they went down the Union for the pool tournament. Joe came back to the present with a bump.

"I'm so sorry." The young lady in front of him looked embarrassed as she crouched down to retrieve some books off the floor between them.

Joe looked at the young lady crouched in front of him almost bewitched by her beauty. She was beautiful, absolutely and utterly beautiful.

"I'm Harri." She said standing and extending a hand. "Harriet McIntosh."

Joe shook the proffered hand, eyes not blinking.

"Well it was nice to meet you." She said after an awkward pause.

"Yes." Joe nodded and watched as the young lady, Harriet, walked away with a brief glance and smile over her shoulder.

"Who was that?" A large hand slapped on Joe's right shoulder and Howard appeared to his left.

"Harri," Joe watched her disappear from view, blinked then looked at Howard standing next to him. "Where's my coat?"

"What?" Howard had not been expecting to be asked about a coat.

"My red one. The one you borrowed for the Northwich game last Saturday."

❖

Seven hours later Howard and Joe walked out the front door of their digs and began the fifteen-minute walk to the union bar.

Joe was feeling lucky. He wasn't sure why but he had a really good feeling about tonight. Maybe tonight he'd win more games than he'd lose. You never know. It wasn't as if he was a bad player it just seemed that everyone at university was better than him.

The two young men walked down the darkening streets towards the student bar, street lights already beginning to warm up and emit a dull orange glow.

"Do you think they'll play the Australia Munster game at the bar tonight?"

Joe shook his head. "Not unless they have feed from Irish TV. Let's hope Munster play better than Leinster did last weekend. That was embarrassing to say the least."

"What about Sky Sports? I hear the uni bar had it installed over the summer break." Howard opened the glass door to the large on campus bar. He followed Joe to the bar where Joe ordered two ciders. Howard took the pint glasses and left Joe to pay for the two drinks while he found some seats close to the pool tables.

Joe swung round to follow his friend and bumped into a young lady standing behind him. "I'm so sorry, I didn't see you there."

"Twice in one day, if I didn't know any better I'd say you were doing it on purpose."

Joe looked up from the floor. "Harri?"

"The mysteriously silent man." Harriet grinned.

"Oh yes, sorry. I'm Joe, Joseph Anderson." Joe hesitated awash with nerves. "Er, would you like to join me, us." He scanned the room and located Howard on the far side of the large room. "I'm sat over there with the Ian Brown look alike, Howard." Joe pointed. "We're playing in the pool tournament." Shut up he said to himself. He seemed to suddenly be infected with a case of verbal diarrhoea.

"Really? That'll be interesting if you get drawn against me." Harriet turned to her friend, who Joe had not even noticed.

"Sarah, Gin and Tonic please. Join us over there with Ian Brown." She linked her arm into Joe's. "Shall we?"

Howard watched his best friend walk towards him with a beautiful girl on his arm, her long elegant legs accentuated by the short red skirt she was wearing. How did he do it? Despite Howard being more handsome, fitter, more confident and less socially awkward it was Joe that always seemed to end up pulling, not that his friend ever realised he had. The amount of disappointed women Joe had left in his wake was astounding without Joe ever realising what he'd done. Or more accurately not done. Howard stood and offered the chair next to him to the lady with Joe. She looked familiar somehow.

Harriet ignored Howard and sat next to Joe. Sarah, Harriet's friend, appeared at that point and took the offered seat with a grin.

"Thank you." Sarah purred.

"So are you going to introduce me to your two new friends?" Asked Howard.

"Of course, Howard this is Harriet, Harriet, Howard."

Howard kissed Harriet's hand then looked to his left. "And you are?"

"I'm Sarah Francis." She pushed Harriet's drink across the table and raised her hand for Howard to kiss.

"A pleasure."

"Ooo it could be." Sarah said under her breath. In a louder voice she said, "So, what are we talking about?"

Howard took several gulps from his cider. "The Autumn Internationals." He said and placed his glass down in front of him.

"What you mean how badly England played against a second rate Canadian team and the fact that the twenty-three thirteen score line flattered them." Sarah looked at the surprised faces of the two men sat at the table. "My dad and two brothers both play."

"So how do you think England will fare against South Africa next month?"

"I'd say it should be quite comfortable."

"Really? What makes you say that?" Asked Howard.

"South Africa are still trying to find their feet internationally and England have a lot of experience with the likes of Martin Bayfield, Will Carling, Brian Moore and Jerry Gusgott not to mention the two gorgeous Underwood boys on the wings."

"Ok." Said Howard wanting to change the subject. "Are we going to play pool or what? Joe you're up first."

CHAPTER FIFTEEN

22:17hrs

Joe sat in the driver's seat of his car, keys in the ignition but the engine not started. The enormity of what he had done suddenly hit him, hit him hard. He screwed his eyes shut and tried to force his mind to clear of all thoughts about the evenings events but the harder he tried the more vivid the images were that swamped his mind. A sense of nausea washed over him and Joe scrambled to open the car door. The door swung open just short of the car parked in the next bay and Joe leaned to his right vomiting on the badly tarmacked floor next to his car. He breathed in and a second wave hit him. Joe vomited again then spat on the floor, wiped his mouth on his sleeve, sat back up and closed the door behind him.

A deep breath followed by a sharp exhale and the engine rumbled into life. Three hundred and fifty miles and about five hours to do it in. Well, he'd better stop messing around and get his foot down.

Tuesday 17th June 2014

Howard stood, hemmed in to the centre of the carriage by the bodies that also stood swaying to the rhythm of the tube train as it hurtled forward along the dark soot clad tunnel like a greyhound after a stuffed rabbit on a track. At six foot two he looked over a sea of heads that bobbed like the silly plastic dogs truck drivers seemed to love putting on their dashboards. The lights flickered as the train lurched to the left, straightened and then slowed as it approached Green Park, the twenty-minute journey seemed to have taken an age surrounded by sweaty odious men in ill-fitting pin striped suits and garish ties. The meeting with Marshal Sterling had gone well. He'd negotiated a good deal for the investment portfolio he was setting up and had got a surprise phone call just before he'd walked in to the entrance to Canary Wharf Tube Station. The caller had just finished a meeting at St Mary's Hospital Paddington and suggested they meet for a drink. Howard had suggested The Footman in Green Park which was about a fifteen-minute cab ride for her.

The doors to the tube carriage opened and he fought his way through the throng of people to get off the tube and on to the platform then was swept along with the crowd as he shuffled towards the escalators. Swept through the barriers and out of the station onto Piccadilly next to M&S Food. He walked the short distance and turned left onto Berkeley Square. Head down he marched forward not looking at any of the shops, bars or offices that he had passed a hundred times before. His head raised sharply startled by the sound of a car engine rumbling next to him, a large Rolls Royce with blacked out windows. Visitors for the Palm Beach Casino no doubt willing to lose thousands for at best a few hours of adrenaline filled excitement. Howard snorted to himself and carried on walking past Starbucks and on to Berkeley Square. Idiots.

Howard turned left and played with the loose change in his pocket, eyes up and looking around for the first time in, he didn't know how long. Trees. There were trees in the centre of Berkeley Square, so many trees. Had they always been there? They must have but he never paid any attention to them like he never paid any attention to most things when he was in London, just travelling from where he was to where he was going. Did everyone do that? Stay in their own little bubble, minding their own business and ignoring the world around them. He heard voices all around him. People talking to each other, on their phones or to sales assistants in shops. So many voices. So many things he just didn't normally see.

Howard crossed Fitzmaurice Place onto Charles Street. Fifty meters in front of him, there she was standing outside the Footman on the corner of Charles Street and Hay's Mews. Wow she looked good in her fitted suit but then she always did. The little blue skirt sitting half way down her slightly tanned beautiful legs made her look like a model. Howard forced his breathing to slow and felt his palms become suddenly sweaty. He surreptitiously wiped them on his trousers as he got closer a grin on his face.

"Harri."

"Howard." Harriet turned and notice the man stood next to her. "You were quick. I was just about to go in and get us some drinks. IPA?"

"Yes, that'd be nice." Howard followed Harriet in through the door to the bar looking at her bottom, admiring the way its shapely form moved gently from side to side. "So, what do I owe the pleasure?"

"What do you mean?" She asked Howard and turned to the man behind the bar. "A pint of IPA and a gin and slimline tonic." She turned back to Howard as the barman started to pull the pint. "I thought it would be nice to catch up. You've been kind of distant for the last six months or so since you and Monica split up and Joe and I have been worried. He told me you were in London today, I was, so I thought that this would be a good time to have a chat, away from the usual people, the usual places, somewhere neutral."

The barman placed the drinks on the bar and Harriet paid before leading Howard to two empty chairs in the window overlooking Charles Street.

"Have you ever noticed how many people there are in London. I mean really noticed. You walk past them all the time and never really see them."

"No. I can't say I have." Harriet looked at Howard. "Don't change the subject. What's going on?"

"Nothing." Howard shrugged. "Nothing. I just needed some time to get my head straight, you know how it is, well maybe you two love birds don't know." Howard took off his jacket and draped it over the back of the chair he was sat on. "I really thought Monica was the one. I know there's been a few girls in the past."

"A few?" Harriet raised an eyebrow.

"Ok, a lot. But this was different you know."

"You said that about Stacey Vaughn back in two thousand three, two thousand four."

Howard nodded. "Four."

"Samantha Farley in oh eight. Every time you get close and think that they might be the one you bail and just run away. Why? Why do you do that? Samantha and I, and Monica and I became good friends while you were dating and they both said you didn't turn up for a date and sent them a text saying it was over. That's pretty fucked up."

Howard sat for a minute and stared out of the pub window drinking his drink, not saying anything. Finally, he decided to talk. To tell her the truth about how he felt about the woman sat next to him. He needed to get it off his chest. It had been sat there for twenty years, since the day he met her. He had tried to tell her the morning of her wedding but his conscience had gotten the best of him. At that moment in time, when he was there, stood in front of Harriet, outside of her parents' house, in that sleepy little village in the middle of nowhere, he had bottled it. His thoughts had jumped to his best friend and how it would have affected him. Telling Harriet how he had felt would have ended their relationship, would have destroyed Joe, destroyed their friendship. Howard hadn't the strength nor the heart to do that to his best friend. The man who had been there for him so many times before that time, and so many times since. But things had changed for Howard. He had realised six months ago that he could never be happy with anyone other than Harriet. He had tried so many times before, so many. Things always started well, in a whirlwind of emotions and lust. As if someone had swooped down, picked him up and carried him along on a rollercoaster ride filled with excitement and joy only to drop him in a lake of freezing cold water. A slap in the face, a cold realisation that what he had was not what he wanted, leaving him empty and alone. Even though there was a person there for him, who loved him, who was committed to him and his future but ultimately a person that he just didn't love and couldn't be with. He knew that he had hurt the women in the short term but better that than living a lie and destroying the women in the long term.

He knew that his story would repeat itself over and over again. He had hoped time and again that he could break the cycle, meet his one true love. But he knew deep down that he had done that twenty years ago and fate had taken her away from him but at the same time left her in his life as a reminder of his lonely misery filled future. He had been successful at everything he had done except with his personal life. Well it was now or never.

Howard looked sideways at Harriet. "The truth is that I'm in love with someone else. I have been for a long time. I try to deny my real feelings and find love elsewhere and for a short period of time I do but as my relationships get more serious, more involved, I realise that it's not what I want, that they don't match up to this other person. The real love of my life." Howard took a deep breath, turned to face Harriet full on and placed his hand on hers on the ledge by the window. "It's you Harri. It's always been you." His eyes slowly moved down. His focus not on the woman in front of him, the woman he loved but on his future a future he couldn't see. He felt warm fingers on his chin gently lifting it up. Warm emerald green eyes peered back at him, peered deep into his soul. It was as if she could read him, knew what he was thinking, what he wanted and for a split second he truly believed that she wanted what he did. But it was just a fantasy, wasn't it? "Harri?"

Harriet looked into Howards eyes. She knew how he had felt about her. She had always known and if she was being honest with herself she had harboured feelings for Howard. Not love, not affection. She didn't like his brash arrogance, his loud aggressive nature, they way he assumed that he was always right, that the world owed him. She hated the way he treated his best friend. Yes, he had helped Joe realise his dreams and get him an amazing job but both were just to serve his own interests, to get Howard what Howard wanted. No, the feelings Harriet had for Howard were not love or adoration but lust. Lust for a handsome man with a body of an Olympic swimmer. She had wondered what he'd be like in bed. His girlfriends had been quite explicit at times and she wanted to know if what they had said was true or just exaggerated fantasies. She knew he was hurting. Could she heal his wounds and make him feel whole, help him get over her or would she just fuel the fire?

"I know." Harriet said. "I've always known. You forget that you turned up outside my parents' house the morning of my wedding and I'm guessing that it wasn't to wish me good luck." Harriet lifted Howards chin a little further and leaned in close to him, her lips brushed lightly against his, barely registering the touch but the hairs on the back of her neck stood on end. Her nostrils were assailed by his expensive perfume, Oud Wood by Tom Ford. The smoky rose wood and amber scent elegant and inviting. Harriet had bought Joe some several years ago for their anniversary but it sat unopened on the dressing table next to the bottle of Joop Homme, the fragrance that he had used for since he was eighteen. He frustrated her. So stubborn and stuck in his ways. Harriet still loved Joe and she had no intention of leaving him, but life was getting dull. She wanted some excitement in her life, something to get her juices flowing, to give her the drive to get out of bed in the morning the way that Joe used to and work wasn't doing anything for her either. Harriet looked into the eyes of the man sat not fifteen centimetres in front of her. She had to admit that he was handsome, physically fit and always well groomed. She knew that he had always desired her, that he thought he was in love with her and for now she would use that for her own gain. As for her, when she had first met Howard her head had not been turned by his good looks or his confidence. They had gone for a drink that same evening and her feelings had soured further as his confidence and manifested as a misogynistic arrogance. She had not liked Howard, but he was Joe's best friend and she had put up with him, making nice, laughing at his jokes, mopping up the mess that always seemed to follow his relationships and pretending that she never noticed the way he looked at her.

Over the years she had realised that behind all that bravado Howard was hiding his real personality. The facade had slowly fallen away over the years, piece by piece and behind it all was a scared little boy who had built up walls to protect himself. From what, she was never really sure. Harriet knew about his childhood and his father but she always suspected that there was something more, something deeper.

Her feelings towards him had softened. Moved from loathing, to tolerance, to affection and dare she say it… love?

Was it love, or was it just a lustful desire to fill the void that had opened up in her life?

Howard's eyes opened slowly and he focused on the beautiful woman in front of him. "Are you sure?" Howard asked, words hardly spoken, hardly heard.

"Does it matter?" Did it matter? Harriet felt aroused. Lust and desire filled her. Joe didn't need to know, he would never find out. She leaned back and picked up her gin, her hand shaking slightly. "If we do this Joe must never find out."

"Never. My lips are sealed." Howard drained his glass.

"Are you ok with that? Lying to your best friend?"

"Are you?" Howard answered the question answered with another question and in that moment, it became real, really fast.

In the scant seconds that followed Harriet knew that she was sure. In this moment this is what she wanted. She stood. "Shall we?" Maybe her brother had been right all those years ago. Maybe she did crave chaos, enjoyed being chased, enjoyed the subterfuge behind affairs or maybe she just craved sex. Something her and Joe seemed to do less and less these days. He was so caught up in her work and she just needed the attention. Any attention other than the regiment sex her and Joe were having, pre-planned to sync in time with her ovulating, same time every month then nothing for three weeks. It had slowly drained the passion from their marriage and she craved that passion back.

Desperately craved it. She knew it was there somewhere but didn't have the energy to chase it anymore.

"I have a nice place booked not far from here." Howard picked up his jacket and casually slung it over his shoulder then gently took Harriet's hand in his. "The Prince's Lodge at The Connaught." It would be the perfect place for a perfect night.

CHAPTER SIXTEEN

22:31hrs

The sound of a car horn brought Joe back to reality, his thoughts fading fast and his head swivelling left to right in an attempt to see what had caused the noise. He realised with a jolt it was him. He was drifting from the middle lane into the outside lane of the motorway pushing the car next to him dangerously close to the central barrier. Joe drifted back to the left and raised a hand as way of apology which did nothing to appease the gesticulating driver of the other car. The car to his right accelerated pulling away to leave Joe alone once again with his thoughts.

Saturday 17th July 2004

Joe and Harriet climbed out of their car and watched the removal van pull onto the drive of their new home. They had spent the past week boxing up everything they owned ready for the movers to arrive early this morning and pack it all into the lorry for the four mile move across town. All the boxes were labelled and would be deposited to their correct rooms by the movers. Joe leaned over and kissed Harriet before they walked hand in hand towards their front door.

"Ready?" Asked Joe.

"Ready." Replied Harriet.

Joe place the key in the front door, waited a second for Harriet to place her hand on his and they turned the key together opening the door to their new home and on the next chapter of their lives together.

They stood holding hands and stared into the house both

having large grins on their faces, neither able to conceal their excitement. It was Harriet's turn to lean over and kiss Joe.

"Hello." Came a voice from behind them. "Excuse me."

The couple turned to see a man with a trolley carrying several large boxes wanting to get past. Joe and Harriet walked into the house, to the right into their kitchen. The Mover deposited the boxes at the bottom of the stairs and exited the house, presumably for a second load.

"Can you believe it? We're finally moving into our dream home." Harriet walked round the kitchen trailing her hand across the work surfaces and randomly opening and closing cupboards and draws as she went imagining what might be there by the end of the day.

Joe saw how happy she looked. It had taken them just twelve years to get here. From meeting in ninety-two, to their first date, getting engaged in ninety-six and married and buying their first house in ninety-nine. Twelve years had vanished in a flash before his eyes and if he could he would do it all again. Twelve magical years. They were trying to start a family and now had their dream home ready for that day.

"It's pretty amazing." Said Joe raising his hand. "Come here, and give me a kiss."

Harriet walked over to her husband, wrapped her arms around him and kissed him passionately.

A cheeky grin crept across Joe's face. "So my darling, are you up for christening this place?"

"What? Now?" Harriet looked quizzically at her husband not sure if he was joking or not. Knowing Joe, he probably didn't realise what he had implied so decided to see how he'd react. "Don't you think the removal men might get a little distracted, what with us going at it on the kitchen counter?"

"What, oh, err, no, I meant later, not now, obviously not now." Joe stumbled over his words as he turned red clearly embarrassed.

Harriet laughed, walked away from Joe looking over her shoulder as she did and winked.

"Oh, you knew I meant later."

Harriet bent down and opened one of the two boxes that had been deposited in the middle of the kitchen floor. "Are you going to help me decide where everything is going to go?"

"Ok." Joe walked over and opened the second box. Mugs and crockery. "Right, mugs can go in the cupboard in the corner to the left of the sink, above where the kettle and toaster will go." He started to unpack. "So is tonight the night?"

Harriet's head came out of the box closely followed by the kettle and lead. "Shall I make us a cup?"

"Yes and you didn't answer my question."

"I know." Harriet was feeling in a playful mood.

"Well." Joe prompted again.

"Well what?" She asked knowing full well what Joe wanted to know.

"Come on sweetie, stop messing me around and answer the question. Is tonight the night?"

"I think so." Said Harriet nodding filling the kettle up. "My last period was about two weeks ago so I should be ovulating."

"Good. The stresses of the move won't have helped over the last few months but I have a good feeling about tonight."

"Amy and Giles. What do you think? Names for the baby if it's a girl or boy."

Joe reached round his wife and placed two mugs on the counter next to the kettle. "I thought we'd agreed on Mary and Hamish?"

"No. you agreed on Mary and Hamish, I didn't." Harriet deposited a tea bag in the two mugs. "*We* hadn't agreed on anything, but that's alright as we have nine months to decide. How about Debra or Andrew?"

The unpacking slowed as the two traded names.

"Jane's nice, so is Walter." Said Joe.

"Laura and Noah" Said Harriet.

"Sheila and Joseph Junior."

"Christine and Luke?"

"I don't think we'll ever agree on names, do you?" Joe

poured hot water from the freshly boiled kettle into the two mugs. "I'm going to ask the moving guys if they want a drink while we're making one."

"Ok, we can pick this up again later. And we definitely did not agree on Hamish and Mary."

"We'll see."

"Yes we will." Said Harriet to Joe's back as he left the kitchen.

Joe walked out of the front door knowing that when they did have children they would not be called Hamish or Mary. He'd resigned himself to that fact years ago when they'd started discussing having a family and the subject of names came up. He would however occasionally suggest the names on the off chance that Harriet might change her mind.

Joe walked back into the kitchen, grabbed his mug of instant coffee and took a sip. Joe pulled a face. "You can tell the difference between this instant shit and freshly ground." Joe turned and leaned against the kitchen counter as he watched his wife unpack a box of glasses and put them in one of the cupboards to the right of the sink above the counter.

"What are you looking at?" Harriet asked over her shoulder.

"Not sure. It hasn't got a label."

"Funny." Said Harriet as she unwrapped another large wine glass.

"Oh," Joe took another sip of his coffee. "Howard messaged me a minute ago. He's going to pop over later with a takeaway and give us a hand unpacking."

"Seriously?" Harriet's hand paused mid-air. Her eyes closed. Why did he have to come and ruin a perfectly good day. Harriet knew that they were close friends but if she didn't know any better she would swear they were sleeping together. It would explain a few things but no, she was certain neither one was homosexual.

"What?" Joe was surprised by Harriet's reaction. He didn't understand what the problem was.

Harriet turned to face her husband. "I was hoping that we could have a few days just the two of us to explore and get to know the house a little bit, if you know what I mean."

Realisation dawned on Joe's face as he suddenly appreciated the inference in Harriet's words. "Oh, I hadn't thought about that."

"No." Said Harriet, he never did.

"I'll give Howard a call." Joe fumbled around in his pockets for his phone.

"Don't worry about it Joe. We'll have plenty of time to get to know the house." Harriet walked over and kissed Joe on his cheek then disappeared into the hallway to get another box. While outwardly she appeared calm and happy, she was anything but. While her feelings towards Howard had mellowed somewhat over the twelve years that she had known him, he was still not one of her favourite people. He was arrogant, brash and loud and the way he seemed to push Joe around annoyed her. She wished Joe would stand up to him, and spend less time with his friend. He was a different person when Howard was with him. His usual friendly, tactile and loving nature gave way to an almost school boy personality that tried constantly to impress and flatter his friend. It was embarrassing and made it hard for her to respect her husband at times.

CHAPTER SEVENTEEN

22:40hrs

Joe switched on the radio and Sarah Cox's voice began to talk at him about a beige motorhome. He listened as Snobbery and Decay by Act started to play.

"Nineteen Eighty-Seven." Joe whispered to himself. He and Harriet always used to try and guess the year that the tracks they heard on the radio were released. Annoyingly she was right more often than he. Well, Joe thought to himself as he absent mindedly sang along to the lyrics, they wouldn't be playing that game together again, would they?

Sunday July 18th 2004

Harriet sat in the bath of their new home, eyes closed and contented. She and Joe had spent yesterday moving in, unpacking and when they'd gotten to bed around midnight making love. The two of them had been shattered and had finally fallen asleep in each other's arms. Harriet smiled to herself, they'd managed to find the energy from somewhere to make love before they'd fallen asleep. It had been wonderful. She had felt almost as nervous and excited as the first time and without the fumbling's of not really knowing what the other wanted or liked.

Harriet sank a little further into the bathwater and her head rested comfortably on Joe's chest, his arms wrapped round her, holding her tight. He made her feel safe, wanted, loved and respected all at the same time. He was there for her, always there for her and she promised herself that she would always be there for him.

"Who's that on the radio?" Asked Joe, he kissed the top of his wife's head and looked at the small portable radio subtly emitting sounds by the bathroom door.

"Vernon Kay, why?"

"I didn't know he presented a show on Radio 2."

"It's Radio 1." Harriet knew Joe was not into current chart music, preferring a more sedate style that Radio 2 presented but every now and again she liked something different. "And before you ask I couldn't find the CD player and the wireless speakers plus you haven't plumbed in the entertainment system yet."

"Oh, ok." Joe sat and savoured the moment. He still marvelled from time to time at the fact that Harriet was with him. He must be doing something right. And judging by the noises she had been making last night he must be doing quite a lot right. "You know I have a really good feeling about this place. I mean this house. We've been in less than a day and it already feels like home."

"It has a really nice vibe about the place. Friendly and welcoming, you did good Joe. This house is perfect."

"It came on the market at the right time, for the right price, in the right location. It just seemed perfect."

"It is." Harriet turned slowly and began to kiss her husband passionately. "It's perfect."

❖

Harriet sat at her dressing table drying her hair. She could see Joe in the corner of the mirror getting dressed, she noticed that he was watching her oblivious to the fact that she could see what he was doing. She loved him with all her heart. He was such a kind, considerate, loving and passionate man. He looked after her, complimented her, gave her little gifts and brought her bunches of flowers at random times all to show how much he thought of her and how much he loved her. It could almost be said that he worshipped her but Harriet never really understand what he saw in her. Yes, she admitted to herself that she was a beautiful woman but he claimed to see beyond that to the beautiful woman inside. And she was glad of that he did see that something because she loved him too, so very much, her husband. He was a beautiful man who deserved a child. She so very much wanted to give him a child, the child they both wanted. They had stopped using any contraceptives a few months ago, not that it counted as really trying, with no luck, but then they both had been stressed at times, had their minds on other things but in the last twenty-four hours they had relaxed, relaxed more than they had for a long time. It helped that they had moved, that they were already ninety percent unpacked. Joe was happy with his job, with his career, it was safe and was now starting to pay very well.

Harriet wasn't quite as happy with her job. Pharmaceutical sales hadn't been on her list of career choices when she had left school. Maybe now things were settling down she could look to follow her dreams. She had done a foundation in acting and got a BA Hons in musical theatre from Guildford School of Acting, part of the University of Surrey. Harriet wanted to tread the boards professionally. She wasn't bothered about becoming a major Hollywood star, she just wanted to be happy. She had the man of her dreams who gave her everything she just wanted to do the job that she wanted. She would wait a few months until everything was truly settled then have the conversation with Joe about her future.

"I can see you looking at me." Said Harriet.

Joe flushed and looked uncomfortable.

"It's alright Joe. I like that you still want to look at me."

"You don't find it creepy?" Joe sat on the corner of the bed and looked over his shoulder.

"No sweetie. I love you." Harriet stood and took the few brief steps to stand in front of her husband.

"I love you too honey."

Harriet leaned down and kissed Joe before sitting back down to complete doing her make up.

Joe smiled, his normal colour began to return to his face. He stood and left the bedroom to head downstairs to the kitchen and put the kettle on. He glanced round the room, Harriet was right. This house already felt like a home and with any luck in about 9 months' time it would be echoing with the sound of tiny feet. Stupid saying. It would take at least a year and a half for that to happen. Why did people say that when a baby was due? Joe's thoughts drifted off randomly as he made himself and Harriet a drink.

CHAPTER EIGHTEEN

22:48hrs

Joe checked his speed and gently came off the accelerator. Ninety-seven miles per hour was a little excessive.

"Nineteen Eighty-Nine." He said to himself. Back to Life by Soul to Soul had just started to play as Joe checked the time. Almost ten to eleven. He sighed and decided that an hour was not enough between stops. He'd carry on until around midnight before he made his next stop. It wasn't as if he needed the loo or was overly tired, it was more the boredom of spending five hours behind the wheel of the car.

Joe had known for about four months that Harriet had been unfaithful, it had turned from a suspicion to a reality that cold November night in Woking. Where he'd sat and watched his wife sit in a hotel bar to meet the man she was being unfaithful with.

His best friend. Howard.

He just wished he'd known why he'd waited four months before he'd done anything about it. No that wasn't true. He knew why. He'd been scared that he'd overreact and someone would get hurt.

Well someone had gotten hurt...

Terminally.

Monday 28th June 1999

"Terminal Three, are you sure?" Joe asked as he followed Harriet into the large airport building.

"Yes. Now come on. The flight leaves in just over two hours and I'd like to spend some time in the Virgin Clubhouse before we have to board."

The couple located a check in desk and slowly made their way to the front of the queue where they collected their tickets and checked in their bags.

"Right then, Virgin Clubhouse it is." Joe pointed to the departures gate and the two lovebirds walked hand in hand through customs and snaked their way through the duty free shops.

They took a seat at a small table and ordered two glasses of champagne.

"So what's up?" Asked Joe as he took a sip from his glass.

Harriet thought for a moment and took a sip herself. "It's Howard." She said.

"What about him?" Joe shuffled in his chair.

"Just something he said at the wedding on Saturday."

"I'm surprised you can remember anything from Saturday the amount you drank." Joe snorted. "Christ I can't remember much past ten pm."

"Joe I'm being serious."

"Ok, sorry Harri, I'm just having some fun. So what did he say?"

"It was about nine o'clock after we'd had the first dance and opened up the bar. You'd gone to the loo or popped outside for a sneaky cigarette and Howard had come up to me to talk. He gave me a hug and told me how happy he was for me and us, then said he wondered what would have happened if that day had been different and he'd taken the proverbial bull by the horns." Harriet paused. "What day, what bull and different how?"

"I'm not sure." Joe's brow furrowed. "The only thing I can think of is the day you and I met back in October ninety-two. He mentioned that to me a few times over the past couple of weeks."

"Oh? Why? How could that day have been different?" Harriet looked puzzled. "You bumped into me and knocked my books flying. You bumped into me later at the uni bar. We had a few drinks. I kissed you. We dated and one thing led to another and here we are."

"Yes but Howard has a crazy idea that when we bumped into each other and started to see each other that it was actually Howard you fancied not me and you were scared to ask him out. He thinks that if he hadn't played it cool and had asked you it would have been the two of you sat here going on your honeymoon not you and me." Joe exhaled finally glad to get off his chest. "There, now you know."

"That Howard has the hots for me? Joe, I already know."

"That Howard fancies you?"

"No that Howard's delusional." Harriet kissed Joe. "Howard's not my type, never has been. I love you Mr Anderson."

"I love you Mrs Anderson." Joe kissed Harriet back and held her tightly in his arms. He pulled back slightly and looked into his wife's eyes. "Harri?"

"It's nothing honest." Harriet sat forward in her chair and clutched her hand bag tightly, her knuckles tuning white.

"It's not nothing, that's for sure. Is it the thing with Howard?" Joe asked.

"*God no!*" Her voice was scathing. "Sorry." She realised that she was being uncharacteristically harsh. "No it's nothing to do with Howard."

"Then what?" Joe watched as two new champagne flutes were placed on the table in front of them.

"It's flying." Harriet took a deep breath. "It's flying." She repeated.

"What about flying?"

"I've never flown before."

"Never?" For the second time in as many minutes Joe's brow furrowed.

"I never flew before we met because my parents could never afford it, besides I don't think my dad would have flown even if he could. He's so racist he hates anyone not born in England. We've been abroad but only as far as Ireland, Holland and France and that was by ferry." Harriet gulped down her second glass of champagne. I've never flown and I'm a little nervous."

"Never flown." Joe was caught slightly off guard. "You've

never mentioned it before?"

"You've never asked?" Harriet replied.

"I never asked because it never occurred to me to ask, besides it's the end of the nineties, I assumed you had flown. I mean everyone's flown."

"I haven't."

"And you wait until we're sat waiting to board a plane to fly to New York before you say anything. Did you not think to say something before, like I don't know, when we were booking the honeymoon?" Joe pulled Harriet towards him and held her feeling the nervous shake of her body.

"I did, think to tell you, but I felt silly. Like you said we're six months away from the millennium and who hasn't flown?"

"What apart from you, oh and your parents? Tell me how are you feeling, honestly?"

"Nervous, very nervous. What happens if we have an accident on take-off or crash when landing?"

"There's not a lot you can do…" Joe didn't get to complete what he was going to say as Harriet talked over him.

"What happens if we get hijacked by pirates mid-flight and the terrorists blow up the plane?"

"I know, what happens if we get attacked by a flock of dragons?" Joe said trying to ease his wife's nerves with humour. "Harri, flying is one of the safest forms of travel in the world and the chances of pirates or terrorist hijacking a plane, especially one going to America, are zero. It's just never going to happen. You've got absolutely nothing to worry about. I promise you. Everything's going to be fine."

"I know, I'm still nervous though." A crooked smile crept across Harriet's face and she gulped down Joe's glass of champagne. "It's a flight or weyr."

"What?" Joe looked confused.

"The collective noun for a group of dragons is a flight or weyr not a flock."

❖

Two hours later the newlyweds were sat in their first-class seats, a glass of champagne in each of their hands. Joe was so happy. He was married to the girl of his dreams flying to New York on his honeymoon. The first class seats had been a gift from his parents.

Harriet sat and stared out of the window to her right and the small roads snaking their way across the countryside beneath her. The nerves of earlier all but forgotten with her mind marvelling at how much the ground below looked like a child's toy. Her gaze left the ground below and took in the first class area of the aircraft. He had said his parents wanted to pay for the upgrade to first class and asked if she'd ever flown first class before. She had said no. She admitted to herself that she should have told Joe then that she had never flown before.

The take-off had been a shock, being thrown back in her seat but after that it had been relaxed and nice. Her gaze wandered back through the window looking at the fields and small animals below.

"This is small." Said Joe in a terrible Irish accent. "And that is far away."

"What?"

"I said. This is small, and that is far away." Joe grinned like a Cheshire cat.

"You think you're funny don't you." Harriet grinned back glad of the distraction that her husband was giving her, trying to take her mind from the big metal tube in which she sat. Flying always seemed so unnatural to her. Like her Nan always said, if God had intended man to fly he would have given him wings.

"How are you feeling?" Joe asked. "Are you ok?" He gently squeezed her hand.

"Yes darling I'm fine." She squeezed back. "It's not as scary as I thought it was going to be."

"Flying first class helps. The positioning of the first class compartment is specifically designed to make the whole flying experience as smooth and as comfortable as possible."

"It's certainly been good so..." Harriet's words got stuck in her throat as the plane hit a small pocket of turbulence. The colour drained from her face and her hands gripped the arm rests tight.

"It's ok sweetheart." Whispered Joe as he gently eased Harriet's left hand of the armrest and placed it in his. "It's just a spot of turbulence, differences in air pressure, hot air rises, cold air falls, that's all. Nothing to worry about. You'll get used to it."

Harriet's breathing sounded laboured for a while but soon began to settle as she saw the coastline fall away below the plane.

"Plymouth." Joe said looking over Harriet's shoulder. "That's Plymouth below us. We have a little over seven hours before we land. I'd suggest getting a few hours' sleep as the time difference will make it a very long day. Plus it'll help with the jet lag."

Despite the nerves Harriet felt safe, felt loved, felt happy, sat next to the man she planned to spend the rest of her life with. She settled down in her chair and looked out of the window at the clouds as they slowly climbed closer to them.

CHAPTER NINETEEN

23:00hrs

"And it seems to have stuck. No Lemons, Noel Edmunds, who'd have thought it." A slight pause came from the radio. "This is BBC radio two, on line, on digital and on eighty-eight to ninety-one FM. This is the news at eleven o'clock."

A new voice crackled out of the car speakers quoting headlines from a pre-prepared script. These words, as those before them, washed over Joe's ears, half heard and half ignored. His thoughts were lucid and vivid in their clarity beyond anything he could remember before. Joe briefly wondered if the events of the day and the early evening in particular had something to do with it. Had somehow sharpened his senses. His continued to wander and his thoughts drifted off in a new direction once more.

Saturday 03rd November 2007

"Well?" Asked Joe excitedly.

"Be patient Joe." The weight of expectation was clear in Harriet's voice.

"I'm just excited, and I have a really good feeling this time." Joe could barely contain his excitement and paced around the bathroom nervously before he came to a stop by the window. He took a deep breath and swung round to face his wife. "Well?" he asked again. "It has to be time now, surely." He began to pace again then abruptly stopped when he saw Harriet staring at him. "Sorry. I'm just excited." Joe's foot tapped expectantly on the tiled floor.

Harriet shook her head. She was as nervous and as excited as her husband and had to admit to having a good feeling too. They had gone through this ritual almost every month for the past five years and so far the results had always been the same. But not this month. She was sure it was going to be different. The signs were all there. She felt sick in the morning. For the past week she had experienced the likes of which she had not had since university. Her breasts were sore and her back ached. But the most compelling sign was that she was two days late coming on to her period and she was never late, never. Joe joked that he could set a calendar by her cycle. Twenty nine days to the day her cycle every month. Well it was day thirty-one and still no sign of her period.

"Well?"

Joe's voice brought her back from her thoughts. "Oh, err, one second." Harriet focussed back on the pregnancy test in her hand. "Um, oh. It's negative." All the positivity and excitement drained from her voice and her face. She was disappointed and upset.

"Are you sure?" Joe asked the stupid question that he always asked and the second part of the monthly ritual started.

Joe would want to see the test to make sure that Harriet hadn't made a mistake. She would get angry with him for questioning her, he would over react as would she. They wouldn't talk to each other all day and go to bed still angry. Joe would say sorry. Harriet would apologise and snuggle into her husband's chest. They'd fall asleep in each other's arms after having amazing sex. Then they'd wake up in the morning and act like nothing had happened and try again for a baby next month. Harriet wished they could dispense with all the crap and just have sex. She didn't want it to be pretty or loving she just wanted to feel Joe.

"Are we to have this dance again?" She asked.

"What's that supposed to mean?" Joe left the bathroom and walked into the bedroom hands on his hips. "Well?" he called.

Harriet walked into the bedroom and sat on their bed. "Sit next to me Joe." She patted the bed next to her. "I love you, handsome man."

Joe paused for a fraction of a second and realised he had been holding his breath, he released it and sat down.

"We're both upset but it's not the end of the world. We can try again next month and the next and the next and as long as it takes, but look on the bright side, you get to have lots more sex."

"I know, I'm just sad. I so desperately wanted it to happen this month. I was so sure this was the month we'd find out we were having our first child."

"It's strange as all the signs are there. It must be psychosomatic. I wanted it so badly that my mind projected the symptoms. Frustrating but it is what it is."

"Next time then." Joe stood and extended a hand. "Come on darling, let's go down stairs and I'll make you a cup of tea."

Harriet nodded and stood, of course everything was always better with a cup of tea. She wiped the tears from her face and followed her husband downstairs to the kitchen.

"Tea?" asked Joe rhetorically as he filled the kettle from the tap over kitchen sink. He turned kettle in one hand, flowers in the other. "These are for you darling."

"Oh Joe..." Tears formed in Harriet's eyes and gently trickled down her cheeks. Guilt washed over her, maybe it was the flowers, maybe it was the hormones. "I'm sorry Joe, I'm so sorry I couldn't give you a child."

"It's not your fault darling. It takes two to make a child not just you. Two... You... and I... Two." Joe took the two steps to his wife and hugged her, stroking her and kissing her neck.

Harriet's tears stopped and she reciprocated the hug wrapping her arms around Joe. He seemed to know how to make her happy, to make her feel safe, to take her pain away. She loved her husband so much and wanted to give him a child so desperately, wanted a baby for herself. They had waited three and a half years after getting married to ensure they were both ready, emotionally and financially before they had started trying. But that was five years ago. Five years since she had her coil removed. Five years since they had begun trying, five years of pain. Month after month of expectation and hope followed by disappointment and pain. The months had rolled into years. How much more of this could she take? How much more could she endure? She didn't want to have to go through this one more time, to go through it again and again, she couldn't.

"Joe, I can't keep doing this. It's been five years and we're no closer to conceiving than we were when we started."

Joe's heart sank. Why was this happening to them? They were good people, they didn't deserve this much heartache. But then they wouldn't have to if they asked for help. "Harriet." Joe lifted Harriet's chin and looked into her emerald green eyes. "We should go to the doctors and see about IVF."

"IVF?" Harriet had not really considered this option, she was sure they could do it themselves. "Why didn't we think about this sooner? We should have gone to see the doctor three years ago. We'd have a baby by now." Harriet started to cry uncontrollably and sank deep into Joe's arms.

CHAPTER TWENTY

23:14hrs

The M6 to Joe was a soulless grey road worse than any other road he'd travelled on in the United Kingdom and that included the M25. It stretched north and south for just over two hundred and thirty miles dissecting the western side of England that had never invited him anywhere. It didn't inspire you to do anything except get off it as soon as possible, a feeling that he had right now.

Tuesday 8th June 1982

Jack Gunn fell through the front door of his house into the narrow hallway of his townhouse and crashed into the small table at the bottom stairs knocking the telephone onto the floor with a loud bang. He stumbled on in a vain attempt to pick the phone up and replace it on the table he'd knocked it off.

"Jack!" Whispered Carol angrily at her husband. "You'll wake the boy."

"Fuck sake woman, stop ya nagging will ya. A little bump's not going to wake Howard." Jack's words were slurred and slow. His face was pale, his cheeks red, the shoulder of his jacket half way down his right arm.

"It's half past twelve Jack. You promised that you'd be home straight from work. It was Howard's birthday and we were supposed to be taking him for a meal together as a family, as a family!"

"He's five." Slurred Jack loudly waving a hand dismissively. "He won't even remember in a day or two."

"Five! Five!" Carol's voice rose in both angst and volume, a venomous undertone bit through. "Howard's ten! Ten. You're a drunken twat. You don't even know how old your own son is!"

Jack pushed passed Carol and staggered into the lounge and on into the kitchen. "Drink!" He slurred to himself as he started banging cupboard doors, going from one to the next in a vain attempt to find a bottle and glass.

"You won't find it." Carol said from the kitchen doorway. "I've got rid of it, poured it all down the kitchen sink, all of it."

"What!?"

Jack's left hand caught Carol on the side of the head as he swung round knocking her off her feet onto the wooden door frame then to the floor behind her. Tears filled Carol's eyes as pain and fear consumed her.

"What do you go and do that for woman?" Jack raised his hand, fist clenched, body towering over the prone body of his trembling wife. "Ya stupid fucking bitch!" For two long seconds he stood over his wife before he moved, still unsteadily, back towards the front door, over his wife, past the broken phone and out into the street beyond. He took a moment to get his bearings mumbling under his breath. "You see what you made me do! God dammit woman." Jack's fists clenched and unclenched his breathing heavy. He made to say something then changed his mind before he staggered out through the hall and off into the night.

Carol pulled herself onto her elbows and then sat in the middle of the lounge floor head in her hands. She started to cry, her tears flowed like rivers down her cheeks as she sobbed inconsolably.

Howard sat in his green and white Celtic pyjamas at the top of the stairs, his chin rested on, and his arms wrapped tightly around his knees. He sat on the top step, rocking gently back and forth as he looked down at the mess in the hall at the bottom of the stairs, telephone strewn across the floor. At the open front door that swung in the gentle breeze. He shivered as he felt the chill of the outside air reach his bare feet then slowly crawl up his legs. His mum had continuously tried to hide what was happening with his dad from him, made excuses for his dads' behaviour and out and out lied but Howard, though he was just ten, wasn't stupid. He had eyes and ears, he could see what was going on, hear the arguments and the noises of his father hitting his mum. He knew what was going on but knowing made it no easier to bear, made it no better because he didn't know how to sort it out, how to stop his father from drinking, how to make his mum happy, how to make his family whole again.

Howard wiped the tears from his face, stood silently and quietly made his way back to his room. He so desperately wanted to have a normal happy family but knew deep down there was nothing he could do to change it. Even so he knew he would try, try everything he could to help resolve a desperate and unchangeable situation. Climbing back in to bed Howard made himself a promise. He promised that he would never hit a woman, never treat a woman in the way his father had treated his mother, like a second-class citizen, as a punch bag for his frustrations. He swore to himself that he would respect women, look after them and love them. Not just women but everyone, everyone deserved to be respected and treated well. He promised himself that he'd never become what his father was. A drunk a wife beater and a hate filled lonely scared old man.

CHAPTER TWENTY-ONE

23:25hrs

Joe sat in the left-hand lane on the M6, mindlessly trundling along at a steady seventy. He so desperately wanted to put his foot down. The road was almost empty and he had so far to go. Joe watched as a blue and white sign sailed passed declaring the next exit in half a mile was junction twenty-five for Wigan. Wigan. The only thing Joe knew about Wigan was that they played the other type of rugby there.

If only he could risk putting his foot down, but the last thing he wanted was to get stopped by the police and have them snooping around his car, especially his boot. He wasn't sure how he would explain what was in there, if it was possible to explain away what was in there.

With any luck in about five hours' time all of this would be behind him and he would be in bed, asleep.

Friday 10th October 2014

Joe rushed through the automatic door sideways barely squeezing through the small gap as they slowly opened into the accident and emergency waiting room pulling in with him a cloud of smoke from the gaggle of people smoking outside. His eyes darted around the large benched room trying to find a familiar face amongst the throng of ailing people.

There she was in the corner by the vending machines.

Joe loosened his tie as he strode forward dodging a child, half his face covered in dried blood, playing on the floor by his parents' feet seemingly oblivious to whatever injuries he might have.

"So, what happened?" Joe asked.

"Shit Joe, you nearly gave me a heart attack." Harriet stood on her tip toes to give her husband a kiss on the cheek. Her attention returned to the vending machine and pushed several buttons then watched as the chocolate bar she selected dropped down to the dispensing tray. "I'm not sure to be honest." She bent, retrieved and opened the Kit-Kat. "I was heading home and I saw a car smashed up in the middle of the Kings College roundabout on Southway just opposite the hospital." Harriet pointed absently mindedly out the front door. "When I stopped I recognised the car, Howard's car." She offered her husband a piece of her chocolate.

Joe took the proffered piece of chocolate, holding it in his hand and looked around the waiting room again. "I thought Howard had meetings in London all day, at least that's what he told me."

"I don't know anything about that. Maybe he was going to the station." Harriet snapped. "Does it really matter at this moment in time? Howard's been pulled from a car and is on a bed being looked at by doctors."

"No, I suppose not." Joe munched on the finger of chocolate given to him by his wife, his thoughts whizzing around his head, right hand in his trouser pocket fingering his brand-new iPhone 6S Plus not two weeks old. Strange the text message he had received at four that afternoon. A text from Howard stating that his meeting had gone well and that he had decided to stay in London for the night to catch up with some old friends and have a few beers. It could be possible that he had changed his mind and got a train to Guildford, for they took a little over half an hour. That was if he was inclined to change his mind which Joe knew from experience Howard rarely was. He'd never pass up a chance for a night in London. Unless he had something to come back for. Joe's thoughts paused, his gaze stopped on his wife. Unless he had not gone to London in the first place. Unless what he wanted was here, had kept him here in the first place. Joe knew of Howard's feelings for his wife, they had been there since the day he had seen her. Joe knew that look he had seen in his eyes that day. He had seen it many times before and many times since in other men but never again in the eyes of Howard, just that once, for Harriet. But never once had Joe suspected that Harriet felt the same way, not once. He did not know for certain but his father had always said trust your gut and his gut was screaming at him. He wished it wasn't true but, in his heart, he knew it was. Had he wasted the last twenty years of his life with a woman that had betrayed his love?

Harriet raised her eyebrows. "Well." Her left-hand gestured slightly awkwardly to the double doors to Joe's right.

"What, oh yes." He took Harriet's right hand with a feyned smile and let his wife guide him through the doors.

CHAPTER TWENTY-TWO

23:37hrs

All things considered Joe had had a pretty good childhood. His parents had portrayed a sense of happiness and togetherness, that they had enjoyed being together as a couple and as a family. They had been married for over thirty years and the nineteen-year age gap had never been an issue for them or any of their friends. It was only at his dad's funeral that he'd learnt a few things that had opened his eyes.

Growing up Joe had wished that he would be as happy as he believed his parents had once been. Have a marriage that was as strong, durable and long lasting. It wasn't until after his father had died that he'd learnt the truth about his parent's marriage or at least his mother's version of the truth.

It was amazing, Joe thought as he pulled out to overtake a lorry, how life seemed to go in circles, how you seemed to make the same mistakes your parents made which were the same mistakes that your grandparents made. Round and round, again and again.

Saturday 26th June 1999

Howard sat listening to Harriet's father talk about his daughter and about how happy Joe made her, how he made a beautiful addition to the family, a perfect partner for his daughter. A perfect partner. His thoughts drifted to earlier that day stood outside Harriet's parents house and wondered what Kevin would be saying if Harriet had said yes to him and if it was him marrying his daughter. He knew for certain that Kevin would never describe him as the perfect partner. He knew Kevin didn't care too much for him and he didn't care, he just cared about Harriet. Why wasn't it him marrying Harriet? He loved her so much his heart ached every time he left her.

He saw Ally sat on the table in front of him, his date for the wedding, one of Harriet's friends and colleagues from work. She was beautiful, sexy, funny, everything he could want except for one small thing, she wasn't Harriet, she'd never be Harriet. They had been dating for a year and she had raised the subject of marriage and kids which wasn't surprising seeing as her friend was about to get married, she saw how happy Harriet appeared to be, at least on the outside because Howard knew deep down that she wasn't happy that she didn't want to be with the man she was with and that it was Howard she really wanted to be with.

Howard smiled at Ally and raised his glass. He knew that in three months he would have ended the relationship and would be looking for someone else to replace Harriet with even though he'd never had her in the first place.

"So, will everyone please stand and raise their glasses to Harriet and Joseph. The bride and groom."

"The bride and groom." Chorused the group of people before him. Howard Morris surveyed the gathered guests before him, his glass raised in salute to his best friend and his new wife. Howard took a large gulp from the champagne flute he was holding. He smiled as the bubbles tickled his nose and a few drops dripped unnoticed on to his tie.

Howard's smile broadened as he looked over at his best friend sat beside him. Who in turn was looking at his best man a slightly drunken smile on his face. The day had rushed by to this point. He could hardly remember the service that had happened not four hours before. The amount of alcohol he had consumed wasn't helping. Howard and Joe had taken their first drink at ten am that morning with the eggs and bacon they'd had for breakfast some seven hours earlier.

Joe stood, slightly unsteadily, shook the hand of his best friend and whispered thanks into his ear. Joe was smiling even more than his best man. Married. Man and wife. Mr and Mrs Anderson. The thought filled Joe with joy. "Firstly, I'd like to thank my best man, Howard." He looked down briefly at the now seated man next to him. "For the wonderful and not *too* embarrassing speech.

"Secondly to the maid of honour, Mary, for all of her support and help today and over the past few months.

"Thirdly to my parents, for everything they've done for us over the past six years helping to get Harriet and I to this point in our lives.

"Fourthly to Harri's parents. Mr and Mrs Macintosh, without them none of us would be here." Joe raised his glass, took a sip of his champagne then looked to his new wife. "And last but definitely by no means least I want to thank Harriet for agreeing to marry me and making me the happiest man alive." Joe sat and kissed his wife passionately holding her hand and never wanting to let go, never wanting the moment to end.

"Right then, I think that was my cue. Time for the best man's speech." Howard stood smiling and raised his glass toasting his best friend. "Doesn't he look good in that suit ladies and gentlemen. You don't want to know how long it took to get him in to that, I tell you it was a squeeze..." Howard's eyebrows raised as he whistled.

CHAPTER TWENTY-THREE

23:55hrs

Five minutes to midnight. Joe stifled a yawn and frantically rubbed his eyes. They felt dry. Six hours in an air-conditioned car would do that. Joe cracked his window and let the chilled night air blow through the small gap onto his face. He exhaled and watched as his breath condensate in front of him. The cold air felt nice on his cold face.

Friday 31st December 1999

Joe sat on the sofa in the living room of his four-bedroom detached house watching the large TV wearing an old pair of pyjama bottoms and a white t-shirt. The TV flickered in the corner of the room with Jools Holland sat playing the piano. He'd contemplated buying one of the new flat screen plasma TV's but he couldn't justify the nine-thousand-pound price tag. The noise from his TV was barely audible above the pops, bangs and whizzes coming from the frenetic cacophony of fireworks that were lighting the night sky outside his house. Joe was uncomfortable, felt bloated from all the snacks and sweats he'd consumed over the past few hours and tried to reach down and open the top button of his jeans without waking his snoring wife who laid across his lap.

Was this really going to be the way he was going to celebrate the new year and see in the new millennium?

Until about an hour ago the two had been at a millennium eve party arrange by Howard at his flat not far from the centre of town. The balcony had a good view of the Rugby club where there was a large fireworks display arranged. They had arrived slightly later than everyone else after Joe had surprised her with a romantic candlelit meal.

They had sat for almost three hours from six talking over a bottle of wine and a four-course meal that he'd prepared. The party had started at seven but it was almost nine when they had realised what time it was and had rushed over to Howard's flat leaving the plates and cutlery on the table to be cleared in the morning, neither expected to even attempt to do it by the time that they planned to get back in the not so early hours of the morning.

The night had been a blur with the two of them consuming a lot of alcohol in a short period of time as they rushed to catch up with their friends.

❖

"Joe!" Howard called from the kitchen across the lounge to balcony door where Joe was stood smoking with several of their friends.

"What?" Joe flicked the dead cigarette butt out of the open door and over the balcony to the street below. He looked over at Howard who pointed to his right.

Joe looked left and saw his wife of six months staggering towards the hall, bump into a table and disappear around the corner. The front door and bathroom where around the corner. Joe headed after his wife hoping that she wasn't leaving the flat. He quickened his pace and rounded the corner into the hall to see Harriet disappear into the bathroom. At least she wasn't doing a runner.

"Harri?" Joe called as the door closed behind her. Joe reached forward for the handle and paused at the door trying to hear what was going on inside. "Harri? Are you ok my sweet?" Joe listened intently. He heard retching sounds from someone being sick and felt suddenly concerned. "Harri!" Joe turned the handle and pushed the bathroom door open. He saw Harriet half sprawled on the floor and half draped over the toilet, head in the bowl.

"Are you ok?" Joe approached Harriet and crouched next to her putting an arm around her shoulders.

She mumbled something incoherent before being sick again. Harriet looked up at her husband a forlorn look in her eyes. She sniffed and took a deep breath. "I'm sorry Joe. I'm so sorry."

"It's ok sweetie." Joe gentle pushed the damp hair out of her face and behind her ears.

"I want to go home." Harriet started to cry quietly. "You stay. I'll get a taxi."

"Don't be silly." Joe pulled Harriet to him and held her tight to him. "Why would I let you go alone? Hey? Why?" Joe stood slowly pulling his wife with him on to her unsteady feet. He caught sight of his and his wife's reflection in the mirror on the bathroom wall and winced. Harriet looked pale, eyes sunken and red, hair matted and greasy, clothes stained. She looked a mess and he needed to get her home. He could not trust that she would be safe travelling the half a mile from Howard's flat to their house.

Jools Holland continued to played the piano on the TV in front of him. Joe looked at the small clock that sat atop the TV set. He had to squint to see the small hands in the diminished light of the room. Four minutes to midnight. His plan for the evening, revised plan, was simple. Sit here for another five minutes. Watch the new year in and then try to get his unconscious wife up the stairs and into bed without waking her. He looked down momentarily, not waking her shouldn't be an issue.

CHAPTER TWENTY-FOUR

00:25hrs

Another thirty miles. Twenty-five minutes or so and he'd be at Southwaite services for his second scheduled stop. He needed some petrol. His activities of seven hours ago seemingly a distant memory. He'd spent most of the drive so far thinking about the past without a thought about the future. About what he was going to do once this night was through.

What was he going to do?

His marriage was dead. There was no life left in it and there was no going back.

His longest and deepest friendship had been ripped apart by betrayal.

He wasn't even sure if he could ever go back to work, or even if he wanted to.

His future for so long had seemed so bright, so inviting now looked bleak and empty.

What was he going to do?

Wednesday 21st October 1992

Joe and Harriet sat and watched as Howard and Sarah sat in the corner opposite them, arms and tongues entangled.

They themselves sat in nervous silence, both trying to think of the next thing to say as they tentatively sipped their drinks, eyes darting here and there. Joe took a deep breath and spoke, his words hesitant, his face flushed and hand clammy with sweat.

"So what course are you actually doing? Howard said it's a performing arts degree but Sarah said you're doing a BA in dance."

Harriet had a little grin on her face. She wasn't sure if it was the room, the alcohol she'd consumed or the man sat next to her but Harriet felt slightly flushed, incredibly comfortable if a little nervous. She looked at Joe and glanced over at Howard who had followed Sarah to the pool table. It looked like she was letting Howard show her how to play, Harriet snorted to herself. That could become interesting later. Howard obviously didn't know that Sarah was the current university pool champion having beaten everyone in the women's and men's leagues.

Her eyes drifted back to Joe as she took a sip from her drink. "I'm doing a BA in Dance, what about you?" Howard was the more classically handsome of the two which was probably why Sarah had jumped on him at the first chance she got but Harriet didn't fancy him. She was warming rapidly towards Joe and hoped that he was feeling the same way and it wasn't going to be one of those one-night stand things. Harriet half listened as Joe explained the basics behind the degree that he and Howard were doing, picking up words like aeronautical, mathematics and physical coefficient. Her chin rested in the palm of her hand as she drank in the view in front of her.

As he spoke Joe saw Harriet glancing repeatedly at Howard. Why? He asked himself. Just for once Joe wished he could meet an attractive girl and that she liked him, that her head wasn't turned by his best friend and didn't just date him to get closer to Howard.

Oh well he had nothing to lose. He stood "Can I get you another drink?" He collected the glasses on the table and looked expectantly at Harriet.

"Please, I'll have another Gin." Harriet stood, straightened her skirt then flicked her hair away from the side of her face trying her hardest to flirt with Joe but he just didn't seem interested in her. "I'll give you a hand." Her voice dripped with hope.

"Don't you worry your pretty little head sweetheart. I'll give this douchebag a hand." Howard had appeared next to Harriet and lightly smacked her bottom. "Come on Joe." He said walking towards the bar.

Sorry, Joe mouthed over his shoulder as he turned to follow his friend to the bar.

Harriet stretched up on her tip toes and gently kissed Joe on the cheek while silently cursing under her breath. She watched the two men retreat towards the bar snaking their way through small groups of other students chatting and drinking noisily. Gosh how she wanted to get into Joe's pants. What? Where had that come from? She wasn't that sort of person; a slut her mum would have called her if she'd been here. Well it was a good job she wasn't. Harriet smiled to herself. The evening wasn't done yet and neither was she. Harriet was sure there was a connection between the two of them. Maybe Joe was playing coy or maybe he was just shy. The night was still young and she had plenty of time to find out.

"What's got you so happy?" Sarah asked as she sat down next to her friend and placed her arm around Harriet's shoulder drawing her closer. "Well?"

"I'm just having a good evening, that's all." Harriet stifled a smile and tried to deflect. "Are you having a good evening?"

"Come on Harri, forget about me for once, it's written all over your face."

"What is?"

"You've got the hots for him."

"What?" Harriet began to feel slightly uncomfortable. Was she being that obvious?

Sarah chuckled to herself. Bingo. She could read Harriet like a book. "I'm not surprised though; Howard is one sexy guy. He's been talking about you nonstop since we got here, so I think you're in there." Sarah turned to face Harriet, waiting for her friend to admit what she already knew but the face that stared back was one of confusion and... disgust.

"Howard? Oh my god, no. Joe..."

The last word hung in the air for several seconds. Harriet wished the world would swallow her. Why had she said his name out loud? Sarah would be relentless, never let it go. Why?

Sarah finally broke the silence. "Didn't see that coming. Err, if you like Joe, do... you... mind... if I, you know, um, have a, err, take Howard back with me?" Sarah looked over at the bar, a dreamy look on her face.

❖

"So then Joseph my lad, when are you going to stop messing around and ask Harriet to go back to yours?" Howard looked at himself in the mirror behind the bar preening himself like a peacock.

"What do you mean?" Joe handed a ten-pound note to the bar man and waited for his change.

"It's so obvious that you like Harri and she likes you." Howard looked at Joe. "Come on man, don't tell me you can't see it?" Joe looked shocked.

"You're serious? You can't be. She spent most of the time we were talking looking at you." Joe took and pocketed his change.

"Yes, to probably see if Sarah had made a move on me." Howard nudged Joe playfully and winked at him before he picked up two drinks from the bar.

Joe grabbed the other two and scuttled after Howard. His eyes focused on Harriet. She liked him, did she like him? Howard said so. He was usually pretty good at these things. She looked so beautiful in her black top and red skirt. His eyes tracked down her body to her long elegant legs that seemed to go on forever.

"You're beautiful." The words just seemed to appear in the air as Joe arrived at the table. He stood, mouth slightly open, wondering what had been going through his head to make him say that. At that moment he thought that any chance he'd had with Harriet had just run out of the door. Harriet's face said it all. Shock. Why had he said that? He was such an idiot. "I..." Joe put the drinks down on the table and began to turn to walk away.

Harriet stood and grabbed Joe's arm. "You're handsome."

Their eyes locked. Their breathing became slower and deeper. In that briefest of moments, their lives seemed to stand still as the realisation dawned on them both. Their soulmate stood before them and nothing else in the world seemed to exist except each other.

Harriet tilted her head upwards as she took half a step forward.

Joe tilted his head downwards as he took half a step forward.

Their lips touched lightly at first, glancing each other then gradually they pushed together.

Joe and Harriet felt a spark, a connection, a joining of souls. Their senses heightened, noises became clearer. In that very moment they felt alive as if for the first time. Was this what true love felt like? Both speculated in the frozen moment in time, neither truly knew.

After several seconds, seconds that disappeared in a flash and at the same time stretched forward into eternity the two of them slowly pulled away to looked deep into each other's eyes. Smiles crept across both of their faces as they sat next to each other and began to talk in hushed tones, the world beyond them gone in an instant, only they remained.

"Told him so." Howard muttered to himself. He looked over at Sarah who was still seated opposite the new love birds. "Come on sexy, let's have another game of pool." With any luck the night might not be a total waste for him either.

CHAPTER TWENTY-FIVE

00:39hrs

Water. Joe desperately wanted some water. His mouth was starting to become dry. He was also getting hungry, very hungry. His departure from Guildford had been pretty rapid and completely unplanned. He hadn't thought to pick up any food or drink before he left nor had he filled up with petrol.

On arrival at Hilton Park he'd thought about it, about getting some on the way out but all coherent thoughts had vanished when he'd been sick.

Joe checked the dashboard. Thirty miles to empty. It was a good job that he had less than ten miles to go before he could fill up.

Sunday 01st August 2004

Joe crept down the stairs carefully avoiding the third step from the bottom that squeaked loudly whenever anyone stepped on it. It was yet another thing he needed to add to his snagging list along with the twenty or so other things that desperately needed to be fixed.

Joe had set the timer on the coffee machine the night before and it was busily percolating away on the counter. It should be about ready. He checked the clock on the kitchen wall and then his watch on his wrist. He figured he had about twenty minutes before Harriet began to wake up at her usual seven o'clock. He had prepared most things the night before and just needed to poach some eggs and toast some bread. He busied himself in the kitchen manoeuvring himself as quietly as he could between the fridge, work surface, toaster and hobs.

Eighteen minutes later Joe loaded up a tray with a plate of eggs benedict, a mug of freshly ground coffee, black and a single yellow rose. He lifted it from the work top with a satisfied breath and made his way out of the kitchen towards the stairs when he heard a screech.

Joe's first thought was that Harriet had woken up from a bad dream either that or there was a spider in the bathroom.

"Honey, are you ok?" he called up the stairs and tried to take two steps at a time while holding the tray as level as possible in a vain bid not to spill the coffee over the eggs. "Honey?" Joe called again. He reached the top of the stairs a moment later and sung left towards the bedroom.

Empty. He placed the tray down gently on the bed and walked to the bathroom. "Harri, what's wrong honey?" Joe looked down as he walked in, his wife sat on the toilet head down, shoulders moving up and down erratically. "Harri?" Concern edged his voice.

Harriet slowly looked up, tears streaming down her face, something in her hand.

"Harri, what have you got there?" Joe asked.

Harriet smiled through her tears. "I'm pregnant Joe."

"What?" Joe took half a step backwards. "Did you just say..."

"Yes, I'm pregnant Joe." Harriet looked up at her husband her grin become broader with each second that passed. "We're going to have a baby." She stood and flung her arms around her husband's neck and kissed him. "We're going to be parents." Joy filled every part of her body. After several years of trying it had finally happened. She let go of Joe and took a step back looking back at the pregnancy test in her hand. The blue line showed dark and clear. There was no mistaking the result. She was definably pregnant. She held it forward presenting it to Joe. "Look Joe, look."

"You're joking." Joe looked down, "You're not joking are you." A statement not a question. Joe couldn't believe it. A multitude of emotions rose up inside him. A mixture of joy, excitement, anxiety and fear and the realisation of what was going to happen in nine months' time dawned on him. Was he ready? Joe asked himself. A little late to be thinking like that now. He had discussed the possibility of having children extensively with Harriet and they had both agreed that it was what they both wanted. But in the briefest of seconds Joe wasn't totally sure it was what he wanted. Maybe he was just scared that he would be a bad parent. He suddenly felt sick and the colour drained from his face.

"Are you ok Joe? You look a little pale." Observed Harriet.

"I'm excited. The rush of adrenaline is making me feel a bit sick, that's all." Joe licked his dry lips, he needed a glass of water. "Eggs..." Joe remembered the breakfast that he had made his wife. Hopefully it wouldn't be too cold. "Shall we go into the bedroom." Joe said. "I have a surprise for you."

"I think that ship has sailed don't you?" Joked Harriet grinning.

"Funny." Joe took Harriet's hand. "Seriously, I have a surprise for you." He guided her to their bedroom.

Harriet saw the breakfast and kissed her husband. The smell of the eggs assaulted her nostrils and she turned and ran back to the bathroom.

Joe stepped out of the bedroom and watched Harriet lean over the toilet as the door slowly closed behind her. The sounds of Harriet being sick rang out around the house and echoed in his ears.

Joe was ecstatic with the news that he was going to be father, he just hoped her pregnancy would be an easy one that her morning sickness would subside quickly and she could settle down to a relatively normal life for the next eight months. He walked back into the bedroom and collected the tray. It seemed a shame to let the eggs go to waste.

CHAPTER TWENTY-SIX

00:48hrs

"Shit!" Joe swore. The exit for Southwaite Services disappeared in his rear-view mirror. Gretna Green would be the next set of services but Joe couldn't remember if they were open twenty-four seven or not. Should he take the next exit and turn around or carry on?

If he went back it would add a good twenty minutes on to his journey.

Joe thought for a moment.

Gretna Green it was. He might be cutting it close but what other option did he really have?

Tuesday 11th March 1986

"That has to be the worst joke I've ever heard." Joe tried to stifle a chuckle as he spoke.

"Then why are you laughing?" Howard asked.

"Because I feel sorry for you." Joe took off his school tie and stuffed it into the pocket of his blazer. "You really are bad at telling jokes."

"You keep saying that but you always laugh."

"Like I said, it's out of embarrassment, not because I think you're funny, which you're not." Joe chuckled again and shook his head. "Not at all."

Joe and Howard turned right off Southmore Street onto

Wolsley Street.

"Isn't that your house? Joe asked.

"What?" Howard was too busy rooting in his ruck sack to pay any real attention to the street ahead of him.

"Where that man is sat?" Joe asked.

"Huh?" Howard stopped and looked up. "Yeah, it looks like my dad".

Joe slowed so Howard could catch up to him.

"But you said your dad was doing a double shift today. That's why we invited Louise Baldwin and Debra Hayes round. Your house is supposed to be empty today."

"He is, it is." Howard stumbled over his words trying to make sense of the unexpected scene in front of him. Two questions popped into his head. Why was his dad home at this time of the day and why was he sat outside the house on the front door step?

"Is he alright?"

"How should I know?" Howard's face was screwed up, his voice was sharp and slightly aggressive.

The boys watched as Jack's right hand slowly rubbed the side of his face, his right elbow slipped off his knee, the arm had been supporting his head which suddenly lurched downwards stopping just short of his knee. Jack's head swayed and hovered above his leg while his right hand seemed to search blindly for his head and knee. Once found he again rested his head in his hand and his elbow on his knee before the cycle started over again.

"Fuck sake! He's drunk!" exclaimed Howard.

"Again?" Joe snorted. "Your dad drinks like a fish."

"This is no joking matter." Howard snapped and angrily stomped off towards his father. "Why!?" he called waving his hands in the air and dropped his bag. "Why dad? Why?"

Jack's head swung up and round in a large looping arch to look at his son. The corners of his mouth raised upwards as he forced a smile. "Howie my boy."

Howard could not contain his anger and frustration. He

kicked a large stone with his battered but highly polished shoe in the direction of his father in the hope it would hit him. The stone flew close to Jacks head and bounced harmlessly in a random pattern of jumps and rolls. Jack moved his head barely noticing how close the stone came to hitting him and how much damage it could have potentially done to him.

"Probably wouldn't have even noticed would you?" Howard muttered under his breath as he slowly approached his father. He looked down frowning. A pair of glazed eyes looked back up at him.

"Howie." Jack tried to stand several times pushing up off the steps and leaning against the wall behind him, his legs wobbled like jelly each time and he fell back down on to his bottom. "Howie, help your old man up will you?"

"Fuck sake dad stop calling me Howie. I'm not five!"

"Watch your language young man. You're not too big to go over my knee." The words were slurred and slow.

"Yeah right. You can't even stand, the state that you're in."

Jack tried one more time to stand, failed and slumped back to the step.

By now Joe had caught up with his friend and moved round to the opposite side of Jack to Howard. Joe nodded to the seated man then to the door behind him.

"No, go home. He's my dad and I'll deal with him." Howard was angry, but above all he was upset and embarrassed that people, especially his best friend, saw his dad like this. Upset that his dad felt the need to drink all the time to the point that he became violent or couldn't stand by himself. That he wouldn't talk to anyone about what was causing him to do what he was doing. That he wouldn't seek help and sort himself out. But most of all that he was letting his mother, his son and himself down.

"And leave my best friend? No. We stick together. We help each other. Look out for each other." Joe reached down and grabbed Jack under his left arm.

Howard let out a sigh and reached down to grab his father under his right arm. He had to admit that he was glad Joe was staying to help. He didn't know what to do and worse still he didn't know who to ask for help or even how to ask had there been anyone he could talk to. Howard stretched and unlocked and opened the door behind his dad as they tried to stop Jack from falling back through the now open door.

"Ready?" Howard crouched again and positioned himself ready to lift his father to his feet. The two fourteen-year olds unceremoniously man handled Jack to his feet then half guided, half dragged Jack in to the house.

"Lounge." Howard answered the unasked question. Jack banged his shin into the phone table as he staggered to his right. Howard and Joe exchanged glances and swear words as they man handled Jack through the hall and into the lounge. The drunken man seemed to trip over or bump into everything close to him and even things that weren't.

"There." Howard pointed with his head at a chair in the corner of the room. The two boys seemed to inhale together to steel themselves for the last few meters.

Finally, Jack sat slumped in a chair by the window. Howard and Joe sat slumped opposite him on the sofa both breathing heavily.

"I hate you." Howard whispered under his breath and watched as his father vomited down his front and on to his legs. "I really fucking hate you." He tried to control his breathing while he stared with loathing in his eyes at his father. It was at that moment that Howard realised that he had no love left in his heart for Jack. The man sat slumped in front of him covered in his own vomit was nobody, not a father, definitely not a dad, a nobody. A stranger. He didn't know him. Didn't want to know him. Didn't want him in his life. Not now. Not ever.

"What shall we do with your dad?" Joe glanced at Jack then looked back at his friend noticing a difference in the way he was looking at his father.

"Leave Jack here. Maybe he'll do us all a favour and drown in his own vomit."

"You can always hope." Joe stood and turned to leave.

Come on, let's go to mine. With any luck we'll see Debbie and Louise on the way and they can come with us there."

CHAPTER TWENTY-SEVEN

00:59hrs

Joe had made a point over the past fifteen minutes to concentrate on exactly where he was. Checking his fuel consumption, how many miles he had left until the car said he'd be empty and how many miles he had left until he reached the services at Gretna Green.

As Joe pulled into the services and up to a pump he glanced one last time at his dashboard.

Two.

That's how many miles he had left before he would have been out of fuel. He let go of the steering wheel with a sigh and wiped his hands on his trousers.

Another two and a half hours and this would all be behind him, just another bad memory to add to the catalogue.

Wednesday 28th March 1990

"So where are we going? The Brewdog?" Asked Joe as he and Howard walked up Meadowside.

"If that's ok with you." Said Howard.

"Well it is your eighteenth after all."

"True, just don't go saying anything to Billy or he'll chuck us out and ban us from the bar." Howard adjusted his thin black tie for the tenth time in as many minutes.

"Why are you so nervous?" Joe looked to his right at Howard in his grey drainpipe trousers and matching jacket.

"It's nothing."

"Really? You're not acting like it's nothing."

"Let's get a drink, find a quiet corner and I'll get you up to speed. I could do with some advice anyway."

The two friends walked into the pub minutes later and immediately split up. Joe walked to the bar and Howard went looking for a quiet corner.

"Hi Billy, two pints of Carlsberg please." Howard leaned against the bar and watched Howard nervously pull apart a beer mat, his eyes looking intently at his hands.

"You two celebrating Howard's birthday?" Billy put the two pints of larger in front of Joe and took the five-pound note from the young man's hand.

"Yep." Joe took the two pounds sixty change and picked up the two beers.

"Wish him happy birthday from me." Billy smiled at Joe then moved down the bar.

"Here." Joe pushed one of the lagers to his friend, took a sip from his and sat down. "So?"

Howard took a long drink and stared at Joe who pulled his tobacco, papers and filters from his jacket pockets then began to roll a cigarette.

"I can't help you if you don't talk to me." Joe licked the gummed strip and finished his rolling. "Damn, got a light?" He lit the cigarette and pulled a stray piece of tobacco from his lips. "Well?"

Howard knew that he needed to talk but for some reason it was difficult for him to start. If he didn't start soon Joe would be at him incessantly until he opened up, plus he knew he'd feel much better for opening up. "Right. Last weekend when you were away with your mum and her new boyfriend in Glasgow I went out for a few beers with Dylan and Hamish. We ended up in the Underground..."

"Why?" Joe interrupted. "That place is a hole. It's like an oven all the time, the beer is overpriced and watered down plus is dirty, real dirty."

"Does it matter why? Really?"

Joe took a drag on his cigarette. "Suppose not." He nodded for his friend to continue.

"We got talking to a few of the uni girls, from Preston." Howard paused to reflect. "Nice they were. One of them ever so, blond hair blue eyes." Howard caught Joe's impatient glance and continued. "Well we were just about to buy them a drink when their boyfriends showed up mouthing off. One thing led to another and I ended up hitting one and before I knew what was going on the police were there. Dylan did a runner but Dylan and I got arrested and charged with affray."

"And you're telling me this now?" Joe stubbed out his cigarette and shuffled in his seat in an attempt to get comfy. "What has your mum said?" Joe started to roll another cigarette. He felt slightly annoyed that it had taken a week for Howard to tell him what had happened. They were supposed to be friends, able to talk to each other about anything.

"You've been away, and I just didn't know how to tell you." Howard took a drink. "She doesn't know and you better not tell her, it'll kill her. You know how she is."

"I do and what do you take me for. If you don't want her to know then I won't tell her. If I did she'd probably blame me anyway even though I wasn't there. What do you think will happen? With the charge I mean"

"First offence and it was provoked. If they press charges, then I'll get a slap on the wrist and a criminal record." Howard sniffed and exhaled sharply out of his nose before taking another sip of his drink. "Could be worse."

"Could be." Joe agreed. "So why are so bothered about it? It's most likely that nothing will come of it."

Howard shook his head, screwed up his face and sighed again. "I'm just worried that it might affect my university application."

"You'll be fine." Joe sounded a lot more confident and certain than he actually felt. "I don't think that you have to declare it, do you?"

"Don't know." Howard's breathing was beginning to get deeper. "I suppose I'll find out in a couple of weeks when all of this is over won't I."

"Have you decided what you want to do and which university's offer you're going to accept?" Joe looked at his friend, he already knew where he was going. He'd gotten his conditional offer from the University of Surrey to study aeronautical engineering.

"I've applied to Glasgow, Aberdeen, Edinburgh and Surrey. I've had unconditional offers from Glasgow, Edinburgh and Surrey. Aberdeen have given me a provisional offer if you can believe that."

It was one thing that they'd agreed not to talk about, their university applications believing that they should do it in isolation of each other so as not to influence their decisions or blindly follow whoever chose first. So that they could follow their own dreams and not each other's.

Joe smiled to himself. "So, what's your preference? Glasgow or Edinburgh?"

"I thought we'd agreed not to talk about applications, at least not until we'd both made our decisions." Said Howard taking a drink.

"We did, but I've already made my decision. I got my conditional offer through yesterday."

"Obviously Glasgow and Aberdeen would be amazing but neither have the exact course that I want to study. Edinburgh is closer to home but Surrey is a better uni, in my opinion. The course is better suited to what I want to do and the support programme is amazing. It has a higher pass rate than Edinburgh and students are more likely to get a job when they qualify. So, I sent off my acceptance to Surrey this morning. Surrey it is."

"I'll see you there then." Joe extended his right hand.

"You? You've applied to Surrey as well?" Howard shook the proffered hand. "My round then."

"Guess so. Oh, and Billy says happy birthday by the way."

❖

Joe stubbed his cigarette out in the quickly filling ash tray. He was smoking too much, but then did it really matter? Probably not in the great scheme of things. He could get hit by a car tomorrow. "My round then." He stood and adjusted his jeans that had been cutting into his crotch for the past twenty minutes. Time for a whiskey chaser methinks."

Howard nodded his agreement and watched his best friend walk off towards the bar and order the drinks.

"Shit." Howard swore under his breath, reached forward and stubbed out his cigarette and pushed the ashtray away from him in to the middle of the table. He recognised the two faces stood next to Joe. The one with the hideous tartan shirt was sporting a rather large black eye. They were the two knob-heads from last week that Dylan and he had had a run in with. Howard shuffled round the table in an effort not to be seen by them, the last thing he wanted was for Joe to get caught up in his mess.

"Friends of yours?" Asked Joe. He set the four drinks on the table and sat slightly further round so he had sight of the bar but more importantly the two English youths stood there.

"What?"

"They clocked you the second they walked in and started mouthing off."

"Hamish and I bumped into to them last week in town. They were unhappy about Tony Stranger's try claiming there was a forward pass in the build-up and robbed them of the five nations title."

"Not sure how that works as we'd still have won nine, seven." Said Joe.

"That's what Hamish and I said."

Joe took a long drink of his beer and placed the empty glass back on the table. "Well Billy's had a word with them and told them in no uncertain terms that if they tried anything the only way they'd be getting out of here was on a stretcher. It looks like it might have done the trick but still, I'd be careful later when we leave." Joe looked at his friend. For the first time in ten years he couldn't tell what Howard was thinking and that worried him more that the two pricks stood at the bar.

"Yeah, well, we'll see won't we. Let's finish these and move on."

"Where to? Asked Joe trying to match Howard gulp for gulp.

"Quite frankly I don't care." Howard felt the need to get up, walk over to the bar, punch those sanctimonious twats in the face and finish what he and Alistair had started the week before.

"Really?" Joe raised his whiskey glass and looked puzzled.

"To us." Howard raised his glass and tilted his head in salute.

"To us." Joe replied and the two young men drained their glasses. "Right then, I'm going for a pee before we head off."

"Ok. I'll be at the bar. I want to have a quick chat with Billy."

Joe picked up his coat and headed off to the gents leaving Howard behind collecting up the glasses.

Barely a minute later Joe was washing his hands when he heard raised voices from the bar. "Howard." He said to his reflection in the mirror above the wash basins and gritted his teeth. What was going on? He rinsed his hands and rubbed them on the legs of his jeans as he hurriedly bundled his way out of the toilets and into the bar area to see Howard, fists raised, being separated from the two English uni students, one of which had a bloody nose, by Billy.

"You two! Out! Before I call the police!" Billy said voice raised. "Now!"

The two students backed away towards the door shouting curses as they left.

"What the hell did I miss?" Joe walked slowly towards Howard. At that moment he realised he had known what his friend had been thinking a few minutes ago.

Nothing.

He had not been thinking about anything. Howard had and still was consumed by rage, by anger and by hatred. Not necessarily towards the two unfortunate English university students who had been in the wrong place at the wrong time.

"What happened?" Joe gestured to the two stools lying on their side next to the bar itself.

Billy raised a hand towards Howard and began to speak. "Your friend here walked over to the bar and the two English kids started mouthing off. One of them took a swing at Howard, so, Howard punched him. Got what he deserved if you ask me." Billy walked back round the bar and put three tumblers down between them. He filled each glass with a large measure and place the bottle of Jura back on the shelf next to the other spirits. "On me lads." He said with a wry smile as he raised one of the glasses.

"Thanks Billy." Joe was not totally convinced with Billy's version of events. By the sounds of his voice Joe didn't think Billy was totally convinced either. He nudged Howard softly in the ribs.

"What, oh, um yeah. Thanks Billy." Howard's attention finally transferred from the door.

Joe looked from Howard to Billy and noticed for a split second the piecing look Billy gave his friend as they all took a sip of their whiskey. His initial hunch had been correct. Billy knew something that he wasn't saying. Joe didn't know what had gotten Howard all riled up and why Billy would cover for him but he vowed to find out.

CHAPTER TWENTY-EIGHT

01:05hrs

Joe stood, eyes closed, shirt sleeves rolled due to the heat of the car. Goose bumps littered his arms and his breath left billows of mist in the air as he pumped fuel into his car. It was at that point he heard a thud. Joe's eyes snapped open, head jerking from side to side scanning for other cars and other people.

"What was that?" Came a voice from behind the other side of the pump, quickly followed by a bespectacled head. "Sounded like it came from the boot of your car."

Joe looked at the smartly dressed man he guesses was in his mid-fifties and nodded then smiled.

"It's just the wife." Joe joked. "It's the only way I could get her to stop complaining about my driving." He replaced the pump and stifled a yawn.

"Wished I'd thought of that." Came the reply and the man nodded towards the front passenger seat of his car. "She's really doing my head in." The man looked at Joe with an air of expectation on his face.

Joe nodded back presuming the woman that was now looking at him was the man's wife. "It's probably just my briefcase falling off my suitcase." Joe shrugged tiredly. "I came around the corner into the petrol station a little fast." Joe walked as nonchalantly as he could off the forecourt to pay. As he walked back to his car he checked for camera's and where the other man was. No camera's looking directly at his boot and it looked like the guy in the other car was getting his wallet from the front of his. Joe made it to the back of his car and pressed the button on his fob to unlock and open the boot. He made a show of looking but kept he eyes closed and held his breath while he did so as he did not want to see what was actually there. Then he remembered his briefcase was actually in there. In his boot with the, the, the other item. His left hand darted in, grabbed his brief case and pulled it out as he closed the boot with his right.

Joe lifted his briefcase as the older man turned making a point of showing him as he walked calmly to the front of his car before climbing into the driver's seat.

Joe felt sick, physically sick.

Why had he said his wife was in the boot?

What if he'd been a police officer and had asked to check.

That was the last he'd have wanted as he'd never be able to explain it away.

Joe started the engine, tried to pull away and stalled the car. In his attempt to appear normal he'd forgotten to release the parking break. "Wanker." Joe muttered under his breath as he restarted the engine, released the parking break and pulled away. Thankfully there was no traffic at this time of night and Joe swung round to drive the wrong way up the road back into the service station car park. Joe found a space away from the service area and killed the engine. He sat in silence for a minute recomposing himself.

Wednesday 03rd December 2003

Stacey Vaughn looked at her small silver watch for what felt like the hundredth time. People busied themselves around her, walking to tables, to the bar, standing in groups talking, sitting at the table laughing, playing pool in front of a black and white picture of Ian Botham while she sat, in the corner, alone. Where was he? It was already eight o'clock. He was an hour late. That wasn't surprising as he was often late but he usually sent her a message, a short text or something. Stacey looked down and adjusted her top around her cleavage before running her figures through her auburn hair. A quick shake of her head at an unwanted admirer and she placed her almost empty wine glass on the table in front of her then picked up her Nokia 6100.

Her phone buzzed in her hand making her jump and nearly causing her to drop the phone back to the table from where she had picked it up from. Howard. Finally. Stacey unlocked her phone and opened the text that had just arrived. The text was only four words. Sorry babe. It's over.

"Fucking arsehole!" Stacey swore and slammed her phone back on the table. Why? Why would he do this? They had been dating for over a year and had been talking about the future, marriage, babies, buying houses, everything not even a week ago. Why would he do this to her? Breaking her heart like this. Sending her a text. He had no spine.

A tear formed in Stacey's eye and slowly rolled down her cheek.

Stacey stood picked up her white leather jacket from the back of her chair and slowly, deliberately put it on, wrapped her scarf around her neck and put her phone in her white leather handbag. She no longer wanted to be here, surrounded by all these people but being totally alone. She needed someone to talk to, with someone who would listen and show her some sympathy. Someone who she could laugh with and forget about this horrendous moment in her life for at least the next few hours. Someone who could help her try and make some sense of all of this. She wiped away the tear and walked out of the Astolat Pub, down the five steps on to Old Palace Road.

Where to? Stacey's thoughts darted around her head. There was only one person that she could think of who would give her what she needed right now. She knew where she wanted to go, who she wanted to see. It was about a mile and a half walk but the air would do her good, clear her head a bit, allow her to get her thoughts in order and start processing what had happened. She walked the forty meters or so to the end of the road and turned left on to The Chase to start her twenty minute or so walk. Heels were not the best thing to walk distances in. She knew that if she went home to change she wouldn't go out again. She'd just spend the night at home, alone crying and wondering why.

❖

Joe's right hand hovered over to the handle of the metallic red pyramid style kettle that sat bubbling away on the kitchen counter. It always seemed to take three times a long to boil when you were stood waiting for it, as if it knew you were waiting and was taunting you. Finally, the kettle started to whistle and clicked off, the water inside its metallic shell rumbled like war drums from an old black and white movie. He poured the boiling liquid over the earl grey tea bag in his mug and watched as the clear liquid started to turn dark brown. The lightly armoured liquid sending a pleasant smell into the brightly lit kitchen. Joe jumped as the front door bell rang. He stirred the tea in his mug and took out the spent tea bag placing it on a small saucer along with the tea spoon. Joe lifted the mug towards his chin and blew across the surface of the tea as he walked out of the kitchen, down the hall towards the front door.

The doorbell rang again as Joe unlocked and opened the door. A cold draft welcomed Joe causing him to shiver in his red t-shirt. "Stacey?"

"Hi Joe. Are you going to ask me to come in? It's kind of cold out here." Stacey smiled and walked in to the hall passed Joe who closed the door behind her.

"Blimey Stacey, it feels cold out there." Joe noticed something in the way Stacey was holding herself, something that wasn't just the cold. "Are you ok?" He asked and then realised that Howard wasn't with her. He and Howard had spoken at work earlier and he has said he was going out with Stacey this evening, that he had a question he wanted to ask her. Howard wouldn't say what the question was but Joe had assumed it was either marriage or moving in together. The two had been dating for over a year and they seemed to be the perfect couple. "Where's How..." Joe didn't finish the question before Stacey burst into tears.

"I'm sorry Joe, I'm sorry. I promised myself I wouldn't start blubbering." Stacey spoke through tears, sharp breaths and quivering lips. "You don't need this. I'm sorry. I'll go."

Joe subtly and softly stopped Stacey in her tracks and gently wrapped his arms around her shoulders pulling her firmly in to his chest. "Let's have a drink. I'll open a bottle of wine and you can tell me what's wrong. Or we can chew the fat about nothing. Anything you want." He led Stacey through into the kitchen. "Red?"

Stacey nodded and pulled off her jacket. "Please." She walked through to the dinning room and hung her jacket and handbag on a brown cushioned oak chair.

Joe lead Stacey through the sliding doors from the dining room to the lounge beyond. He sat in his usual spot in the right corner of the three-seater sofa opposite the bay window. Stacey walked past Joe and sat on the smaller sofa to Joe's left and placed her glass on the coffee table in front of her. Her shoes slipped of her feet which came up on to the sofa tucked to her side. Joe sat silently and watched the plethora of emotions wash over Stacey's face, not wanting to rush her and afraid that she might at any moment burst into tears again. What had happened to cause her to be so emotional? Had Howard asked her to marry him and had she realised at that moment it wasn't what she wanted? He would find out soon, he would be as supportive as he could, be the emotional crutch she apparently needed this evening but his loyalty lay with his best friend of thirty years. He liked Stacey, they got on well but he always felt a little awkward around her as she was so confident and outspoken. Completely different from how she seemed now. How he wished Harriet was here and not on one of her overnight sales trips. She would be better at this than he. She could talk to her, would probably know what to say, to sympathise with her, plus Harriet was not one of Howard's biggest fans so would not have to fake any reaction. He continued to watch as she tentatively sipped her wine and he noticed her cleavage for the first time and immediately felt even more awkward than he had only seconds before.

"How's the wine?" Joe asked breaking the ice.

"Nice. Malbec?"

"Sangiovese, Chianti. I thought I'd try it for a change. I'm not sure I like it, it's a bit too peppery for me. But it's moreish. I'm really not sure."

"It's nice." Stacey reply.

The two of them sat in silence for another minute sipping their wines and seemingly waiting for the other to start talking.

"Right." Stacey spoke first. "So, as you probably know Howard and I were supposed to meet tonight. At the Astolat. It's the only place he'll go. I don't know why as there are plenty of other places in town but he never wants to try anywhere. It's the same with food. He always orders steak when he's in a restaurant, Rogan Josh if we have Indian, Pepperoni if it's pizza." Stacey took a breath as she realised she was rambling. "I'm sorry."

"Don't be. Take all the time you need. I'm going nowhere."

Stacey composed herself and unconsciously adjusted her top before taking a sip of wine. The dark liquid slowly moving down her throat to her stomach followed by a warm feeling that spread to her fingers and toes. A grin spread across her face for the first time in more than an hour and she felt relaxed and unburdened in the company of a man she felt comfortable with. "We, Howard and I, had been looking at a flat near Farnham Road Hospital and a house on Castle Hill. He had been subtly asking me about my thoughts on marriage. He said he wanted to meet this evening as he had an important question to ask me. It was obvious what he was going to ask me. He was going to ask me to marry him and I would have said yes, without hesitation. Howard was, is, the love of my life. We clicked the moment that we met, complimented each other and the sex." Stacey's breath slowed and became deeper as she remembered.

Joe cleared his throat, again feeling awkward and uncomfortable with the talk of sex especially that concerning his friend. He tried to hide his embarrassment, stood and retrieved the open bottle of wine from the kitchen.

Stacey chuckled to herself. It was funny how a man in his early thirties was made to feel so uncomfortable by the talk of sex. "You make me laugh Joe. You're so sweet and innocent."

"I'm glad I can make you smile." He said refilling Stacey's glass.

Stacey continued to talk but moved on from the talk of sex. "I don't know what happened, why he decided not to join me and why he sent a text. A text of just four words, just four words. Sorry babe. It's over. That's it, four words. He didn't have the decency to tell me in person, to do it face to face." Stacey looked up at Joe. "Why?" Those four words would be engrained in her heart forever more. Forever more. Tears welled in Stacey's eyes and she began to sob quietly.

"I don't know why he did what he did. I really don't." He truly did not know why Howard had ended the relationship but he had form from numerous relationships before, of not showing and not facing the women he hurt. That was the one thing that Joe hated about his best friend. His lack of respect for women and he knew not for where it came. "As far as I knew," Joe continued, "he was going to ask you to marry him. He'd bought you a ring just last weekend. I was there when he chose it, a diamond solitaire." Joe regretted talking about the ring as it just made Stacey cry even more. "I'm sorry." It was Joe's turn to apologise. He moved on to the small sofa next to Stacey and put his arms around her for the second time that evening. "It's going to be ok. I'll talk to Howard and find out what's going on. Why he did what he did. He's probably just nervous, just needs some reassurance."

"No. No it's over. For everything I feel for him, as much as I love him I don't think I could ever forgive him." Stacey wiped tears from her eyes and stood sliding her shoes on her feet. "I... I." She walked past the large sofa, into the dining room to retrieve her jacket and handbag, scurried to the hall and placed her hand on the handle of the front door.

Joe arrived a fraction of a second after her, his hand raised stopping the door from opening.

Stacey stood there by the front door, her leather jacket in one hand, her handbag in the other. The walk home to Weston Road would only take her about ten minutes or so but she didn't want to be alone tonight. Her eyes drifted up to Joe's soft face and her lips opened slightly, her voice quiet and almost inaudible. "I don't want to be alone tonight Joe."

Maybe there was something there between them in that moment, maybe it was just the wine, Joe didn't know what it was but he leaned forward and kissed Stacey lightly on her lips. "Then don't be." He said taking her coat and hanging it on a spare hook on thc wall by the door.

CHAPTER TWENTY-NINE

01:10hrs

Coffee bought, Joe walked back towards his car, keys in his right hand and coffee in his left. As he walked back to his car he scanned the car park for other people. He suddenly felt the need to actually check the boot and make sure everything was ok.

He reached the car, walked around to the back and scanned the car park one last time. Convinced he hadn't been followed and wouldn't be seen Joe unlocked the car and went to open the boot. He wanted to peer inside, to see the large space empty of almost anything with just usual rubbish he kept in there, screen wash, a coat and his emergency first aid kit. Joe knew if he looked he would see something that he didn't want to see. Something that had made him take this journey north, something he wished he could just walk away from, he could run away from, leave it all behind and start over.

The boot closed moments later with a dull, barely audible thud. Somewhat calmed and resigned to his fate, Joe carried on with his seemingly never-ending journey north.

Wednesday 12th March 1986

Are you going to tell me what's going on in that pea sized brain of yours? You've been quiet ever since we left your house." Joe and Howard walked through the gates of Morgan comprehensive school on Forfar Road. Joe watched as his friend shrugged but said nothing. Joe pressed on undeterred walking fast to keep up. "Well?"

"Leave it, alright. I don't want to talk about it." Howard sounded tired and grumpy, his hands stuffed into his jacket pockets.

"No Howard, I won't leave it. I'll keep pestering you until you talk to me. Something's wrong and I want to know what it is. Maybe I can help, maybe not but we won't know until you tell me. Plus, I can get quite annoying you know." Joe stopped and grabbed his friends arm causing him to stop and turn. Joe raised his eyebrows. "Well?"

"Ok, ok, you want to know what's up, well I'll tell you. Jack lost his job. Gross misconduct. He's been missing shifts, turning up to work drunk and yesterday they caught him drinking on the production line. Fucking idiot didn't even try to hide what he was doing, just pulled the bottle out and started boozing. I heard him and mum arguing last night." Howard breathed heavily through his nose pushing down the feeling of nausea that had been slowly growing inside him over the past sixteen hours. "Jack has drunk almost all of mum's money, the money she'd been saving over the past eight years. Apparently, we were going to go to America this summer." Howard almost growled. "Well not anymore." He spat the words out through gritted teeth. "Not... any... more..." Howard pulled his arm free.

Joe was a little confused. "You're this upset because you're not going to get to go to America?"

"Yes, but no. For someone who has an IQ higher than Einstein you can be pretty stupid."

The comment elicited a wry smile from both boys.

"I'm pissed off that my dad's drunk. Again." Howard stared with hate in his eyes. "That's my life. I have a father that's a drunk, so much so that he's lost his job, spent all of our money, not that there was a lot to begin with, but still. It's the principle. Mum's had to cancel the holiday as they now can't afford to pay for it. Plus, I'm pissed off that he hit my mum. He hit my mum and that's unacceptable."

Joe watched as Howard's pale face turned red with rage, his hands became tight balls by his side. Then as quickly as it had started it stopped. Howard looked like nothing was wrong.

"What did you do?"

"Nothing." Howard's rage turned to shame and he stopped walking to look at the back of Joe's head. "Nothing, I did absolutely nothing. I stood there and watched my father hit my mother and I did… nothing." Howard choked back tears looking up to the sky in a vain hope that gravity would stop them creeping out. "He hit her so hard man, so hard. He sent her flying across the living room and I just stood there like a dick. Why Joe, why?" Tears slowly seeped out of his eyes and ran down his cheeks. He sniffed and angrily wiped the tears from his face with his white shirt sleeves. "Never again Joe, never again. If he raises a finger against her, hell, if he even thinks about it I'm going to knock his fucking head off his shoulders."

Joe watched the scared sad little boy in front of him disappear and in that moment a fire seemed to light in the heart of his friend. He knew the words that Howard said were the truth, that Howard would protect his mum whatever it took. "I'm there for you Howard, whenever you need me, whatever you want. You know where I am." Joe looked around the school yard at all the other kids making their way off to registration.

"What you got up first?" Howard's voice was flat and calm almost devoid of all emotion.

"Maths." Came Joe's reply.

"English. See you at first break." And with that Howard marched off.

CHAPTER THIRTY

01:17hrs

Second time lucky. Joe actually managed to leave Gretna Green Services car park this time. Last time with his mind on what was in his boot he'd forgotten to go to the toilet until it was almost too late. He'd double checked the boot again just to be totally sure that everything was as it should be before setting off again.

Joe gently increased his speed as he cruised down the slip lane and joined the A75M doing sixty-five. Joe continued to accelerate until he reached seventy-five and hit the cruise control. The police north of the border seemed to be less tolerant of speeding on motorways than they were south of it.

Friday 23rd March 2018

Joe walked back into the deserted reception area of Guildford Engineering Technology and Aerodynamic Systems. He was surprisingly calm despite the activities of the last hour or so. Howard was sat in one of the chairs used by the company's many visitors, head in his hands mumbling to himself, rocking slightly backwards and forwards.

"Oy! Howard." Joe's tone was curt. He needed Howard's attention. "Are you ready?" Joe looked down at his friend.

Friend.

The actions of Howard over the past months had made things awkward.

Those of his wife had made things difficult.

Their movements over the past ninety minutes had

changed the whole dynamic of their relationship and Joe doubted whether their friendship would last out the night. Thirty-eight years thrown away over two stupid mistakes.

"Yes, I'm ready. I'm on the 19:30hrs flight. If I leave now I should get to the airport in time to check in, even with the usual Friday night traffic." Howard stood, stretched and walked slowly towards the door. His tie that he always wore was nowhere to be seen and the two top buttons on his shirt undone.

"Aren't you forgetting something?" Asked Joe to Howard's back.

"What?"

Joe raised an eyebrow.

"Oh yeah, sure."

"We need to get it into the boot of your car while it's still quiet. Security won't be on site for another..." Joe checked his watch, looked up then back at Howard, "half an hour so we'd better get our skates on just in case they're early." Joe ran his fingers through his rapidly greying hair before disappearing through the door at the back of the reception area.

"My car?" Howard's words were flat and emotionless. "How will I get to the airport?"

"The train will be quicker." Replied Joe "You won't get stuck in any traffic and miss your flight do you? You can walk to the station in ten minutes and at be at Gatwick Airport forty-five minutes after that. Besides you'll need your car to get home afterwards."

Howard stood and stared at the entrance for several seconds. If he walked out now he could be anywhere in a few hours and nobody would know, nobody would be able to find him. Howard turned towards the exit.

No, he couldn't do that to Joe, it was not Joe's mess to sort out or in his nature to leave Joe to it. Yes, he was partly responsible for creating it but Howard had to take responsibility for his own actions. Besides if he was being totally honest with himself, how far could he actually get? Howard turned back towards the entrance and followed his friend into the corridors towards the factory area.

"How will you get back if you take my car?" Howards head was foggy. He could barely see beyond the next few minutes.

"I'm meeting Harriet up there so we'll bring her car back." Joe smiled. It also meant that if he got caught speeding or any CCTV cameras spotted him then all they would see was Howards car and hopefully assume it was Howard driving.

❖

Joe looked into the boot of Howard's car at the large bundle wrapped in a plastic sack while he rubbed his sweaty palms on his trousers. Howard stood just behind him to his right gazing over his shoulder. Neither man knew what to say so they just stood there in silence.

Howard sneezed breaking the tension just for a moment, long enough for Joe to slam the boot shut.

"We should get a move on if we're to hit our rendezvous." Joe walked round to the right-hand side of the car, opened the driver's door and looked at Howard. He still didn't know what to say. He climbed in to the driver's seat, started the engine and pulled away as he fastened his seatbelt.

Howard watched as the saloon rumbled into life and slowly pull away. He checked his watch, half past five. He needed to get to the airport and catch his flight. Howard's right hand slipped into his jacket pocket looking for his car keys. Where?... Oh yes, Joe had them. He had a little over two hours before his flight took off and he needed to check in, ideally, an hour before then.

Howard nodded to himself, his head finally beginning to clear and a smile slowly creeped across his face. "Better get a move on then, hadn't we?" He said to himself.

CHAPTER THIRTY-ONE

01:59hrs

The last forty-five minutes had flown by. Joe was more awake and more confident that he had been during the whole journey so far that everything would go according to plan.

The pips on the radio sounded as Joe saw the road signs declare that he was no longer on the A74M but the M74. That meant give or take a mile or two he had about one hundred miles left of his journey tonight. After that a whole new journey would begin. A journey without the woman he loved or his best friend. He felt betrayed by the two people that were closest to him. That used to be closest to him. For the past few years they had been drifting further away while he had played along with them and kept up appearances, allaying any suspicion that he was aware of their duplicity. It had not been easy and at times he just wanted it to all be over but he wanted to hurt them as much as they had hurt him. He just needed to figure out how he was going to do that. The best way would be if he could get Howard to take the fall for this whole debacle but that wasn't going to be easy. Joe had had quite a bit of time to think about things trapped in his car alone and he had come to the conclusion that this whole journey had been a mistake. A big mistake.

What had he been thinking? Well he hadn't, had he? Again, he'd rushed in to try and get his friend out of a fix without thinking about the consequences or how it would affect him personally.

He was taking the most risks driving north and Howard had simply hopped on a plane. But maybe that could work in his favour. There would be evidence of him travelling.

Ok so he had stopped and paid for petrol using his credit card but he could explain that away with the visit to his mum's house. He'd get there while she was asleep so no one could prove exactly what time he'd arrived. While Howard had no reason to be going to Glasgow. He'd told everyone he was going to spend the weekend in London visiting friends, and the last-minute change of plans could look suspicious. Maybe, if anybody thought to ask. Well he had another ninety minutes or so to try and figure something out.

Tuesday 26th October 2004

Joe turned right off Stirling Road into the main carpark of the Royal Surrey County Hospital. The short drive from the house had taken a little over twenty minutes due to the early morning commuter traffic. Joe lightly stroked Harriet's right thigh as he manoeuvred round the carpark looking for a suitable space to park in.

"Hmmm." Joe mumbled under his breath head swivelling from left to right and back again.

"What's up sweetie?" Harriet asked, her left hand resting gently on her slightly swollen stomach, eyes closed. The smooth cool cotton fabric between her hand and her stomach felt nice to the touch and oddly comforting.

"Sorry?" Joe swung into a free space making appoint to reverse park and to leave more space on the passenger side than the drivers, so his wife could easily get out of the car. "Oh, nothing really. I was just thinking it might have been easier and cheaper to get a taxi, when you factor in how much it'll cost to put two hours on the car park."

"Maybe."

"Ready?" Joe looked at his wife and took a deep breath suddenly feeling nervous and excited. "I don't know why, but I'm nervous." Joe said and clutched Harriet's hand tight.

"Really?" Harriet shuffled round to face her husband and

leaned forward to kiss Joe. "It'll be fine Joe. Trust me."

"I know. But I am. I know it's illogical and I'm being silly."

Harriet shuffled back around and bent forward as best she could to inelegantly retrieve her hand bag from the foot well in front of her. "Shall we?" She asked.

Joe took another deep breath. Nodded. Then exited the car and swiftly made his way round to help Harriet out. "I'll grab a ticket from the machine over there, I'll catch you up."

"Don't forget to lock the car. You know what you're like." Harriet smiled cheekily. For such an extremely organised and intelligent man Joe could be so forgetful about the stupid little things.

"Ok." Joe pressed the fob to lock the door and hurried off to get a ticket. A minute later he had caught his wife up just as she was getting to the entrance to the maternity wing of the hospital.

"Why did you have to wear that coat?" She asked looking sideways at her husband.

What?" Joe peered downwards. "My brown leather jacket. Because I like it. Why? Don't you?" He pulled the front down slightly and squared his shoulders. It had cost him two hundred and fifty pounds in the sales at the start of the year.

"No." Harriet snorted in reply. "It looks like you're going through a midlife crisis. You just need the Saab convertible to go with it."

Joe stopped himself from speaking. He'd been at the Saab garage at the weekend and was considering trading in Harriet's RAV4 as a surprise early thirtieth birthday present. He'd have to have a serious rethink.

"What time is it?" Harriet's voice had become soft again.

A quick check of his watch. "Quarter to. We have fifteen minutes. Plenty of time." Joe was frantically trying to calm himself. His palms were sweaty and his stomach was churning. For some strange reason he had a terrible feeling about today. Something was playing on the back of his mind and he couldn't figure out what it was. Plus, he'd just found out that Harriet didn't like his new coat nor the car that he was thinking of buying her. Could the day get any worse? Joe berated himself, he was being overly dramatic, something he never usually was, in any situation.

Ten minutes later they had signed in and were sat in the waiting room of the maternity wing holding hands, Harriet's head resting on Joe's shoulder as she gently hummed an unrecognisable tune to herself.

"Alice, Emily or Grace." Harriet cooed softly.

"Jemima, Margaret or Charlotte." Joe replied.

"How old is she going to be when she's born? Sixty?" Harriet laughed. "You're convinced that she's going to be a girl?

Joe shrugged. "Yes." He sounded confident, his early nerves and uneasiness was a distant memory.

"Ok, but just in case shouldn't we consider boys' names?"

"No. But ok if you want to." Joe paused for a moment then continued. "Anything as long as it's a boys' name and not a name that could be either like Carole, Beverly or Leslie and definitely not Joe. Other than that, I don't really mind. It's entirely your choice."

"Really?" Harriet sat up. It was unlike Joe to relinquish control of anything. He always had to have an input and feel like he was at least having some influence in the outcome of everything. A cheeky grin crossed her face. "How about Zane?"

"If that's what you want. Ok"

"Hmmm." It wasn't but they had another six months to choose a name be it a girl or a boy and if it was a boy she had free reign to decide what the name would be." Harriet's head rested back on to Joe's shoulder and the fell back into silence as they waited for their appointment.

"Harriet Anderson." Called a voice.

Harriet jumped slightly surprised then stood. "Err, hello." All eyes upon her for the briefest of time Harriet she felt like she was back at school.

"Hi Mrs Anderson, I'm Becky. Would you like to follow me please?" Came the rhetorical question.

"Joe." Harriet reached for Joe's hand.

"Huh? Oh yes." Joe briefly watched the worm on his phone run into the edge of the screen then pocketed his phone and switched it off as he stood next to his wife catching the subtle scent of her perfume. He followed his wife who in turn followed the sonographer, a young woman in her mid-twenties, down a short corridor and into a dimly lit room.

"Can you get on the bed for me, and you'll need to lift your dress up so I can see your stomach." The young sonographer pushed a few buttons in front of her on the sonogram and picked up a large tube of lubricating gel which she shook several times vigorously.

"I said you should have worn trousers." Said Joe watched as Harriet unceremoniously pulled her dress up under armpits as she climbed clumsily onto the bed that was positioned in the middle of the room. She was wearing a small pair of black lacy knickers. Strange choice he thought then his focus shifted on to the ultra sound machine.

Becky placed a large square of blue tissue over the top of Harriet's legs and second piece over her chest to leave her stomach exposed before squirting a large blob of the gel just above her belly button.

"Ooo, that's cold." Harriet exclaimed squirming slightly.

"Let's take a look, shall we?" Becky passed the transducer from her left to her right hand and pushed it firmly into the lower part of Harriet's belly. "Is this your first?" She asked. A grainy green image appeared on the screen of a twelve-week old child. "There we go." Becky mumbled as she shifted the transducer around slightly. "You can clearly see the head, two arms, two legs." She pressed buttons, taking measurements. "Let's see if we can get them to move slightly shall we, this might be a bit uncomfortable." Becky continued to manoeuvre the transducer then suddenly stopped. "Hmmm." She looked intently at the screen.

Joe leaned forward trying to see what Becky had seen on the screen but not fully understanding what had caught her attention.

Becky placed the transducer back into its holder on the ultra sound machine. She stood. "If you'll excuse me for a minute." And without further explanation Becky left Harriet and Joe in the room without any clue as to what was happening.

Several minutes passed with the couple sitting in silence. Joe kept looking at the screen of the ultra sound machine but seeing noting and pacing impatiently around the small room.

It was Harriet who spoke first and broke the silence. "Joe?"

"Everything is fine sweetie, I'm sure." Joe waved a hand dismissively at the door the nerves and uneasy feeling he had on arriving at the hospital returning with a vengeance. "She probably just needed the loo."

"Probably."

Neither of them believed it for a second and they returned to sitting in silence waiting for the sonographer, Becky to return.

Several more minutes passed before voices could be heard in the corridor outside.

Joe looked at Harriet and she returned his pained, scared stare.

"Can you hear what they are saying?"

Joe just shook his head.

The door opened a fraction, closed, then opened again and Becky came back in the room followed by a tall grey-haired lady in blue scrubs.

"Hi, this is Sheila. She just wants to have a look at the ultra sound if that's ok?" Becky said and took half a step to the side to allow Sheila to sit down.

"Let's take a look, shall we?" Sheila's voice was calm and reassuring, it exuded experience and tranquillity. She mirrored what Becky had done some five minutes or so before, even what she said. "Yes." Sheila turned to face Harriet. "Becky has asked me to come in and have a look at the ultra sound as we cannot detect a heartbeat from the foetus." She raised a hand to stop the obvious questions and continued to talk in her calm reassuring tone. "This is not as uncommon as you may think and does not necessarily mean that there is anything wrong. This can be caused by a number of possibilities. The scan is showing that you are about nine and a half weeks along so it could be that your dates are a little off and you are not as far along as you thought. It may be due to the position of the foetus in the uterus. The baby is laying towards the back and is not presenting as we would like and that can cause issues."

"What are you saying?" Joe asked looking in horror and disbelief at the two medical professionals in the room.

"There is no easy way of saying it but there is a small chance that you have suffered an early gestational miscarriage. We won't know for sure until we do another scan in about a weeks' time. In the meantime, I would advise that you go home and take a day or two off work. We'll book you in for another scan in a week to re-check and we'll know more then."

"Ok." Harriet sat in shock barely able to speak.

"In the unlikely event that it is a miscarriage then you may suffer some bleeding that could become heavy in the next few days along with cramping. If this happens you need to get to your GP as quickly as possible and they will get you referred to us." Sheila looked at the couple. She hated these ones. Miscarriages were so hard on couples. Everyone rallied around to help and look after the expectant mother but the father was always left to look after himself and men had a habit of locking their emotions inside. "Is there anything that you want to ask me?"

"Harriet?" Joe could not think of any questions. His mind had gone completely blank.

"No. Nothing. Thank you." Harriet wiped the gel of her stomach and stood. "Thank you."

"Like I said if you need anything..." Sheila was cut off before she could finish the sentence.

"No. It's ok. Joe, I want to go home." Harriet grabbed Joe's hand and pulled him to the door.

Joe could not believe it. After the years of trying it may still not have happened for them. He followed his wife crying inside. Knowing now that the feelings he'd had earlier had been because of this, because their child was not alive. It would destroy Harriet. He would do everything he could to be there for her but would he be able to do enough?

Harriet marched out of the maternity wing, through the corridors and in to the car park. Dragging Joe behind her to their car and quickly got in to the passenger seat. It was only then that she let it out. All of her emotions, all of her fear. She wept with Joe sitting beside her not knowing what to say or do.

CHAPTER THIRTY-TWO

02:24hrs

Joe took the slip road to leave the M74 behind him and slid seamlessly on to the M73. Joe did not know why but for some inexplicable reason he hated the M74.

Joe could count the number of vehicles he'd seen in the last five minutes on the fingers of one hand. They had progressively thinned the further north he'd travelled and the later, or earlier depending on how you looked at it, it had got. What fool would want to be driving at half past two in the morning if they didn't have to and when they could be tucked up in bed asleep. Joe knew where he'd rather be right now.

His phone buzzed in the phone holder stuck to the bottom right of his windscreen making him jump slightly.

Number withheld.

Joe answered anyway.

"How long?" Two words crackled at him.

"Just over an hour give or take." Joe replied and hung up. His right hand fished into the door well to his right. He needed a cigarette.

Friday 23rd March 2018

Howard walked down a long corridor, a plain beige wall to his right broken only by expensive pieces of modern art every two meters that the CEO, Mr Smith, seemed to like to indulge in.

To his left was a floor to ceiling glass wall punctuated by several glass doors behind which were empty meeting rooms occupied by large oak tables and black leather chairs. Another indulgence of Mr Smith.

Howard stopped suddenly, a figure sat alone in one of the large meeting rooms, their back to the glass wall but Howard recognised the man instantly. He would know him anywhere. But why was Joe sat alone in a meeting room at this time of day by himself? Would he mind being disturbed? Maybe. Joe had been less than his usual cheery self of late and no matter how much he coaxed him Howard could not get Joe to tell him what was up. Even Harriet had become strangely quiet. Not answering his phone calls, taking an age to reply to text messages, cancelling their rendezvous at the last minute or just failing to show up when they had arranged to meet.

Howard reasoned that something was amiss at home but just couldn't find out what. He could try and guess but Howard was never one to speculate, he liked cold hard facts. A philosophy he liked to live by 'information not postulation'.

"Sod it." Howard said under his breath. He couldn't just stand around, he needed to know what the hell was going on with his friend. "Joe." Howard said in a loud a jaunty voice as he entered the room. "What are you doing in here all alone at this time on a Friday?"

"Waiting for you." Joe said not looking up from the notes he continued to scribble with the expensive fountain pen that Harriet had got him for their tenth wedding anniversary nearly nine years earlier.

"Why?" Asked Howard perplexed. "What's going on?" He suddenly felt and sounded nervous as he stood behind the chair, one down from his oldest friend.

"Remember last year when you went and saw your mum, just after she'd moved in to the nursing home?"

Howard sighed and walked slowly round the conference table so he could see his friend's face. Friend? Yes, even if things had gotten a little strained between them Howard considered

Joe to be his friend. His best friend. Howard sat opposite Joe and rubbed his face with his hands. He remembered the day vividly. His mum had been upset but didn't know why. She was in the later stages of dementia and didn't know where she was most of the time or who anybody was. She called Howard by his father's name more often than not, half the time her voice filled with love the other with venom and hatred. She'd spent most of the day talking gibberish.

"How could I forget the day I put my mother into a nursing home? It's not the sort of thing you can ever forget." Howard was unsure where this was going.

"You'd asked me to go with you as you said you didn't want to be there by yourself." Joe continued. "Do you remember what your mother said that day?" Joe was quiet and calm almost detached.

"Which bit?" Howard was getting more and more confused. "It was a load of tosh. She was ranting about dad leaving her then reminiscing about the wedding as if it was just the day before. A lot of nothing."

"Yes, most of it was."

"Most?" Howard's sat up straight his interest pricked.

"Yes, most of it." Joe repeated and shuffled some papers around in front of him.

Howard's curiosity quickly turned to frustration at Joe's procrastinating. "You said that already. What's your point?"

"Your mum mentioned a few things about your dad and his job at Timex."

"So? She says a lot of things and hardly any of it makes any sense. What's to say she actually knew what she was talking about this time or wasn't getting confused again?" Howard asked surprised at how irritated he was getting. "What's your point?"

Joe could see Howard's frustration bubbling away and that was fine with him. He decided to carry on drip feeding Howard the information he had. Everything didn't have to happen straight away as the build-up of tension added to the mood of the conversation. As good a negotiator as Howard was he'd be even better if he had a little patience when he wasn't holding all the cards. "It's not so much what she mentioned but who, a name. James."

"And?" Howard interrupted, his perpetual impatience continuing to manifest itself even in the simplest of conversations.

Joe waited a few seconds for his friend to settle and to add to his annoyance at the same time. "James MacDonald."

"So? What's your point?" Howard asked through gritted teeth, his frustration turning to anger.

Joe knew it was because his friend felt like he was not in control of the situation. Should he point it out Joe asked himself. Normally he wouldn't dream of saying anything, just let the slight annoyances of his friend wash over him but he'd had enough of being the nice quiet friend. Fuck it he thought. A brief inward grin at his unexpected internal profanity.

"You do know that everyone can always tell when you feel that you're not in control or things are not going the way you want them to as your demeanour changes. You look uptight plus you become short tempered and aggressive." Joe sat back in his chair, top lip resting on the tips of his steepled fingers as he surveyed the man opposite him. They had been friends for over thirty-five years. It was amazing how quickly things changed. As Joe watched he saw Howard struggle to relax and contain his anger as it flashed behind his eyes. It was followed by the expression of a lost child, then a steely determination slowly washed over him that was replaced by a placid calmness that encompassed his whole body. Joe was impressed. In that moment he knew two things. The first that he would not win in this continued battle of patience so decided to knock it on the head. And secondly that his friendship with Howard would never recover. There was no going back for the two men, it was just whether or not Howard had realised it as well and if Howard cared as little about it as Joe did. The past was the past. You couldn't change it any more than you could change the path of the sun. The future was a different matter, he could influence that, could help guide it one way or the other and with what he was going to tell Howard he hoped he could eliminate two issues in his life.

Joe took a deep breath and a sip from his rapidly cooling coffee. "You must have heard your mother talking about James MacDonald before?"

"She's mentioned the name on numerous occasions but never expanded or explained anything about him." Howard's voice was calm, his eyes neutral giving nothing away. He was the perfect negotiator, the perfect poker player.

"In what context did she mention him in?"

"To be honest I never really paid much attention, but I do know she never seemed to be very complimentary about him. I just figured it was an ex-boyfriend or something, someone who had upset her or such like." Howard shrugged not sure what else to say.

"I figured the same until last year. Your mum mentioned the name and your dad in the same sentence. And that he worked at Timex. At first I thought she meant your dad but she actual meant James MacDonald."

"What?" Howard sat up straight his calm exterior slipped slightly. "Where they made Spectrum Computers?"

"Yes."

"So? Dad worked there before he got fired and hung himself."

Joe sighed. It looked like he would have to spell it out as Howard wasn't putting two and two together. "I've done some digging and James MacDonald worked with, well more precisely for your dad in the development team at Timex from 1982. After your dad lost his job guess who got promoted to development manager?"

Howard took a stab in the dark. "James MacDonald?"

"Yes." Said Joe. "I've spoken to a few people who worked there at the time and the story goes that your dad was working on some new coding for the operating system on the Spectrum Plus two but could never get it to work. Then proof was presented to the directors that your father had actually got the code to work but had sold them to SmarTech Computer Systems for the SmarTech S87 which was launched a year later."

"I am aware of that." Said Howard matter of factly.

"Well what you don't know is that James MacDonald was the one that presented the proof to the directors at Timex and that there was a theory that James MacDonald was actually the one who sold the code and framed your father." Said Joe.

"Even if that is true, what can we do about it now? We don't know where this James MacDonald is. He could be anywhere."

"That's not exactly true." Said Joe. "We've been working with James MacDonald for the past eight years." Joe looked to see how Howard would react to the news, but he just looked perplexed so Joe continued. "You've been on several business trips with the Big Mac. I checked with HR and John is actually his middle name."

"Son of a bitch. John MacDonald is James MacDonald." Howard's face drained of colour.

"Yes. James John MacDonald." Joe let the information sink in. Joe's curiosity started to twitch. He wanted to know what Howard would do with the information.

"That asshole." Howard slammed his fists on the table making Joe jump slightly. He looked across the table head swaying from side to side.

Joe knew what was going on inside Howard's head. The calm demeanour had fallen away and his thoughts were written all over his face. He was wondering how Joe had worked it all out, how long he'd known, why he'd told him now. Then Joe saw the anger slowly slip away as the next step in Howard's thought pattern kicked in. Why had John done it? Had John understood the consequences of his actions before he'd done it or cared afterwards?

Howard's eyes became wide, his pupils dilating and Joe knew that the third stage of his questions had been reached. Did John know who Howard was and if he did what was his agenda?

Joe nodded and decided that it was about time he filled in the gaps. He felt he owed him that much for the years that they had been friends. "I started doing some research about seven months or so ago after that bigwig from BAE was over. He called John Jim and they talked about the old days at SmarTech and I started to put the dots together. It took about three months of digging to get it all confirmed." Joe paused and pushed a manila envelope that had a large number one drawn on in marker pen across the table then leaned back. "It's all in there. It confirms that James, John MacDonald, started at Timex in eighty-two, stole the operating system for the Plus Two, framed your father, got him sacked then took his job. Six months after that John took a senior job at SmarTech. Here's the twist. John coded the operating system for the ZX Twelve-Eighty and convinced Timex to invest heavily in it but it never worked properly. John jumped before he got the push himself and Timex never recovered from the money they pumped into a product that bombed in the market." Joe took another sip from his now cold coffee, his mouth becoming dry. "John doesn't know who you are, he doesn't know that your mum changed your surname back to her maiden name. You're Howard Morris, your dad was Jack Gunn. I doubt if he's ever thought that there is a connection there, you never talk about your dad or what he did so why would he?" Joe looked at then man in front of him, once his oldest friend. He felt sadness creeping into his heart for what had happened to him and how he must be feeling to finally understand what had led to his dad's drinking and ultimately his suicide. All they had been through together and Howard had thrown it all away for a woman, a woman that he should never have had. That was in the past now as was their friendship.

Howard took a moment to absorb the information. "Why tell me now? Why the hell did you leave it three months to tell me? Why did you not tell me when you made the connection, so we could look into this together?"

Joe stood and pushed his chair under the table. "Together." Joe snorted with contempt. "To be honest I just didn't want to spend any more time with you than I had to." Joe pushed a second envelope across the table. This one had the number two written on it.

Howard took it and opened it pulling out the contents. On top was a large picture of Howard passionately kissing a woman. The woman's face could not be seen due to how she was stood. Howard slid the top photograph to the back to reveal a second large print. This one the face of the woman could be seen.

It was Harriet.

"How? When?" Howard stuttered and looked up at Joe's back.

"I've known for about seven months." Joe said as the conference room door swung closed behind him.

CHAPTER THIRTY-THREE

02:30hrs

Joe left the M73 behind him for the M80. All roads merging into one in his mind. Traffic was light, as he had expected with the majority of vehicles being lorries hauling freight from one warehouse to another, to factories and supermarkets. A continuous yet almost ignored life blood travelling down the arteries of the country.

Saturday 14th November 1992

Joe could feel the blood pulsating through his arteries, his ears were thumping, blocking out all but the loudest of sounds. His heart pumped hard and fast. He made such an effort to keep his breathing deep and slow. Joe wiped the sweat away from his forehead and eyes with the back of his left hand as he stared forwards. He tried to steady his breathing again and watched the blond haired, mud-covered man running towards him with intense focus. Joe took a last deep breath in and exhaled slowly mirroring the side step to the left as he started to walk backwards trying to anticipate the next move.

Joe lifted his left arm and feigned going to the right trying to draw the onrushing man to his left. It worked and Joe smiled as the mud-covered man took the bait and sprang the way he wanted him to. Finally, he launched himself forwards wrapping his arms around the pair of legs kicking up trying to escape the hunters snare.

Caught, Joe brought his man down to the damp muddy grass and used his momentum to swing his body round over the fallen man. Joe released him for a fraction of a second as he stood then stooped over the prone assailant and hooked the rugby ball tight into his chest not allowing him to release it then steeled himself for the inevitable hit and at the same time tried to strip the ball away causing the opponent to hold on tighter.

Hours seemed to pass but in reality, it was seconds before the referees whistle finally blew to stop the passage of play. The referees right arm raised signalling a penalty, his left pulling into his chest. Not releasing.

Joe released his man and pumped the air as he let out a yell.

Howard came running over to his best friend. "Amazing mate!" He exclaimed.

"Amazing, Bollocks!" The blond-haired winger barged passed Joe giving him an unfriendly shove. "You were fucking lucky!"

Howard reacted first giving the retreating figure a heavy shove in the back causing him to stumble and fall forwards back on to the grass. "Watch your mouth knobhead!"

Joe pulled Howard back away from the advancing opposition players as he tried to lose themselves in the midst of their own players. A sea of light blue shirts of the University of Surrey's Rugby Football Club engulfed the two young men.

"How much longer have we got?" Joe planted his hands on his knees as he watched the fly half kick the ball towards the opponents twenty-two. He stood and started to jog after his team mates as they made their way forwards. "Ref! Ref, how long?" He called. "Ref?"

"Less than a minute." Came the reply.

"Right lads. We're going long, back in a rolling maul, out wide, back into the centre. At that point both wingers, be ready we'll make a decision on the fly depending on where their defence is but we're going hard and fast from the off." The captain looked at his team mates. “If we keep the ball alive we can do this. We’re only two points down so nothing stupid, ok? Keep your heads on your shoulders, no fancy stuff, keep it simple but keep it moving. Clear the ruck, stay on your feet and Howard,” All eyes turned to Howard. ”Don’t go in from the side! Right, let’s do this.”

The forwards lined up facing the hooker holding the ball above his head. Joe and Howard watched as the lineout ball was launched long over the line of waiting men, too long, over the expectant man at the tail and into the arms of a surprised Oxford University player. At that point Joe knew it was over. They would lose the last match and finish third in this year’s university competition.

Twenty-nine players charged forwards from either end of the pitch. The Oxford players in an attempt to kill the ball and the game and the Surrey players tried to steal the ball to push for the try line and win the match.

Arms flailed.

A boot spiralled through the air.

Mud churned.

A scrumcap rolled towards the side line.

The sound of the whistle echoed around the pitch.

Half the supporters cheered.

The players pulled themselves one by one from the ruck.

Howard looked up.

Joe stood and turned towards the referee head down.

A free kick, to Oxford.

Howard swore.

The Oxford players knew that they had won. All they needed to do was kick the ball in to touch and the game was theirs.

❖

“It was a close game.” Harriet snuggled into Joes’ arms and stole a quick kiss before they both took a sip from their drinks.

“Still fucking lost though, didn’t we!” Howard stood and

skulked off towards the bar for another round of drinks. The university bar was almost full but had a quiet subdued mood that covered everyone there.

Harriet looked slightly hurt and forlorn as Howard's back retreated away from her. "What's Howard's problem? Whenever I say anything he's always short or dismissive with me. Why?"

"He fancies you." Joe finished his pint, watched his friend order more drinks then looked down and kissed his girlfriend. His shoulder was sore. He knew that he'd be paying for that in the morning and that it would hurt even more because of the loss. He surveyed the bar and wondered how long everyone would stay before they started to head home. Term had finished a week earlier and it seemed that half of the students had stayed to watch the last match of the season only to have it end in a loss. They'd been there for about forty minutes and he figured it would start to thin out soon.

"Sorry?" Harriet leaned forward pulling away from Joe and blinked several times. She turned to look her boyfriend in the eyes, her brow furrowed and creased. "He what?!"

"He fancies you." Joes' voice was flat and emotionless as he spoke. "Can't you tell?" Joe paused and watched a cacophony of thoughts and emotions wash over the beautiful face in front of him. "He flirts with you constantly. His emotions are all over the place and he's nervous whenever he's around you. Haven't you noticed?" He asked.

"No!" Harriet sounded shocked. "You're joking? Please tell me you're joking?"

"Joking about what?" Howard place a tray of drinks on the table.

"Sarah has the hot's for Bill Clinton." Joe said without missing a beat.

"What have I missed?" Sarah returned to the table wiping her hands down her skirt, a large grin on her face. She glanced down and back up. "Oh, the hand dryers in the ladies are rubbish." She sat and reached forwards grabbing a pint of beer.

"So, how's Bill?" Howard sat and distributed the rest of

the drinks.

A glazed look came over Sarah's face and she squeezed her hands together in front of her chest. "He's a dreamboat and so funny, I loved his last film. Have you seen it?"

"Seen his last film?"

"Groundhog Day?"

"Oh, Bill Murray, not Bill Clinton." Howard turned to face Joe and Harriet, neither of whom could barely contain their laughter.

"Let's leave these two to get to know each other a little better." Said Harriet. "I'm sure Bill Murray has nothing on our Howie." Harriet patted Howard on the shoulder as she led Joe away towards another table leaving Sarah and Howard standing in awkward silence.

"You seemed in a bit of a rush to get away from Howard after I told you that he fancied you." Joe watched for a reaction from Harriet but was disappointed that there wasn't one.

"It wasn't because you told me that he fancies me, I just needed to get away from that arrogant knob." She paused and scanned the bar making sure that none of Joe or Howard's friends were in ear shot. "Thinking about it, it kind of makes sense. The way he looks at me and the inconsistent way he acts when he's around me, all tongue tied and nervous one minute the loud, brash and arrogant the next. I know he's your best friend but I have to say that I'm not sold. He's not my cup of tea."

Joe raised an eyebrow. "Are you always this forward?"

"Yes." Harriet leaned in and kissed Joe passionately on the lips.

"Good." Joe could hardly contain himself. He was dating a beautiful girl, a girl he really liked, who couldn't be more perfect if she tried and for some inexplicable reason she seemed to like him. He just hoped that he didn't screw things up or even worse that she would run off with Howard as the girls he knew always seemed to do. They fell for his good looks, his charm and his bravado. But maybe Harriet was different. She seemed to see Howard for what he really was, a man hiding behind a front, hiding the real Howard, an insecure and frightened little boy. It was what Joe loved about him and what drove him crazy all at the same time. They had been friends for almost ten years and would be for many more years to come.

CHAPTER THIRTY-FOUR

02:36hrs

Joe motored down the M80 and yawned, his eyelids felt heavy, like lead weights above his eyes. He rubbed his face. Stirling. About ten miles to Stirling, another thirty-five to Perth and a further twenty-five to Tay Rail Bridge just south of Dundee, his ultimate destination this evening.

No. Joe made a snap decision, checked his mirrors quickly and pulled the steering wheel to the left, crossed and empty lane and clattered over the rumble strip. Maybe he shouldn't leave it until the last second next time before he decided to take the slip road.

Sunday 20th October 2002

Harriet stirred, vaguely aware that there was someone sat next to her. She shuffled and rolled on to her right side slowly opening her eyes to look at the man sat next to her, his head buried in a novel.

"Morning Joe." Her words were soft and gentle. A smile creeped across her face.

"Coffee darling?" Joe asked rhetorically as he placed his novel carefully on his bedside table and picked up a mug of fresh coffee. He swivelled back and offered the mug to his wife.

Harriet took the mug as she manoeuvred herself into a seated position while trying to keep the duvet from falling off her chest.

"Cold?"

"No, just, well, comfortable." Harriet inhaled the deep rich aroma of the coffee and took a sip, savouring the flavour. For how much longer she thought briefly. It was time. She was ready.

"Joe." Harriet looked up from the mug. "I'm ready."

"Ready?" Joe was confused. "Ready for what?"

"For us." Came the cryptic reply.

"For us? What are you talking about?"

Harriet giggled as the perplexed look that sat on Joe's face. "I'm ready to start trying for a family. You and I." She paused for a moment to let the news sink in. "I want to have a baby Joe. With you."

Joe sat in silence, stunned by the enormity of the statement. He picked his coffee mug up and immediately put it back down. His mouth opened and closed several times as if he was going to say something then changed his mind. Joe swung his legs out of the bed and stood walking to the closed curtains. "Are you sure?" He asked back to his wife.

"I've never been so sure of anything in my life."

Joe turned. His eyes met his wife's. they were both grinning like Cheshire cats. Joe walked back to the bed and climbed over his side to kiss his wife.

They embraced and kissed passionately, starting the next chapter in their life together.

CHAPTER THIRTY-FIVE

02:41hrs

The M879 became the M9. Joe tried to stretch his body as he sat in the driving seat without banging his head on the roof or pressing too hard on the accelerator pedal. He couldn't say that his journey had seemed like a good idea because it hadn't. It had been an impromptu foray north. A journey that, had he planned it in advance, would have started at eight in the morning. Had he have really planned it he would have only been in the car for the drive to and from the airports.

What had he been thinking?

Well that was the point wasn't it.

He hadn't been thinking at all.

He had reacted to a situation, a situation that technically he had manufactured, though he never expected it to play out the way it had. He had stepped up and taken charge of the aftermath, taken responsibility for what had happened, and was resolved to finish what he'd started.

Saturday 27th June 2015

"What were you thinking?" The look on Harriet's face was one of disbelief and anger.

Joe mumbled a few words under his breath, head tilted slightly forward.

"Well?"

"I..." Joe gestured in the general direction of the car sat on the drive way, the driver's door still open. "Don't you like it?" He felt like a child again being berated by his father. An old man that showed him little to no affection and had to have everything just so.

"Like it. Like it! Does it matter if I like it or not? It might have been nice to have known in advance that you were going to spend sixty thousand pounds of our pension on some fancy car that we don't even need."

"A hundred and twenty." Joe mumbled.

"What?! A hundred and twenty thousand pounds!"

Joe gestured again. "It's an S class Coupe, leather interior, sat nav, cruise control, twenty-inch alloys the works."

"I don't give a shit if it's got gold leaf panels. Why the fuck, do you think it's ok to waste our pension and money set aside for when we have kids and they go to uni on a stupid fucking mid-life crisis car."

A switch seemed to flipped inside Joe. Harriet was being unreasonable again. The past few months her temper had become shorter, she was getting more unreasonable, snappier, less tolerant of him and anything he did. "Stop being overly dramatic! We don't have any kids, yet. And as for the pension, it's still there if we ever need it. I paid for the car with half of my bonus. I decided to do something for me, for us for a change.

The couple stood looking at each other, hands by their sides, neither wanting to make the first move, both daring the other.

The seconds seemed to tick by slowly.

Eyes darted left, right, up, down.

The corner of Harriet's mouth turned upwards just a fraction.

"Draw!" Harriet whipped her right hand up two fingers pointing at Joe, dropping her thumb forwards. "Bang!"

Joe feigned getting shot and fell to his knees a big wide grin on his face.

Harriet walked to her husband and helped him to his feet.

"You got my trousers dirty." Joe brushed at two dusty stains on his knees.

"Forget about your trousers. Come on. Show me what

you've wasted our money on."
Joe grinned like a Cheshire cat excited about the brand-new car sat on his driveway, choosing to ignore the little jibe from his wife.

CHAPTER THIRTY-SIX

02:42hrs

Joe blinked rapidly in a vain attempt to wake himself up as the M9 became the M876 once more. He would have to stop soon for a comfort break before he got cramp in his right calf. He could already feel it building up. He let out a long sigh and berated himself for not using the cruise control a little more. For the sake of about one mile per gallon on the consumption and an irrational sense of not being in control he would have felt a whole lot better than he did now.

Thursday 30th April 1992

Joe was bored, so very bored. He tapped the end of his pen on the notepad in front of him and watched the lecturer stalk back and forth on the small stage at the front of the hall. He knew he should be here listening to what was being said but nothing Mr Brown was saying was new to him. He had read all the course material in the first term he had been at university. He could have sat all the exams and come away with a first at the end of February but then he would have missed all of this. He wondered, not for the first time why university courses were created the way they were. One or two lectures a week, so little information given to the students by the lecturers, so much more had to be researched by the students themselves. But even then, they didn't need three years for what could be, no should be completed in a year at the most. He knew it was down to economics. Universities and their local economies wouldn't get anywhere near the amount of money that they did now. Cities like Oxford and Cambridge would go bankrupt with their income dropping by almost three quarters. Joe wondered if it was just him that thought like this, thought there was a conspiracy to keep the lower classes away from further education due to them not being able to afford to go. He needed to think about something else. But what? He'd already spent the last twenty-five minutes planning his meals and writing a shopping list for the next month as well as his exercise regime. Regime implied he actually exercised and did anything other than do a few stretches before a rugby game, well May was going to be the month he started.

Definitely.

Maybe.

Joe leaned towards Howard. "Did you hear about the riots that happened in LA last night?" He asked in a whispered voice.

"No." Howard's reply was short and sharp. His attention fully immersed in the lecture.

"Yeah, apparently the four white police officers that beat up the black taxi driver have been found not guilty of using excessive force and it's caused massive civil unrest."

"Joe, please. I'm trying to concentrate. Unlike you I'm not a sponge and need to listen in order to learn this." Howard pointed to the projection screen behind Mr Brown. It was at that point Howard realised that Mr Brown had stopped talking and was looking in their direction. "Sorry, my pen's out of ink and I'm just getting another from Joe." Howard held up the biro and instantly felt stupid.

"Well then Mr Morris if it's ok with you then I'll carry on." Mr Brown brought up the next slide showing an exploded technical drawing of Concorde. "We all know what this is, Concorde. From its first flight in 1969 it still took a further seven years before it came into service. The budget of seventy million pounds was slightly over spent and it eventually cost Sud Aviation one point three billion. That's the equivalent of four point two billion today."

Joe watched as the lecturer scanned the faces in the lecture hall. Most sat with mouths open wide as they tried to comprehend the numbers they had just been told.

"Can anyone tell me what happened to Sud Aviation?"

Eyes again darted, heads turned this way and that.

"Anyone?" Asked Mr Brown. "Not even you Mr Anderson."

"They formed a consortium with British Aerospace to complete the project." Joe spoke, his chin rested on his palm, voice flat and emotionless, eyes half closed.

"Correct, and can anyone else tell me how they were able to do this on the back of an already extortionate development cost?" Again, Mr Brown looked around the room, a look of hopeful expectation on his face. "No one?" He paused and took off his tweed jacket, made a show of brushing some unseen dust or lint from the sleeve then placed it on the lectern in the middle of the small stage area he was on. "No? Ok Mr Anderson, please regale your fellow students with the answer."

Joe straightened himself, looked up to the ceiling then began to talk. "It was a state-owned corporation, Sud Aviation. The French government and ultimately the French tax payers paid for the initial development costs."

"Correct! In the short history of avionics there have generally only been two types of company that services this industry. Those that are state owned and funded by their respective governments and private corporations that sell to governments, so are, in effect government funded as well. The latter generate most of their money through military applications and advancement of military hardware. This may change in the future with increased consumer travel but all advancements in this area are on the back of military advancements.

Fortunately, or unfortunately depending on your point of view, you will find that all technology exists as a by-product of government requirements to better their military capability. Weapons manufacture and development has been, and will most probably in your life time, continue to be the driving force for all technological advances."

Mr Brown checked his watch.

"Right then. It looks like time has beaten us. Before next week I want all of you to see if you can find something of a technical nature, that is used in everyday life, that hasn't been developed or bastardised from something that was originally developed for a military application. I doubt if any of you can, but it will be interesting to see your thoughts." Mr Brown retrieved his jacket from the lectern. "And," he continued. "I do not want any of you to just say there are none. I want to see some proper thought and research in to the matter."

With that a buzz erupted as fifty or so students stood and started talking at the same time.

"Microwave ovens?" A voice questioned from behind Howard.

"Radar." Said Joe in matter of fact tone. "Microwaves were developed from radar."

"Joe! There's no need to patronise the beautiful young lady." Howard smiled at the blond haired, blue eyed young woman and extended a hand. "I'm Howard."

"I know exactly who you are." The voice cold, eyes ablaze, brow furrowed. "You don't even remember do you?" The young woman turned away, "Fucking Asshole!" and stormed out of the lecture hall.

Howard watched as the woman disappeared out of the far door a blank look on his face. "Was it something I said?" He asked and turned to Joe.

Joe shook his head in disbelief. "You really don't remember do you?" It was Joe's turn to ask a question. "Oh my God Howard, you're unbelievable."

"What?" Howard stood transfixed searching his memory for the answers that would not come. "Joe!" He called after his retreating friend while he hurriedly collected his things. "Joe!" he called again and raced after his friend. "Joe, who is she Joe? Joe..."

Joe stopped, turned and waited for Howard to catch him up. As his friend drew close he started to walk again towards the library.

"Where are you heading?" Howard panted as he tried to

keep pace with Joe. "The student union is the other way." He pointed for effect more than anything. Both were quite familiar with where on campus the student union bar was.

"Library." Came the one-word reply.

Howard grabbed Joe's arm and swung him round so they were face to face. "What is up with you man? You're acting all weird. Did you catch something of what's-her-face in the lecture hall?"

Joe pulled his arm out of Howards grip and shoved an accusing finger towards Howards face. "You *really* are unbelievable." He turned away then turned back, thoughts swimming around his head. Howard was his best friend but he was also a chauvinistic pig and a serial womaniser, He treated everyone except him the same. Badly. "Her name is Debbie Shaw."

Howard's forehead scrunched, eyes turned slightly upwards. "That name's familiar."

"That's because you dated her last year for about six weeks, did the deed and then never called her."

"Huh." Howard grinned as he vaguely remembered some details. "Did the deed, that's funny."

"Seriously? That's what you focus on?" Joe air quoted. "Did the deed." Joe loved his friend very much but he could exasperate him so much at times. "You really are infuriating. You date her and as soon as you sleep with her you treat the poor girl like shite." Joe started walking towards the library again then stopped and turned yet again to face his friend. "How many girls have you dated in the last two and a half years since we've been here. Doesn't have to be accurate, a rough ball park figure will do."

"I don't know." Howard ran some names through his head and tried to count at the same time. "Some... where... in the region of... thirty, or so. I mean, do you want me to count one night stands as well?"

"And you think that's acceptable? Ok let me ask you another question. How many of them are you still talking to?"

"Why would I want to talk to any of them now we've split

up?" Howard wasn't sure why Joe was getting so touchy. You met a girl, got to know them and if you found that you didn't like them then you moved on to the next until you found the one. It was simple. Joe seemed to want to be friends with everyone, be all nice and sweet. That's not what won girls hearts or got you ahead in the world. There was no point in arguing with Joe. He'd tried so many times before and the stubborn fool just wouldn't listen to him. "Library?"

"Sure." Joe knew that Howard would never understand how to treat a woman right and would ultimately end up either alone or unhappily bouncing from one failed relationship to another. "I need to work out Mr Brown's problem."

CHAPTER THIRTY-SEVEN

02:44hrs

Joe started to count down the minutes. He figured he had about forty-five before he reached his destination. The nine hours and fifteen minutes that lay behind him were a foggy blur of continuous dull grey landscapes and sleep deprivation. Maybe sleep deprivation was a little extreme but he would normally have been in bed asleep about four hours earlier.

Three twenty-nine.

That's when he figured he'd arrive at the bridge.

Joe knew it was a mistake to think about his arrival time as he he'd only get obsessed with arriving at three twenty-nine and get upset and annoyed should he arrive earlier or later than that time even if it was only a minute.

His phone buzzed on the passenger seat beside him. Joe reached over and picked it up as he drove on to the Clackmannanshire Bridge that crossed the river Forth.

A text message.

Two words.

One question.

"How long?"

Joe typed two numbers. "4" and "5". Then pressed send.

Wednesday 16th January 2002

Joe stood outside the back door to his parents' house casually smoking a cigarette. A dark grey jacket sat open on her shoulders, a black tie tied, but loose around his neck. He'd left Gatwick with Harriet early in the morning, landing just before ten. They'd pick up the hire car and raced up to Dundee arriving at the house just before twelve.

They had a good two hours before the funeral cars would be arriving to pick him, Harriet and his mother up from the house.

Harriet squeezed passed her husband her black dress almost hidden by her thick black coat pulled tightly around her neck. "Gosh it's cold."

"It is January in Scotland, were you expecting a tropical rainforest?" Joe handed his wife the cigarettes and lighter that hand been nestled in his left hand.

"No, it just feels colder than the last time we were here." Harriet lit her cigarette, took a long draw and passed the packet back to her husband.

The couple stood in silence for a minute starring down the white frost covered garden slowly smoking their cigarettes.

Howard appeared in the door way behind them. "Room for one more?"

"Two more?"

Harriet turned. "Margaret?" Her name a question. "I didn't know you smoked." She sounded surprised.

Margaret placed four mugs of tea on the windowsill just outside the door and pulled her jumper up round her chin. "Yes." She said a took the cigarette offered to her by her son. "Just don't tell Trevor, he'd be dead upset."

"Mum, really?" Joe closed his packet and lit his mum's cigarette.

"What? Too soon?" Margaret's softly accented voice dead pan.

"It's totally inappropriate. Come on mum, we're here for dad's funeral for Christ's sake." Joe's skin began to flush. He turned and paced away from his mother shaking his head.

"Not yet Joe. We have another two and a half hours before

the funeral starts."

"Oh!" Said Joe as he flung his arm in the air. He turned to face his mother. "That's alright then."

"Calm down sweetie." Harriet walked towards her husband and casually flicked her cigarette on to the grass. "We're all dealing with this in our own way. It's just your mum's way of coping."

Joe shrugged off his wife's advance. He could feel his blood beginning to boil. A finger pointed forwards. "You! You never really loved dad. You stayed with him because it was convenient and for his money." Almost twenty years of anger and rage finally began to spill out from the recesses of Joe's mind. It had started when he was in his early teens when he had started to notice how his parents actually acted around each other, cold and robotic. A dissociative state of unloving and uncaring animosity. The evenings when his mother had been seeing 'friends', his dad's 'golf trips'. All lies, all a façade.

"Joe!" Harriet raised her voice.

Howard stood by the back door in stunned silence, cigarette halfway to his open mouth. This was totally out of character for his best friend.

"Joe nothing." Joe looked from his wife stood beside him back to his mother stood calmly sipping at her tea next to Howard. "Come on mum, tell them. Tell them the truth." Joe's nostrils flared, his breaths short and shallow. For twenty years he'd been carrying a secret around with him, one that had nibbled away at his conscience and his soul. Well no more. He could no longer hold on to it, he no longer wanted to hold on to it. He wanted everyone to know what his mother was really like. Why she had married his father and what she had been doing, most probably, ever since that day. "No, fine mother. I'll tell everyone."

"Is this really time or the place for this? Shouldn't we leave this now and discuss this after the funeral?" Harriet didn't know what Joe was talking about but they were here to bury Joe's dad. It should be a sombre time of reflection not one of angst and arguments.

"This is exactly the right time. The time for everyone to know the facts. That you married dad for his money. That you had at least one affair, that you treated him like shit, that you were and still are disrespectful of him." Joe paused to catch his breath. "Well? Deny it. You can't can you? Because it's all true!"

Margaret's demeanour did not change throughout her son's rant, she stood calmly watching her son. "Ok." She took one final drag of her cigarette then flicked the end onto the lawn. "Please." She gestured to Howard who lit a cigarette and passed it to Margaret.

"Well?" Joe stopped pacing and looked at his mother hands thrust in his pockets. What was he expecting his mother to say? She would try to plead with his sensibility, say she had no choice or talk to him like he was a child as she always did.

"Your father and I had a ... a very complex relationship. One that towards the end was compounded by a nineteen-year age gap." Margaret raised her hand to stop her son interrupting her. "An age gap that I was fully aware of when we met and I thought I fully understood." She took a draw from her cigarette and coughed. "Trevor pursued me from the day started work as an admin at the club in nineteen-seventy. It was a whirlwind romance and we were married after dating for seven months. But this you already know. What you don't know and what I didn't know at the time was that Trevor's first wife had died of cancer six weeks before we met and he never got over her. I was the rebound, nothing more."

Joe, Harriet and Howard all stood in silence, the same look of stunned disbelief on their faces.

"Dad was married? I mean before you?" Joe could not believe what he had just heard. It must be a lie. It couldn't be true, could it? She was just saying it to justify her actions. "I don't understand. Why didn't either of you say anything before now?"

"Your dad was twenty when he married Joanne. Eighteen years later she died of cancer. That was at the end of November nineteen sixty-nine, six weeks before we met. Eight weeks before we had our first date and eight months before we were married. Your father was such a gentleman, he never rushed me or forced me to do anything but I fell head over heels in love with him and I thought he had with me. It wasn't until after we were married and living together that I found out about his first wife. He lied and said she had died a long time before met and he had grieved for her. The truth was that he never stopped loving her, never. I was the rebound, always the other women in the relationship despite *her* being dead. Your father treated me like a glorified house maid. I was there for sex, to keep the house tidy and to cook his meals for him. He starved me of affection and attention throughout our marriage but we kept up appearances for the sake of his job, the club board and his friends. He liked having the hot young wife on his arm until we got home. Your dad wasn't the great man you thought he was. He was hard and selfish in the boardroom and worse in the bedroom!" Margaret spat the last words out, years of contempt and hatred finally being allowed to be released but she felt good. It had been too long bottled up. Joe had the right to know exactly what his father had been like, there was no point sugar coating it any longer. Margaret knew that Joe would need some convincing, that he would take his father's side knowing that a dead man could not defend himself. "You need convincing. Ok. The picture on the mantle. The black and white one of the young couple getting married. Your father told you and always maintained that it was a friend of his, didn't he?" The question was rhetorical. "You should take a proper look at the picture. Oh, and maybe take it out of the frame and have a look at the back of the picture." Margaret's voice followed her son back into the house.

Joe emerged several minutes later photo in hand. "This doesn't prove anything other than dad was married before." Joe passed the picture to Harriet.

"He was married." Harriet looked at the fifty-year old photograph. She had seen it on numerous occasions before sat on the right-hand side of the mantle and like most people she suspected did not pay it any attention nor notice that it was there. She remembered asking Joe about it the first time they had visited the house together in the summer of ninety-three and his father had interrupted his son's reply, snapping off three words 'it's a friend'. Nothing more, just those three words. She had thought it a little strange at the time and Joe had told her to leave it, that he would explain everything to her later. He had said it was the wedding photo of Trevor's best friend Douglas from school taken when he was only eighteen back in nineteen fifty-one. It was just before he went to Korea with the Royal Marines. Three months later he had apparently been killed in action. Harriet turned the photo over in her hands and looked at the back. Beautiful calligraph adorned the back giving two names and a date. 'Trevor Joseph Anderson and Joanne Mary Campbell, Saturday 14th July 1951'. Harriet scrunched her eyebrows as her mind raced. "Erm, Margaret. Where are your wedding photos?" Had she ever seen pictures of Trevor and Margret's wedding day?

"They're in the loft somewhere. They've been there since we got married. Trevor said he couldn't be doing with all that romantic nonsense. So, no he wasn't a great man, a romantic man or an affectionate man. He starved me of affection and intimacy unless he'd been drinking then all I could hope for was that it was over quickly." Margaret took one final draw on her cigarette and threw it into the garden. "So yes, I looked elsewhere for the affection and attention I needed." As soon as she had uttered those words she regretted saying them. Joe was so like his father, so Victorian in his belief's at times. She hoped he hadn't heard her properly but hope slipped fast.

Joe swung around, eyes rising from his feet. "It's you." He said face animated. "You're her."

"Her who?" Asked Harriet not sure what was going on. Her eyes darted from mother to son and back again. Joe's face red with rage, Margaret's red with embarrassment and fear.

"You're the boardroom bike!" Joe's voice was almost a shout. Spit jumped from his mouth as forced the words out.

Howard stepped forward, forgotten for the past five minutes, a spectator in a face paced exchange he could barely keep apace with. "Now Joe. That's no way to speak to your mother, no matter how much you're hurting."

Suddenly everything made sense to Joe. Every time he'd gone to see his parents at the club there had been whispered conversations that stopped whenever he was seen. The giggles and always being asked the same old question, had he brought his bike with him? He'd overheard people talking about the boardroom bike but had been so naive to understand what had been meant and then the comments had seemingly stopped and Joe had forgotten about them. "How many mum?" He asked, voice dead pan. "How many of the players did you sleep with?"

Joe stared at his mum all emotion washed away from his face.

"Well, how many?" He asked again.

"I don't know." Margaret swallowed, her head tipped forward slightly, tears formed in her eyes and started to slowly trickle down her cheeks. There was no point lying anymore, her secret was out and Joe deserved to know the truth. "Thirty, forty, maybe more. You lose count." She shrugged.

Howard's tea involuntarily spat out of his mouth as he looked at his best friends' mother in a new light. Who'd have thought it. Obviously, no one here. A grin began to spread across his face. "Kudos Mrs Anderson."

Joe erupted. "Shut the fuck up Howard. How dare you!" He glared at his best friend then back to his mother. "Thirty or forty! You slept with thirty or forty people. Took advantage of young vulnerable men."

"None of them were vulnerable, and I didn't take advantage of any of them." Margaret's tears streamed down her face, makeup running.

Harriet stepped forward towards Joe. "What's wrong with you? That's your mother, she deserves some respect and for you to listen to her without jumping to ill-informed conclusions. Besides what's wrong with her sleeping with thirty people? Howard must have slept with that many girls in the first two years that I knew him."

"That's different." Said Joe.

"Different? How?" Harriet looked at her husband perplexed.

"Well for a start he's not married and for another he's a man."

Howard spat his tea out for a second time."

Joe realised from the changing expressions on his wife's face that he'd said something wrong. He looked to Howard for support but all he got was a shake of the head and a raised hand.

"I mean, it's not the done thing." Joe spluttered. "Is it? I mean a woman doesn't act like that."

"But it's ok for a man." Harriet strode into the house. "Double fucking standards."

"Harri..." Joe called to his wife's retreating back. "I..." but it was too late. Harriet had completely disappeared into the house.

"Shit Joe!" Howard could barely believe what he had heard. He had been expecting a quiet sombre funeral not a full-on scene from a soap opera.

"You young men really need to think before you speak." Margaret's calm had returned and her face was clear of streaking mascara.

"Well I'm sorry mother but it's not every day that you discover that your mum's a whore. What would dad say if he was here?"

Margaret shrugged for the second time in as many minutes. "Not a lot actually He knew everything and didn't care. I mean you can't keep something like that secret in the small close-knit community at Dundee United. Like I said he was still in love with Joanne. I was the trophy wife that gave him two children. He never forgave me for your brother's death even though it was no one's fault that he died from leukaemia. He compared me to Joanne all the time and I never lived up to her standards." Margaret mimicked her dead husbands voice. "*That dress would have looked better on Jo. Jo had a better figure than you could possibly wish for.* On and on, always comparing and I was always second best." Margaret paused for a few seconds to let the information sink in before she continued. "How would you feel? Trapped in a loveless marriage. Constantly being belittled? Well?"

Joe began to pace again. He couldn't answer the question, he had no experience of that to draw on.

"You need to understand that everyone wants to be loved and I took what little love I could from whomever was willing to give it to me. Your father never really gave me anything I needed. And towards the end I was nothing more than a glorified nurse-maid anyway."

Joe stopped in his tracks and looked up slightly, rolled his neck and cleared his throat. A thought popped into his head, a disturbing thought. He swung around and looked his mother deep in the eyes. "Is dad, dad?" He asked. "I mean is dad actually my father or was it one of the other countless men you're saying you've been with?"

"Joe! I can't believe you'd even ask that question."

"Don't deflect. Answer the question." Joe snapped at his mother desperate to know but scared of what he might find out.

"Of course he is."

"Are you sure?"

Margret took a breath and frowned brow wrinkling. "I was twenty when you were born and twenty-two when your brother Hamish was born. And that's pretty much when sex with your father stopped. He got what he wanted, two sons to carry on the Anderson name. He wanted you or your brother to take over as chairman of the club and after Hamish died hoped that your job in Guildford wouldn't last so you'd come back home.

Joe felt sick, it was his mothers' word against, well no ones. His dad was dead and couldn't defend himself but he didn't not believe her. He had come to Dundee today to say goodbye to his father, pay his respects to the man he looked up to and revered but wasn't sure how he now felt. None of this felt real. Part of him just wanted to find a whole and crawl inside.

"You need to apologise to your mum." Howard stepped forward out of the metaphorical shadows. "I'll give you some space." With that Howard walked into the house leaving Joe alone with his mother in the backyard.

Joe looked at his feet, he wasn't sure he could forgive his mother for what she had done to his father, for betraying him. He knew he was probably being unsympathetic to the pain she'd felt for the past thirty years but it was a lot to process.

"I know what you are thinking and I'm not expecting you to forgive me for my life choices. Look Joseph I just want you to be happy and if you don't get your backside into that house and say sorry to your wife you're going to be very unhappy for a long time."

A tear formed in the corner of Joe's eye. He took a few tentative steps forward and met his mum as she slowly moved towards him. They embraced.

"I love you mum."

"I know Joe, I know."

CHAPTER THIRTY-EIGHT

02:47hrs

"That was hopelessly devoted to you by Olivia Newton-John." The voice from the radio was barely audible over the hum of the car engine.

Hopelessly devoted. That sort of summed up his marriage and his whole life for that matter. Joe had a go at himself for being so morose. He needed to move on with his life. The events of earlier may have thrown a proverbial spanner in the works but they had also given him the proverbial kick that he'd needed to move his life off the course it's been on for the past twenty years.

Things he knew would be a little trickier than he'd like for the next few months and yesterday evening hadn't helped but he was sure that his current course of action was his best, even if it had been thrown together in a minute of madness.

Joe had a sudden desire to stop and check the boot of the car.

No, it would serve no logical purpose. Nothing had changed in the past few hours and wouldn't until he got to where he was going. He needed to get there and get this night over and done with as quickly as possible. A stop would cause an unnecessary delay.

Friday 20th June 2014

"You want to go straight over and stay on the A46." Harriet tried to stifle a yawn behind the back of her hand. She checked the time on the clock on the dashboard. Quarter to eleven. "Just over three and a quarter hours."

"Not bad, and we stopped for breakfast at Toddington Services." Joe indicated left and pulled of the roundabout. "Do you think James and Olivia will be up yet?"

"Um." Harriet thought about it for a minute. Her brow furrowed slightly, they should be up. "I assume so. Why?"

"What time did they get home last night?" Joe asked "I honestly can't remember what you said."

"Last night?"

"When you called your brother. Last night. What time did he say they had gotten home?"

"Last night he said that they should be getting discharged this morning."

Joe glanced to his left. "What? Should be getting discharged this morning?" He scratted his head. "I thought you said they'd be home. Does he know that we're coming up?"

Harriet nodded a little uncertainly. "Erm yes, yes of course. You don't think I get us up at half past six and drive almost two hundred miles without James knowing that we're coming up do you?"

"No, I guess not." Joe breathed in through his nose and pursed his lips. "Um, does Olivia know we're coming?"

"James said that we should come up and stay for a few days, help out around the house, do some cooking so James and Olivia can get some rest."

"Ok, if you're sure." Joe nodded his head lightly and checked his mirrors. The car behind him was annoying him, it was so close it might as well be in his boot. Joe tapped his breaks causing his break lights to come on and he saw the nose of the car behind him dip as the driver hit his breaks making Joe laugh quietly. "Ok, so what happens if we get there and they're not home?"

"I figure we grab some lunch at the Six Bells." Harriet weighed up her options. "I suppose I'll give James a call."

"I think maybe you should drop him a text sweetie, he might be driving still and not in a position to answer his phone.

We're about thirty minutes away, the last thing I want is to get there and them not be in or worse that James hasn't told Olivia and we're a surprise."

Harriet fished in her handbag, an invariable black hole of makeup, pens, keys and other bits and pieces. "I really need to get an upgrade." She said as she pulled the iPhone 3 from her bag.

"As interesting as that may be, and as interesting as that was every time you've said over the past three years you still need to send your brother a text. We can look at getting you a new phone when we get back to Guildford. Let me know what he says."

"O... K..."

Joe glanced to his left again and felt a warm glow wash over him. His wife was a beautiful woman and he loved the way she stuck her tongue out when she was typing a text message.

"What are you grinning at?" Harriet looked sideways at her husband.

"You, the way you stick your tongue out when your texting." Joe checked his mirrors, indicated and pulled out to overtake a lorry.

The couple jumped as Harriet's phone beeped.

"James?"

"Yes."

"That was quick." Joe indicated and pulled back into the left lane. "What's he say?"

"Give me a sec to unlock my phone." Harriet squinted at her phone.

"You know you should put your glasses on, or get a new phone with a better screen so you can at least read what it says." Joe chuckled to himself.

"Not funny, you know I've left my glasses at home."

"Check the glove box. Don't you usually leave a pair in there for emergencies?" Joe applied the brakes as he approached the roundabout and indicated left.

Harriet dived into the glove box and retrieved a pair of glasses that she put on, adjusting them to sit comfortably on her nose. "They're about 2 minutes from the village. James has asked that we give them an hour or two to get in and settled." Harriet looked up. "I'll tell him we'll grab lunch at the Six Bells and pop round for about two o'clock, you ok with that?" Harriet started to text, tongue sticking out, as Joe replied.

"Sounds like a plan. I'm starting to get hungry anyway and I doubt James or Olivia will be in any sort of state to make us lunch." Joe pulled off the roundabout on to the A15, his speech seemed to slow and then speed back up as he traversed then exited the roundabout. "Do you think we should call ahead and book a table?"

"Call ahead? Why? It's Friday lunchtime at and a local pub in a small village, we're not in Guildford anymore."

"No, I suppose not." Joe scanned the horizon watching the road snake towards him round a slow right-hand bend, he liked this part of England. It almost reminded him of being home in Scotland. The countryside around Dundee had the same rugged open feel to it with small villages and farms littering the winding roads. Joe and Harriet had often spoken about the future. About where they would settle down when they retired. They could not decide but had narrowed it down and both agreed that it would be one of three options. Guildford or just outside where the two of them had made their home for the past twenty years, Dundee where Joe had grown up or the Lincolnshire Wolds which had been Harriet's childhood home.

Neither really wanted to stay in Guildford, they had friends and work there but for all the years they had lived there, it had never really felt like home, to either of them. Joe knew that Harriet was not sold on the idea of moving to Scotland despite what she had said. He could tell by her body language whenever they spoke about it. If he was being honest with himself Joe was not overly bothered about moving back. His dad would have been almost eighty-one had he not have passed away and his mum's health was not the best. He did not expect his mum to be alive when he retired and he had no other family there.

Joe knew that Harriet wanted to move back to Lincolnshire, to or near her childhood home. Her brother was currently stationed at Coningsby and had bought a house in Hopton on the Wolds, the village where they had grown up which was about half a mile from their parents' house. The rest of Harriet's family, of which there was quite a few, all lived with ten miles of each other. He had to admit that he always felt welcomed whenever they visited, being accepted in as part of the family from day one. No one had any airs and graces, they treated everyone the same. It was nice. It was somewhere that he felt he could live. Besides with the money they'd get when they sold their house they could pretty much buy anything here. Houses were so cheap compared to where they lived. They could buy something twice the size and have money left over.

As the miles past by them Joe listened to Harriet as she regaled him with a story about a night out in Lincoln during the summer holidays of nineteen nighty two before she started University. It was a story he'd heard countless times before and would undoubtably hear again every time they came to see her brother or parents in the future.

"Next left." Harriet said. "On to Main Street."

"Same as last time then?" Said Joe slightly cheekily. "Is the Six Bells still on the left just before the crossroads?" He continued as he pulled off the A157 on to Main Street.

"I hope so otherwise we're in the wrong place." Harriet retorted. She peered in to the side mirror then swivelled her head and looked over her shoulder.

"What's up?"

"Ambulance. Approaching fast from behind us with his blues and twos on."

Joe manoeuvred the car as far to the left as the road would allow, slowed and tried to pull onto the pavement. He was thankful nothing was coming in the opposite direction as the ambulance passed them on a sweeping left-hand bend barely slowing.

"I wonder where they're going in such a hurry?" Harriet mused to herself.

"Yeah." Joe was also curious but quickly resigned himself

to the fact that he'd probably never find out. "I doubt we'll ever know." He pulled back on to the road and checked his watch. "Twenty past eleven. Will the Six Bells be open yet?"

"Used to open at eleven so unless something's changed we should be fine. We can have a drink before we eat." Harriet squinted as she tried to stare forwards. "I think I can see the ambulance stopped up ahead."

"Knowing our luck, the pub will be on fire and we'll have to find somewhere else to eat."

"Joe!" Harriet hit her husbands' arm. "That's not very nice."

Joe rubbed his arm and slowed to thirty as they drove into Hopton on the Wolds. He had to admit he liked the village and the houses. If he and Harriet did decide to retire here they could do a lot worse besides.

The village playing field passed them on the right and Joe pulled off the main road in to the pub car park opposite the church that sat imposing opposite the pub, both about a hundred meters from the crossroads ahead.

Joe parked up and both he and his wife exited the car.

"Do you think they purposely built the pub opposite the church?" Joe looked to his wife, distracted by something.

"What, oh sorry darling. Looks like something's going off at the crossroads."

"I hope it's clear by the time we finish lunch, the other way to your brother's house is not a quick two-minute drive."

CHAPTER THIRTY-NINE

03:00hrs

Joe stifled yet another yawn, rubbed his eyes for what felt like the thousandth time. A coffee would go down a treat right about now. But he had neither the time to spare, the inclination to stop nor knew of anywhere that would be open at this time of the morning. He was driving on autopilot, almost oblivious to the countryside that was passing him by. If he'd been asked there and then where he was he'd say Scotland but couldn't be more specific than somewhere near Dundee.

Joe glided the car round the roundabout off the A997 and on to the M90 and instinctively he knew where he was. He had driven this road more times that he cared to remember and would be on the motorway for only three miles before he left it for the more familiar roads from his youth.

He picked up his phone and checked the road for any headlights before clumsily typing then sending a text. Two numbers and two words.

"Three zero want coffee."

Saturday 10th February 2018

Joe hadn't realised when it had started but he felt nervous.

He placed the phone next to his ear waiting patiently for what seemed like an eternity before it started ringing.

Well at least he had the right number. Had he though? It was ringing but that didn't mean it was the right number and he didn't know who would answer. For all he knew he'd called a takeaway or a plumber's merchant.

Four, five, Joe counted the rings becoming impatient and worried that there would be no-one at there to answer the phone.

"Hello." The voice, female, sounded old with the familiar accent of home.

"Hello, Mrs Stuart?" Joe's voice shook slightly, his nerves almost getting the better of him.

"Yes." Came the one-word answer.

"Hello Mrs Stuart, my name is Joseph Anderson. I was wondering if you had a few minutes please?" He asked tentatively.

"I don't have any PPI, and I wasn't involved in any accident." Came the disgruntled reply. "Please stop calling me." Her voice became hard and uncompromising.

"I'm not calling about PPI, accidents or anything like that. I'm trying to find out some information about the father of a friend of mine who I believe you worked with back in the mid-eighties."

"Oh, who?"

"My friend is Howard Morris, his father worked at Timex, Jack Gunn." Joe passed his phone to his left ear, his right suddenly felt like it was on fire from the pressure he was inadvertently applying to the phone. He flexed his right arm, all the muscles felt tight and sore like he'd been to the gym lifting weights, well that's what he thought it'd feel like never having actually been to the gym to lift weights.

There was an awkward pause before the old women spoke. It was not what Joe was expecting or what he wanted to hear.

"I have nothing to say."

"Please. It's really important." Joe pleaded. "I know his wife, Carol, Jack's wife Carol, she's in a nursing home in Dundee with Parkinson's. This has nothing to do with her. I'm sorry for rambling I just need to know a few things, please." Joe pleaded again. He paced around his kitchen, then headed towards the coffee machine to refill his mug. Why was this so hard, why was he so nervous? Deep down he knew why, the answers to his questions could change Howard's life immeasurably or it could be another dead end. After this he did not know where to go, so much depended on this woman. This Fiona Stuart.

There was another long pregnant pause and Joe wondered if Fiona Stuart would ever say anything. He could hear slightly laboured breathing down the other end of the phone as he walked to the back door. He decided he needed a smoke. He knew Harriet had started again and if he was being honest with himself he had never wanted to stop.

Joe wondered if he should prompt her to try and say something or just wait. Joe would rather have been doing this face to face but he didn't have the time to go all the way to Dundee and back. The conversation, even with all the pauses, shouldn't take more than about ten minutes and a thousand-mile round trip was a little excessive even for the information he needed. Joe lit a cigarette and began to twitch impatiently as he opened the back door. It felt like an age since he or Mrs Stuart had said anything. "It's going to rain." He said under his breath. A chilly breeze greeted him. It couldn't have been more than six or seven degrees outside but he liked the cold air. It reminded him of home. The phone was passed back to his right ear as he looked at the grey clouds drifting slowly overhead.

"It is."

The two words startled Joe.

"Why do you want to talk about Jack and what do you want to know?" Fiona Stuart asked, her voice sounded tired but Joe heard something else there, an inflection of fondness. Could it be she had been reminiscing, did she or had she had feelings for Howard's father? There was only one way to find out. Joe watched the smoke from his cigarette drift out into the dark evening sky. What did he have to lose? Everything really, she might clam up and say nothing, hang up and then where would he be?

"I know about you and Jack." Joe took a stab in the dark and continued to talk before Fiona could react. "But that's not why I'm calling." He scrunched up his eyes, an almost pained look crossed his face. Several seconds passed and Joe realised that he was holding his breath.

"Good, what Jack and I had was special and nobody's business but ours." Fiona Stuart's voice was hard again and Joe decided to leave that there and move on to the real reason he had made the call.

"I agree, your private life is your business and no concern of mine. The reason for my call is to ask about Jack's time at Timex, his relationship with John MacDonald and the real reason he lost his job in eighty-six. I've heard rumours, lots of rumours. It'd be nice to know what actually happened."

Another pause.

"Mrs Stuart, please, if you can shed some light on things." Joe decided to push. If he didn't this call could take all night. Time wasn't something he had a great deal of. Ideally, he wanted to be done before Harriet got back from the gym at quarter past ten so he didn't have to field any obdurate questions before he decided to tell his friend what he had learnt.

"Who did you say you were?" Fiona asked.

"Joseph Anderson." He replied.

"Is that supposed to mean something to me?"

"No. Probably not." Joe flicked his dead cigarette into the yard and picked another from the packet he'd left on the kitchen surface just to the left of the back door. Well, he thought, in for a penny in for a pound. "I'm the best friend of Howard Morris, Howard Gunn before his mother changed their surname in eighty-nine after the unfortunate incident with his father. Howard just wants to know what really happened with his father but couldn't bring himself to make the call hence me calling you."

"So why now?" Fiona's answers seemed to be getting shorter and they hadn't started long to begin with.

"John MacDonald has come back on the scene."

"Stay clear of him. Whatever you do stay clear. That man's bad news, he's evil." Fiona suddenly started talking. "Him and Jack used to work together. They were developing a new operating system, some sort of code for the plus two but they couldn't get the logic to work. But when a similar code turned up, working, inside the SmarTech 7 the managers at Timex assumed that someone had sold the code. Then when John MacDonald confirmed their suspicions they sacked Jack.

Jack always denied the accusations until the day he died. Six months after Jack was sacked John resigned moved south and guess where he got a job?"

Joe knew where but decided to humour Mrs Stuart. "Where?"

"SmarTech!"

"So, John sold Jack's code, sold Jack as a scapegoat, got him sacked and then ran off for a job at the firm where he'd sold the code to."

"Exactly. The only thing was Jack could never prove that it was John. It sent him mad and drove him to drink and depression. He never recovered and took his own life. I..." Fiona began to cry quietly barely audible over the phone line.

"I'm sorry for upsetting you." Joe suddenly felt awkward. He had the information he needed from Fiona.

"I... I hope..."

The line went dead and Joe slowly lowered the phone from his ear. That was that then. He was glad she had ended the call so quickly once he had gotten the information he needed if he was honest. He didn't have to make pleasantries or try and console her.

Joe started to wrack his brain, he needed to remember the name of the man he had met while he was contemplating his PhD at university. The one who had been working at SmarTech in the eighties and joined the University of Surrey as a lecturer in ninety-one.

Beazley. Professor Beazley. Malcolm. That was it. Professor Malcolm Beazley. A few calls to the university and Joe could probably get a number for Malcolm. Then he could confirm Fiona's version of events. Once he had that Joe needed to tell that supposed friend of his. Joe's ultimate hope was that Howard would do something stupid and get himself sacked or possibly worse.

CHAPTER FORTY

03:03hrs

As he approached junction eight that would take him to the A91 Joe took a precursory check of his mirrors and it felt like his heat had suddenly jumped into his mouth. Blue flashing lights were approaching fast from behind.

They couldn't be for him, could they? He'd come so far.

Who knew where he was. Howard. He was the only one who knew what he was doing tonight as his journey had started as he'd left Howard behind. He knew as he had been the one who'd sent him the text minutes before, but he wouldn't, would he?

Joe pulled into the left-hand lane and followed the slip road as it swung first to the left then round to the right and up and over the road he'd left a moment ago below. The blue lights seemed to have disappeared from view. His heart skipped a beat, his breath held. Then they appeared again to his left coming out from beneath him as they raced north along the empty motorway.

Saturday 26th June 1999

This was really happening. It really was. He was getting married today. He, Joseph Leon Anderson. He never really thought that this day would happen, that he'd be so lucky to find a woman as perfect as Harriet and that she would agree to marry him. Today he truly felt blessed. Blessed. Such a strange concept and Joe was not sure why he had thought it. Was he blessed? He was not a religious man. He believed in science, logical thought. But he also believed that the universe was too big a place to expect that the human race was the only sentient species to inhabit its unending void. That it was more than likely that one or more of those beings may have at some point in history travelled through the cosmos and visited earth. These beings could have and probably would have been mistaken for gods to the primitive beings that had inhabited the earth at that time.

Joe pondered the concept of religion again as he often did in the shower. For some reason his mind always seemed most clear during his morning ablutions, as if while he was washing his body his mind was also washed clean of all the clutter from the past twenty-four hours to leave tenuous thoughts of religion and unsubstantiated facts created in a bygone age. He felt most at peace during this half hour every day. Was this how those first scholars had felt, trying to find answer to questions they had neither the preconceptions or experience to solve thus leading them to believe in superbeings. Or maybe it was a way to justify their actions. 'God made me do it.' 'He appeared to me in a vision.' 'They are unbelievers, we must kill them and take their lands.' Joe was not naive enough to be aware of all the good that religion had brought to the world nor all the bad and he was not sure how it balanced or if in fact it did.

A lot of very intelligent people believed in God of one kind or another but he could not bring himself to take that leap of faith himself, not fully. His parents were Christian and had dragged him to church until he was twelve and he had started asking some awkward questions they could not answer. The next eight years had been religion free unless you counted his belief in physics and science as a religion. Then he'd met Harriet. She went to church, not every week but enough. She had forced him to go with her just that one week and he had enjoyed the community that it brought with it. It helped that the bishop at Guildford Cathedral, which was right next to the campus, was not the sort to force religion upon anyone. They let you follow your own path which suited both him and Harriet.

Harriet had wanted a white wedding in church. They had agreed to have it at her local church in Hopton on the Wolds, a small picturesque church in a small picturesque village in rural Lincolnshire. The only issue had been finding a venue that was big enough for all the guests and had accommodation for everybody close to the church. It wasn't going to be a massive event, but there would be about eighty people attending. Just under half, Harriet's family and old school friends, could stay locally. It was their friends from Guildford and his family from Dundee that needed the rooms. There were several hotels in nearby Market Rasen but not enough for all of the guests. Harriet and he had decided that they wanted to keep everyone together so had looked a little further away. The two options had been the White Hart Hotel in Lincoln's Bailgate or the Petwood Hotel in Woodhall Spa. Both were about twenty miles from Hopton church but Harriet had fallen in love with the Petwood the moment she had seen it. It also appealed to Joe as it had been the home of the famous 617 squadron during World War II.

Joe stepped out of the shower his thoughts of religion and a higher power left behind like the remnants of the water slowly draining down the plughole. He towelled himself dry and dressed quickly in front of the full-length mirror near the window. The service wasn't until two. The coach was booked for one and he had two full hours before he needed to leave. A cup of tea, that what he wanted, a cup of tea. Joe picked up his jacket from the Fallston Chaise Longue at the end of the large four poster bed, stepped out of his room, locked the door behind him and walked down the corridor, past the beautifully impressive red carpeted staircase to the bar.

"Tea, please." Joe waited patiently while the young girl brought him a pot of tea. "Thank you." He said and took the drink to an empty small round table by the window where he sat, lit a cigarette and stared absently at the pictures and news paper pages hung on the wall depicting the history of the building and its links to the 617 squadron.

❖

Harriet laughed. The joke wasn't that funny but the

champagne she had been drinking since breakfast at about nine had made her light headed. She needed to stop drinking, get some water and something to eat. She adjusted her dressing gown and looked into the mirror her hair finally ready for the big day. She stood slightly unsteadily on her legs and took a sip from her glass. No more. Harriet walked into the kitchen from the dining room.

"Mum, where's the coffee?" She called looking into a cluttered cupboard in the corner of the kitchen above the kettle. She was sure her mum kept the coffee there. Harriet made a vague effort to look further in the cupboard moving a few mugs and tins form side to side.

"It's on the side next to the kettle." Came the slightly muffled reply from her mum Jean. "Make me one as well please sweetheart."

Harriet looked down. There it was, next to the kettle.

Harriet's phone buzzed and beeped in her dressing gown pocket making her jump so much that she nearly dropped the mug in her hand. She had forgotten that it was there.

"Who's texting you?" Asked Jean.

"How am I supposed to know, give me a chance to get my phone out of my pocket." Why did her mum still talk to her like that? With that tone of voice, belittling, asking questions that were none of her business. Why were her parents like this? They treated her like a little girl, like a five-year-old. For Christ sake it was her wedding day. Her and Joe had a house and a mortgage, had jobs and careers that were blossoming and taking shape. They were talking about starting a family in a few years' time. All the things that made her a woman apparently gone unnoticed. She looked down at her phone, a text message, two words I'M OUTSIDE. Why would he be here? Now? Today? Surely, he should still be at the Petwood, the bus wasn't due to pick everyone up until one. Harriet looked over her shoulder and wondered what her mum would say if she knew he was here, outside, now. What did he want? She was getting married in a little under three hours. Well, she said to herself, there was only one way to find out. "I'm just going to pop outside for some fresh air." Harriet called over her shoulder. "I'm feeling a little claustrophobic."

"Ok sweetheart, don't mess your hair up."

Harriet grabbed her cigarettes by the front door and walked into the street. She looked around and stopped half way down the driveway. Howard's car was parked just down the road facing away from the house on her side of the street, she could see his hands dancing nervously on the steering wheel. Harriet walked slowly towards the car her cigarettes forgotten about in her hand. She slowed further as she neared the driver's window and stopped on the curb just behind the driver's seat looking in through the window. Her right hand came up and tapped the window.

Howard jumped, startled by the unexpected sound. He inhaled deeply and opened the door looking up and back. "Hi." Howard waved and immediately felt awkward and embarrassed. He shook his head as he climbed out of the car. He had spent the whole of the previous evening and half of a sleepless night going over what he would say and trying to figure out how this moment would play out and in the five seconds that had passed since Harriet had tapped on the window everything had disappeared from his mind.

"Hi." Replied Harriet waiting for Howard to talk to her and explain why he was here. "This is a surprise."

"I know. I, err." Howard stumbled over his words. "I shouldn't have come."

"But you did. You're here now and there must be a reason." Harriet remembered the cigarettes in her hand and offered one to Howard before lighting one herself. She waited patiently for Howard to start talking. She was not in a rush.

"Nice dressing gown."

"You're deflecting." Harriet looked down at her pink dressing gown and adjusted the front to cover her chest a little more. She wasn't sure why but she felt a little uncomfortable. "I haven't got all day Howard. I need to get back inside before my mum comes out looking for me. God knows what she'll do if she sees you here." Harriet raised a finger. "Don't piss about or try and deflect again, just tell me why you are here. Tell me now!" Her voice raised slightly, face flushed.

"I just wanted to check you were alright." Howard's words fell out of his mouth as he said the first thing that popped into his head. "You seemed a little nervous and unsure that this is what you wanted. It was nothing you said just a feeling I got, the way you were speaking and what you didn't say. It's what you didn't say." Howard looked at the woman in front of him his eyes scanning every line on her face, the contours of her neck and shoulders. God how he wanted her to tell him how she really felt. That she didn't want to go through with the wedding that it was him she had feelings for. He knew how she felt, he'd known it since the day they had met back in ninety-two, the one night they'd spent together in December of the same year. He just didn't know what had gone so wrong and why their relationship hadn't followed the path that it should have. They should be together now, it should have been their wedding day not Joe's. He loved his best friend but Joe had stolen his life from him.

Harriet leaned forward and kissed Howard on the cheek. "I'm fine, yes a little nervous, but who wouldn't be on their wedding day. You're a sweet man Howard. You always have Joe's best interests at heart." She turned to walk away. "I don't know what he'd do without you."

Howard climbed back into his car and watched in the rear-view mirror as Harriet walked away. Her shapely figure disappeared up the driveway and in through the front door of her parents' house. Howard's hand gripped the steering wheel tightly turning his knuckles white before he started to bang it with the palm of his right hand. "Howard you fucking idiot" he whispered to himself through gritted teeth, eyes screwed shut tight. Howard knew Harriet fancied him back in '92 and knew she still had feelings for him. If only he had the courage to tell her how he felt and he knew that she would declare her undying love for him. Something just wouldn't let him do it. He knew that this was his last chance, he wouldn't get another. This love story was just not meant to be.

❖

Harriet watched from behind the horrible brown curtains of her parent's front room window as Howard turned the car around in the street and pulled away. She hoped, back to the Petwood otherwise the conversation with Joe later might be a little awkward with his best man nowhere to be seen. She couldn't call Joe and tell him as it'd just cause him to panic and ask a lot of questions she couldn't answer like why Howard had actually come to see her. She felt a shiver down her back and pulled her dressing gown tighter around her shoulders and again felt a little uncomfortable. Her mind darted trying to put the pieces of a puzzle together when she had no picture to work with and about four of the thousand or so pieces that she would need to complete it.

"Harriet are you ready?"

Her mum's voice pulled he back into the room. "Yes, I'm just going to go for a pee then I'll be right up."

CHAPTER FORTY-ONE

03:19hrs

Joe opened his window wide and felt the chill night air hit his face. He was finally on the A91 and at most fifteen minutes away from the Tay Road Bridge. In about an hour, and before the sun rose on the coming day this nightmare of a night would be over.

Joe's phone beeped. He glanced down at the message on the screen.

Coffee ready in ten.

Great, he just hoped it wasn't instant or Startbucks. In his opinion there was no difference, both tasted like sludge.

Friday 10th October 2014

The couple walked through the double doors into a corridor. They beared right followed it briefly to its end and walked into the ICU.

"Howard Morris?" Asked Joe.

The nurse on at the nurses' station didn't look up from her paperwork. Her voice matter of fact, disinterested and tired. "They've just transferred him upstairs to Bramshott Ward. Level C."

"You go up and find Howard I'm just going to have a quick chat to the nurse. I'll join you in a few minutes." Joe watched as Harriet walked down the corridor towards to the lift and turned back leaning over the counter of the nurse's station. "Hi Stacey."

"What?" Stacey looked up. She sat back in her chair and

brushed several strands of loose auburn hair behind her ear as she looked at the tall slightly chubby man in front of her. "Do I...?"

"Joe, Joseph Anderson." Joe tilted his head and raised his eye brows. "Don't tell me you don't remember me?" Joe looked slightly crestfallen at the blank look staring back at him from Stacey's face. "Two thousand and three, you had been dating Howard for about fourteen months when he failed to turn up for a date and sent you a text saying he was ending the relationship. You turned up on my doorstep and spent most of the evening crying into a glass of wine in my kitchen."

"Oh my god, Joe." Stacey stood, walked round the counter and gave Joe a hug. "It's been a while."

"It has. How have you been?" Joe kissed Stacey's forehead and looked down and the beautiful red-haired nurse stood before him.

"How have I been? What since that arsehole stood me up and broke my heart, yeah good. I met Fred in oh six, we got married in oh eight and have two lovely girls Isla and Ava. You?" Stacey walked back round and sat back in her chair.

"Good. Harriet and I have been trying for a child for the last ten years or so but... Anyway, I just wanted to ask if you knew what had happened with Howard, I mean with regards to the crash he had." Joe was suddenly nervous. He wasn't sure if Stacey could actually tell him anything but if she could he wasn't sure he wanted to know. An uncomfortable pause hung in the air. Joe coughed and wondered if he should say something. "I know that Howard hurt you and seeing him here today must have opened up some horrible memories. I'm sorry I asked. Please forget I asked."

"No, it's ok. Water under the bridge." Stacey looked up pain behind her eyes. "He was apparently driving too fast and not paying attention and clipped the curb as he approached the roundabout rolling the car into the centre island. He sustained multiple fractures to his ribs, his right arm, cracked his skull and punctured a lung. He's been taken up to Bramshott Ward where he's been made comfortable. We're waiting for the surgeon to arrive and he'll be taken to theatre."

Joe bit his bottom lip and nodded several times. "Thank you."

"He certainly wasn't as lucky as his passenger." As Joe turned to walk away Stacey began to talk again. "The police say that she walked away with only a bruise on her left shoulder from the seatbelt. A woman with deep auburn hair apparently."

Joe hesitated in his step before continuing down the corridor to follow his wife up to the ward. What was Howard thinking? Why wasn't he paying attention, it wasn't in his nature. For all of his faults Howard was a very safe driver. He liked his flashy cars but drove them like an old man.

Bramshott Ward.

Joe walked in through another set of double doors, hospitals seemed to have so many, and for the second time in half an hour surveyed the room in front of him for his wife. There, at the far end of the room sat next to a bed. She appeared to be frantically talking to the man lying in the bed with numerous tubes coming from his arms. His eyes narrowed and breathing slowed. This was not the time to be asking questions. His best friend was lying in a hospital bed after a horrendous car crash. He could leave it to another day. His breathing picked up as did his pace. As he neared the bed Harriet's head lifted and she spun to face him a forced smile on her face.

"Hi sweetie." Harriet stood and kissed her husband. "You'll have to get close to Howard as it hurts when he talks so he's having to whisper." She lowered her voice. "Just be warned, the sound of gurgling is a little off putting so be nice."

CHAPTER FORTY-TWO

03:31hrs

Joe took his foot off the accelerator and allowed the large Jaguar to glide down the bay road and gently slow as the Tay Rail Bridge came into view. Two very familiar, but not so friendly faces stood by the side of the road waiting for him.

One face expected.

One face, not two.

What was she doing here? Joe swore under his breath. Presumably she was there to hold Howard's hand.

"Fuck Sake!" He swore again as he brought the car to a stop under the bridge and killed the lights and engine in quick succession.

The driver's side door opened and Joe climbed stiffly out. He stretched, sore and uncomfortable from his long drive. "Right, let's get this over and done with as quickly as possible. I don't want to stay here any longer than we need to."

Howard pushed a coffee into his friends, former friends hand noticing that there was neither eye contact nor pleasantries from the man he'd known and had counted on to be there for most of his life. "Ok." He replied with one word, clearly Joe was not in a talking mood. Then neither would have been if the shoe was on the other foot.

Joe walked round to the boot leaving Howard and Harriet where she stood.

"You got the rope?" Joe asked, the plastic coffee cup resting on the car roof.

"Already in place." Howard replied advancing slowly.

Joe's face popped from around the side of the raise car boot, eyes scrunched, mouth open, a perplexed look on his tired face. "What? What do you mean already in place?"

Howard continued to walk slowly forward, arms bent at the elbows, palms open and fingers pointing upwards.

"Harriet!" Joe hissed loudly barely containing his anger and frustration. "Why in god's name did you tell her and what the hell is she doing here?"

"Keep your hair on and don't shout. We don't want any of the locals waking up do we?" Howard waited a few seconds for Joe to calm slightly before he continued, watching him pace back and forth. "Just listen please. Look we can't just string him up. It wouldn't look right. He's been in the boot of the car for nine hours. All the blood will have drained to one side of his body. Rigour mortice will have started to set in. If we string him up then it will look like someone has put him there. Plus, his neck's probably broken and his heads been caved in. He wouldn't be able to get himself up on to the bridge to hang himself in that state."

Joe had to admit that Howard might have a point, or two there. "Go on."

"It needs to look like he's tried to hang himself and it's gone wrong. I've tied a piece of rope around one of the rail lines on the bridge so it looks like it's been cut by a train and he's fallen. We get another bit of rope with a frayed end, tie it round his neck in a make-shift noose and throw the body under the bridge. The rocks will explain the injuries and the water will explain away the lack of blood."

Joe thought about what Howard had said and weighed up all the options. It all made sense. It concerned him slightly that Harriet had had the idea but then she did read a lot of murder mystery novels. It crossed his mind that she had thought about killing him and getting rid of the body. He looked past his old friend at his wife still stood in the shadows by the wall at the side of the road. A smile drifted across his face as he forgot about the past six months and remembered all the good times they'd had together, the pain and heartache they'd got through, the reason he'd asked her to marry him. And just as quickly as it had come the feeling passed and he remembered why he was here and what had led him to this point in time.

"So, are we going to stand around here all night or are we going to get this body moved?"

Joe watched Howard as he took the final steps towards the car and noticed that his hair was ruffled and out of place, not the usual well-groomed side parting that he always had. He had the beginnings of a black eye most probably from a blow landed by John before his fall, back at the factory. There was also some blood on his tie and shirt. From John? He couldn't see any obvious signs that it had come from Howard. It was strange seeing him so dishevelled. Normally he would notice the tiniest speck of dust or lint and remove it straight away, preening himself like a peacock but not tonight. Tonight, he had been rattled and he was, possibly for the first time, not thinking about how he looked but about what he'd done and how he was going to get away with it.

Howard removed his tie and placed it on the roof of the car followed by his jacket, not sure why he had left them on and not changed there was no point getting either of them dirty. The tie had cost him nearly two hundred pounds and the suit a Tom Ford pin stripe that had cost him over two thousand pounds. He removed the cuff links from his shirt cuffs, they were gold, engraved with his name, H Morris and the number seventy-two. He remembered when Joe had given them to him as a gift on his fortieth birthday six years before. Was it poetic or just fate that these would be the only thing that would survive his thirty-five-year friendship with Joe? He placed them on top of his jacket and rolled up his sleeves as he prepared to get to work.

❖

Half an hour later Joe and Howard stood by the boot of Howard's Jaguar, the boot lid still open as Joe looked inside for any signs that there had been a body in side only thirty minutes before. Satisfied he closed the boot and looked up in to the relieved eyes of his once best friend.

"Right you take the tarp and dispose of it, I'm going to have one last look around just to make sure we've not missed anything."

Said Joe.

Howard grabbed his jacket and tie off the car and Joe saw his friends cuff links fall on to the floor next to the rear tyre.

"Howard." Joe said before he stopped himself saying anymore. Howard hadn't realised that he'd knocked his cuff links off the car when he had retrieved his jacket and tie.

"What?" Howard asked walking towards Joe.

"I'll see you in the office Monday." Joe's voice was like ice, cold and emotionless.

"Monday, right." Howard continued walking past Joe. "As if nothing has happened." Harriet joined him by his car and both climbed into the front seats. "See you then."

"Keys?" Joe asked in a loud whisper and a hand appeared from the still open passenger door. Joe walked round the car collected the keys to his wife's car from her outstretched hand and watched as the large Jaguar rumbled into life then pulled away. That was that then, hopefully he wouldn't have to see either of them again. Forty-five years and his life was going to start over again, Joe had to admit that he was feeling nervous and excited about his future. One last look at the now empty road where Howard and Harriet had just been, then at the body still half concealed by the lifting darkness. Well he couldn't stand around he all night, could he?

Friday 23rd March 2018 – 17:00hrs

Howard stalked down the second-floor corridor past empty offices fists clenched by his side. Everyone had gone home, everyone that is except Joe, who he had just left behind in one of the conference rooms, himself, obviously and John McDonald. The man who he'd just found out had worked with his dad back in Glasgow in the eighties. Who had caused his dad to lose his job, had forced him to move to Dundee and had ultimately led to his father's depression, alcoholism and death. His dad had never been happy in Dundee, never. A day didn't go by without him bemoaning him and his mum's choice to leave Glasgow and move to Dundee. Howard had wanted to stay in Glasgow too, yes he had met Joe and they had had an amazing friendship but deep down he'd hated moving, hated Dundee. It was so small, had no real character and he'd never wanted to go back once he'd left, he even hated visiting the place to see his mum as it always stirred up emotions and memories of his dad. And now he'd learnt the truth behind it all, it had all been the fault of John McDonald! If he hadn't have stabbed his dad in the back they'd have stayed in Glasgow and perhaps Howard would have settled down and had a family instead of searching for years for something that in his heart he'd known until very recently he'd never find.

Howard's strides widened as he got closer to the double doors to the factory in front of him. Behind them, a mezzanine, from which he should be able to spot John. He tried to restrain himself, trying his hardest not to run despite the overwhelming desire that built up inside him. A desire to confront the man who had caused his father to kill himself. All these years he'd blamed his father not fully understanding the reasons behind his choices. His father had still been a coward in his eyes, taking the easy way out, leaving his problems behind him for others to try and sort out, but he could finally put things in to context. He finally understood what had led his father to the decisions he had made and while he could never forgive him for what he'd put him and his mother through he could understand it and get some sort of closure.

His pace finally slowed as he came within the last few meters of the door. He stooped, right hand raised and resting on the door in front of him, to catch his breath. Was he doing the right thing confronting John? Was he in the best mood to confront him if it was the right time?

Why prolong the inevitable? The confrontation was coming, he knew that for a fact, whether it was today or next week it didn't really matter so he might as well get it over and done with. He knew he'd feel better for it and hopefully that snake would up sticks and fuck off. Howard didn't care where to as long as it wasn't near here.

A final breath and Howard pushed the door open and

stepped on to the mezzanine.

He stopped.

John was there. In front of him. Suit jacket draped over his shoulders, tie loose around his neck. He hadn't been expecting that. His heart seemed to skip a beat then he snapped. His adrenaline surged through his body. Almost thirty years of pent up aggression and anger flooded his body, a veiled mist descended and all he could see was red.

"Bastard!"

Howard threw a punch which connected with John's chin.

"You fucking bastard!" Howard screamed as he threw a second punch.

John stumbled backwards, blood erupting from his nose. His face a mix of pain, shock and disbelief.

"You killed my father!" Howard push on, fists clenched, punches raining.

John continued to stumble backwards and stopped as he hit the railings at the edge of the mezzanine but Howard continued forward. John tipped backwards trying to get away from the onslaught coming his way. His feet came off the floor and as John realised that he was going over the edge his arms reached, his hands grabbed at thin air.

"Nooo!" Blood sprayed from cuts above his eye, from his mouth and nose.

Howard took one last swing, it barely connected but it was enough. Enough to push John over the edge. Over the railings and send him to the factory floor below.

Howard stood. Arms still raised. Fists still clenched. Breath coming short and sharp. His eyes began to focus, to take stock of the empty mezzanine floor before him.

Where had John gone? He had been there only a moment ago.

Realisation dawned. What had happened. What he had just done. Howard inched forward slowly holding his breath. He reached the railings and swallowed taking several breaths before he peered at the floor below. Maybe he was ok.

"Shit." Howard whispered. What was he going to do? The body below was lifeless, the head at an awkward angle to the body, eyes starring lifelessly at him. Boring into his soul. Howard thought he'd feel better, that he'd get closure, be able to move on but he felt worse. John had destroyed two lives now...

"Howard!"

A voice called from behind him, he turned, his face white, mouth opening but finding no words.

Joe looked as the fear washed the anger and rage from Howard's face.

"Howard?" Joe asked. "What have you done?"

CHAPTER FORTY-THREE

24th March 2018 – 04:07hrs

Harriet pulled her seatbelt across her chest and plugged it in with its familiar click. "So?" She said. "What now?"

"What now? What do you mean? Howard looked a little perplexed. We have the rest of our lives together ahead of us."

"My God Howard, you're unbelievable at times. I'm not talking about the next ten or twenty years I'm talking about the next ten or twenty hours. It's four in the morning, we both came up here last minute, we can't go to Joe's mums which is where I should be for obvious reasons. I know you have a hotel booked for the weekend but I want to get home sooner rather than later and get some things together as I don't want to be there when Joe gets back. I don't suppose you've given it much thought."

Howard looked to his right and watched Harriet start the car. "I'm happy to go back to the hotel get a few hours sleep, check out at about half nine and head south."

"Did you remember to plant the memory stick I gave you in John's jacket?"

"Yes." Howard paused before he continued. "You never did tell me what was on it."

"Oh, just copies of some files I downloaded from Joe's laptop a few weeks ago. He asked me to copy a few technical drawings of his latest engine modifications for a meeting and I took a copy of

them as a backup. He's always misplacing things so I took an extra copy just in case and I've had it in my bag ever since." Harriet slowly pulled away as Howard nodded. Well, she'd made her choice and now it was time to live with the consequences.

❖

Joe put the keys into the ignition of Harriet's car and pressed the start button.

A sigh.

He checked his mirrors.

He replayed the image of Howards car as it slowly pulled away from the side of the bridge, Howard sat in the drivers seat next to his wife. Rage boiled inside of him. The betrayal of his wife and his best friend. He knew he would never be able to forgive either of them but knew that he needed closure, needed to move on and he would only get that if Howard paid for his betrayal and by doing so it would hurt the women he loved as much as she had hurt him. Seeing her tonight had made him realise how much he still loved her and just how deep her betrayal had hit him. He would have to try and move on but was not sure that he could, not sure that he wanted to.

He needed closure.

Harriet's car finally disappeared out of view along the snaking road and Joe took a breath, lowered the drivers' door window and killed the engine. He opened the driver's door and stepped back out into the early dawn air. The light from the moon that hung in the early morning sky to the East gave an eerie almost satanic glow to the proceedings. He had one last thing to do before he left the Tay Road rail bridge. He had to be quick, if he stayed too much longer he risked getting caught near the body of one of his work colleagues and it would be difficult to explain what he was doing there.

Joe walked round to the passenger side of the car, reached back into his car and pulled his gloves out of his coat pocket on the passenger seat then headed back down the rood the twenty or so feet to where Howards car had been. One last look around as he put his gloves on and he bent down to collect the cuff links that were laying on the floor next to the curb. Howard had not noticed that he had knocked it off the roof of his car when he had retrieved his jacket and in all the excitement must have forgotten that he had been wearing it in the first place. Joe quickly made his way across the road, over the low wall and careful picked his way over the rocky river bank making sure he avoided stepping on the mud so he wouldn't leave any foot prints or evidence that he'd been there.

The body of John McDonald lay peacefully under the bridge and if he ignored the frayed piece of rope around the neck he could just about believe the man was asleep. Believing that somehow made this whole experience slightly easier. Joe stuffed one of the cuff links into John's left trouser pocket then casually dropped the other a few feet closer to the river bank. He could see that the tide was already starting to come in and he knew that he didn't have time to waste. He made his way back to his car, climbed in and keeping his gloves on pulled a phone from the well in the drivers' door. John's phone. His iPhone 7. It was locked and by the looks of it only had about twenty percent of its charge left but that didn't matter for what he needed it for. He pressed the screen at the bottom activating the emergency call function and the phone dialled nine, nine, nine.

It rang.

It rang again.

Then a voice spoke those all to familiar words. "Which service do you require?"

Joe cleared his throat and in the worst Glaswegian accent he could muster replied. "Police. There's been a murder. Tay railway bridge, Bay Road Wormit." With that he tossed the phone as hard as he could over the road and heard it clatter on the rocks near to where John's body lay. With any luck the police would find the body before the tide came in and washed away the evidence that would tie Howard to the crime scene.

Well. That's that then.

His heart raced and felt like it was about to explode out of his chest. Had he done the right thing? Doubt washed over him. He and Howard had been friends for over thirty years. He and Harriet had been together almost twenty-five. They had both betrayed his trust and hurt him in the worst way possible but still there was so much history between them. So many good memories.

Either way it was a little late to change his mind now.

He started the engine and took one last precursory look over to where the body lay but the wall on the other side of the road blocked his view.

What now?

He had no idea where he should go or what he would do beyond getting a few hours of sleep. He knew he'd have to go back to work Monday and act as if everything was normal for a month or so before he handed his notice in. Beyond that he had a new life to plan and look forward to.

Joe pulled away trying to work out where he could go at four in the morning for some food and sleep.

THE END?

This chapter of the story concludes in **The Journey: It Leads Us Here**. Find out where Joe's journey has taken him. Has he been able to forgive the woman he still loves? Who will Harriet find true happiness with? And can Howard live with the life he has taken?

Chapter One

Saturday 24th March 2018 – 08:12hrs

"So why the hell am I here?" Detective Inspector Roy Galloway called out to the group of people that milled about in front of him as he lifted the tape that surrounded the crime scene over the receding dark reddish-brown hair atop his six-foot 2-inch frame. His tubby but once athletic body now, rounded through a combination of a lack of exercise and poor diet, moved slowly forward as he surveyed the area between himself and the waters edge. He scratched his left cheek, the burst capillaries caused by his somewhat excessive drinking habit tingled. Galloway had transferred from CID in two thousand and two to the Major Investigation Team in the Metropolitan Police based in Hendon before moving three years later to Dundee in search of a quieter life. And for the best part of thirteen years it had been quiet, sometimes too quiet. The local papers had a few years earlier called Dundee the Murder capital of Scotland with ten percent of all murders in the country happening in Dundee, but ten percent of sixty was still a small number.

Galloway stopped and shuffled a cigarette out of the battered packet he'd just pulled from the inside pocket of his jacket then place it between his lips before lighting it with his old brass zippo. Roy had stopped smoking when he'd gotten his promotion to DI and started again within three months of moving to Dundee.

"Inspector Galloway." The slight figure of PC Kayleigh Ransome gestured to her left and led the senior officer towards the water line. "This way sir."

My God, Roy said in his head, she must be at least a foot

shorter than him, even with the slight decline in gradient of the land they were walking down he'd be able to see over the PC without any fuss. He'd be interested to see how she handled a gaggle of football hooligans on match day. He'd be very interested.

"So why am I here..." Roy asked again as he stopped just short of the body lying on the ground. "It's clearly suicide." Roy casually gestured at the body as he looked up to the bridge approximately twenty meters above him. His gaze then slowly tracked quickly along the four-and-a-half-kilometre length of the bridge to Dundee at the other end.

"That's what I thought at first sir." Detective Sergeant Patrick Fraser stood, brushed the knees on his dark brown suit trousers and stretched a hand forwards towards his senior officer. At just over five foot six he had to look upwards to meet the Inspector's eyes.

"Patrick." Galloway took the proffered hand.

"Hi Roy, sorry sir. We've completed a precursory look around the area and at the victim but we're awaiting the coroner to confirm time of death." DS Fraser tilted his head to the right. "Victim is approximately six-foot-tall and in his late fifties, due to the discolouration of the skin I'd estimate time of death between twelve and eighteen hours ago but that's just a guess, the coroner will confirm that when he gets here. Hopefully," DS Fraser checked his watch, "he won't be too much longer."

"What makes you think it wasn't suicide?" Galloway looked down at the body lying face down on the rocks by his feet, the body of a suited man in his mid to late fifties. Roy could see a tie poking out from the left side of the body and a rope, approximately twelve millimetres in diameter tied around his neck. The rope was almost neatly coiled close to the head with the end frayed as if it had been roughly cut by something not very sharp. "Look he has a rope around his neck. It's frayed like it's snapped from the weight of the body." Roy pointed upwards.

"That's what I thought at first, but look a bit closer." Patrick Fraser waited a few seconds for Roy to look around. "Don't see it? No?" He nodded to himself. "Move a bit closer to the head and look directly upwards."

Fraser indulged his DS, moved around the body to the head and looked up. "What am I looking for? I don't see anything."

"Where's the other end of the rope?" Fraser raised a hand to stop Roy before he could speak. "We've already had a look at the bridge by the rails and the other end is wrapped around the tracks. Its end is also frayed and looks to match the end around the victims' neck. However, and this is where it gets strange. The rope is tied to one of the inside tracks not one closest to the edge."

"So?" Galloway was getting impatient and his frustration was beginning to show.

"Think about it, why would the victim use an inside track and not just tie the rope to the railings. It would be simpler and a lot easier. This guy would have had to have dug the gravel from under the track to get the rope tied off, plus with the amount of freight trains that use the line at night there's no way he could guarantee being finished, so to speak, before a train came and cut the rope. When you arrived, I was checking the victim's hands and they're clean. Completely clean, not even anything under his nails. Even if he washed his hands you'd think there would be some marks. Besides what man in that state of mind washes their hands before topping himself?" Patrick coughed and cleared his dry throat. "The other interesting things, the first is the length of rope that's attached to his neck. Just over two and a half meters."

"And I'm supposed to understand the significance of that how?"

"Because the width of the gauge is one point four five meters and the distance from the outside rail to the edge of the bridge is another two meters meaning if he had tried to hang himself with this rope he wouldn't have gotten over the railings."

Galloway let the information sink in and flicked his unsmoked but dead cigarette away to one side. "That is interesting." Roy rubbed his chin thoughtfully. "And the second?"

Patrick's face lit up. "This is a real peach. We recovered the victims' phone over there by the road side about six meters away from the body. The screen's cracked but the number matches one that made a 999 call this morning at just after four claiming there had been a murder." DS Fraser pulled his mobile from his pocket and extended his arm out between the two men. "Listen."

"Emergency services, how can I direct your call?" Said a female voice.

"Police. There's been a murder. Tay railway bridge, Bay Road Wormit." The voice was that of a middle-aged male with what sounded like a fake Scottish accent.

"A murder at Tay Railway bridge. Can you please confirm that you are on Bay Road, Wormit and not in Dundee? Sir, sir?"

The call ended with the caller hanging up their phone. Miserable

"Ok." Galloway rubbed his cold nose with the back of his hand leaving a thick glistening trail behind. "So, someone, obviously not the victim, then made the call, which means there was at least one other person here last night."

"I take it you've canvassed all the houses in the area and what? Everyone was asleep and saw nothing." Galloway watched DS Fraser nod his head. Oh well, it wasn't the end of the world, he'd cracked cases before with no witnesses and sometimes someone suddenly remembered something, he'd have to wait and see what turned up. "Have you checked the victim's pockets?"

"Not yet, I had been waiting for forensics to finish first." Patrick looked to his left and called out to a man and a woman standing face to face deep in conversation. "Mary, Peter! Have you finished with the body?"

"For now. We're waiting for the meat waggon to arrive and take the body back so we can do an autopsy." Came the reply from Mary.

"Tactful as always." Roy smiled.

"Well I guess when you've been dealing with dead bodies for as long as she has." Patrick left the sentence unfinished and pulled a pair of latex gloves from his pocket. "Shall we?" The question was rhetorical and the two men converged on the prone body.

"Do we know anything about the victim?" Galloway pulled a wallet and rifled through the contents. "Several bank cards, three credit cards, Tesco club card, Nectar Card, All Star Fuel card all in the name of John McDonald. Driving licence also for a John McDonald. Date of birth sixteenth of September nineteen fifty-nine. Lives in Godalming Surrey. And... about... one hundred... and... fifty pounds in cash, all tens and all English bank notes so it's likely he's not been in Scotland long."

Patrick pulled his hand out of the right trouser pocket. "Car keys, Porsche, if the key fob can be believed, and a yellow memory stick." He stood and looked around as he placed the keys and memory stick into a clear evidence bag. "Why would he have car keys on him. There's not a Porsche, that I've seen, anywhere near here." The DS paused, a thoughtful look on his face. "Several things just don't add up. How did he," Patrick pointed at the body, "get here in the first place? He couldn't have driven, if he did where's the car? If someone drove him where are they and why does he still have his car key? Why did he come all the way from Surrey to hang himself? It must be almost five hundred miles, there's got to be a lot of places closer to home that he could have tried to kill himself. Lastly and most importantly, how did a man hang himself with a rope that couldn't reach the edge of the bridge from where he'd tied it off, let alone allow him to dangle from it."

Roy Galloway walked slowly round the body staring at the prone figure. "Has the body been moved at all?"

"No." Patrick look a little perplexed at the unexpected question. "We'd just finished taking pictures and completed the precursory look at the area around the body. Why?"

"The body is lying on the rocks on his chest, face pointing down but slightly to one side, the right cheek is lower than the left. But look at the discolouration of the skin around the left ear. After the heart stopped beating the blood stops pumping around the body and gravity pulls it down where it settles. One half of the body becomes pale and the other a scarlet red. Strange that the discolouration is on the upper side of the face." Galloway looked up at DS Fraser. "And you're sure the body hasn't been moved."

"Definitely not. Let's get the keys and the memory stick to the lab and see if there are any finger prints that we can use and then let's see what's on that stick." Patrick turned and started to walk back towards the road and his car.

Galloway gave a half-hearted wave to the retreating back of the Detective Sergeant. He had decided to have a look around and stay while the body was taken away, it might shed some more light on the situation. Roy checked his watch, just before half past eight. Scotscraig golf club was just five miles down the road at Tayport, once the body was taken away he should still be able to get there for the time he was booked in to tee off. He'd head to the station once he'd finished his round, technically it was his day off.

Printed in Great Britain
by Amazon

80675425R00142